*As a child and young woman, I was especially blessed to have a number of beautiful women in my life — women gentle in love, fierce in battle. They taught me so many lessons along my journey. Those who have passed on will remain forever in my heart. The others continue to inspire me every day. I love you all dearly.*
*This one is for you:*

*Peggy*
*Stella*
*Cora*
*Blanche*
*Gwendolynn*
*Joleen*
*Patsy*
*Murle*
*Wanda*
*Anita*
*Tracie*
*Carolyn*
*Linda*
*Holly*
*Elizabeth*
*Leslie*
*Mona*
*Bobbie*

A SAVANNAH REID MYSTERY

# WICKED CRAVING

# G. A. MCKEVETT

**KENNEBEC**
**CHIVERS**

This Large Print edition is published by Kennebec Large Print,
Waterville, Maine, USA and by AudioGO Ltd, Bath, England.
Kennebec Large Print, a part of Gale, Cengage Learning.
The text of this Large Print edition is unabridged.
Other aspects of the book may vary from the original edition.
Set in 16 pt. Plantin.

---

**LIBRARY OF CONGRESS CATALOGING-IN-PUBLICATION DATA**

McKevett, G. A.
  Wicked craving : a Savannah Reid mystery / by G.A.
McKevett. — Large print ed.
    p. cm. — (Kennebec large print superior collection)
  Originally published: New York : Kensington Pub., 2010.
  ISBN-13: 978-1-4104-2535-5 (pbk.)
  ISBN-10: 1-4104-2535-5 (pbk.)
  1. Reid, Savannah (Fictitious character)—Fiction. 2. Women
private investigators—Fiction. 3. Overweight women—Fiction.
4. California, Southern—Fiction. 5. Large type books. I. Title.
PS3563.C3758W53 2010
813'.54—dc22                                        2010004765

---

BRITISH LIBRARY CATALOGUING-IN-PUBLICATION DATA AVAILABLE
Published in 2010 in the U.S. by arrangement with Kensington Books,
an imprint of Kensington Publishing Corp. Inc.
Published in 2010 in the U.K. by arrangement with Kensington
Publishing Corp.

U.K. Hardcover: 978 1 408 49106 5 (Chivers Large Print)
U.K. Softcover: 978 1 408 49107 2 (Camden Large Print)

Printed and bound in Great Britain by
CPI Antony Rowe, Chippenham, Wiltshire.
1 2 3 4 5 6 7 14 13 12 11 10

# ACKNOWLEDGMENTS

I want to thank all the fans who write to me, sharing their thoughts and offering endless encouragement. Your stories touch my heart, and I enjoy your letters more than you know. I can be reached at:

**sonja@sonjamassie.com**

# CHAPTER 1

Savannah Reid rolled down the window of the rented pickup, breathed in the fresh sea-scented air, and decided it was a perfect day in sunny California. But then, barring earthquakes, mudslides, and brush fires, most Southern California days were pert nigh perfect.

She vacillated between being deeply grateful she had moved from rural Georgia to the picturesque seaside town of San Carmelita, and being bored to death with "perfect." She missed the drama of an old-fashioned, southern thunderstorm, complete with all-hell's-done-broke-loose lightning crashing around you and the scream of tornado sirens going off, warning you to shake some tail feathers and get your tail — feathers and all — into the nearest storm cellar.

*Ah, yes,* she thought, watching the palm trees glisten in the tropical noonday sun.

9

*There is nothing quite like huddling with your granny and eight siblings in a spider-infested tornado shelter at two in the morning, storm raging above you, to bring a family together.*

"And we are close," she whispered, thinking of her loved ones in Georgia, so far away. "So close it's a wonder we haven't murdered one another yet."

"Murdered who?" Dirk asked as he guided the pickup truck away from the downtown area and headed toward the poor side of town. The part of San Carmelita that didn't have perfectly matched palm trees lining the streets. The part where windows had bars, not flower boxes, and the only fresh paint on the building walls was gang graffiti. The part where you were more likely to see a pit bull chained to somebody's front porch than a Chihuahua poking its head out of somebody's purse.

"What?" she said to the guy sitting in the driver's seat next to her. Detective Sergeant Dirk Coulter was still with the San Carmelita Police Department.

She wasn't. And on most days, she was grateful for that. Occasionally, she waxed a bit bitter about the fact that she had been dismissed. But those days only came along about once a month . . . like most of her truly dark moods. And a bar of chocolate or

10

a dish of ice cream usually put her world right again.

"You were talking to yourself," he told her.

"Was not."

"Were, too."

"Well, do you have to bring it up and make me feel like a nitwit who's losing my marbles?"

"Don't snap at me. You told me to tell you . . . said you wanted to break the habit."

"Oh, right. Sorry." She sighed and wondered if she could blame her forgetfulness on perimenopause. After all, now that she was solidly in her mid-forties — and if she didn't admit that she'd been forgetful her whole life — it could float, excuse-wise. And it would carry her through to menopause and past to senility.

"I'm forgetting stuff lately," she said, "because I'm approaching the 'change o' life.' You wouldn't know anything about it. It's a woman thing."

"I know it's not why you're talking to yourself. You've been doing that for twenty years." He slowed the truck down to drive over a particularly deep drainage dip in the road and checked his cargo in the mirror. "But that might be why you've been extra irritable lately."

She shot him a look. "Ever consider it

11

might be because you've been exceptionally irritating?"

"No."

"No, you haven't been irritating?"

"No, I haven't considered it might be me. I'd rather blame it on you and your hormones."

"A dangerous thing to do, blaming anything on a woman's hormones."

"You brought it up."

"True."

She didn't like this — him winning two arguments in a row. She decided to just keep quiet and say nothing for a while.

That never lasted long.

"It's just that I've been bored lately," she said, fifteen seconds later, as they headed deeper into a valley that stretched from the sea into the dry, brown, scrub brush–covered hills.

The tattoo parlors, pawn shops, porn stores, and junkyards had given way to tiny, dilapidated stucco houses and yards covered with dead, brown grass, surrounded by sagging fences.

Many of the inhabitants sat on sagging sofas on sagging porches, wearing saggy clothes and saggy facial expressions — much like many of the inhabitants of the poor, rural town where she had been raised.

Savannah understood despair. She knew, all too well, the toll it exacted on the human spirit.

"Do you miss being on the job?" he asked. "Is that why you're bored?"

She considered his question honestly before answering. Did she miss being a police officer? The constant adrenaline rushes? The camaraderie with the other cops? The fascinating view of ever-changing human drama? Having drunks throw up on her shoes?

"I do sometimes," she admitted. "Mostly when I don't have any clients. Private investigation can get pretty mundane when you don't have a single case to investigate. It's been a bit lonely at the Moonlight Magnolia Detective Agency lately."

"And that's why you hang with me," he said, giving her a grin and a poke with his elbow.

"That and all this philosophical, mind-expanding conversation." She looked him over, taking in the Harley-Davidson T-shirt that had, in a former life, been black, but had gone through a navy blue stage and was now a muddy chocolate brown. "And your sense of style."

She glanced at herself in the truck's side mirror and saw a woman who wasn't exactly

13

a fashion plate herself. Her thick, dark hair had a mind of its own, so she pretty much let it do its wayward-curls thing. Clean skin with a bit of lip gloss and mascara, hastily applied, were the extent of her daily beauty rituals. And her wardrobe was only a notch above Dirk's on any given day — a light-weight blazer over a simple cotton shirt with jeans or linen slacks. The blazer hid the Beretta strapped to her side. And the cotton and linen kept her cool under the California sun.

Years ago, when they had first met, both Savannah and Dirk had turned heads, especially when they were in uniform, before their detective days. And even though Dirk's T-shirt might be faded, and they both had gained some extra poundage here and there, in Savannah's mind, Dirk was still a stud, she was a babe, and as a pair, they were both pretty darned hot stuff.

On the seat between them lay the empty sack that had recently held two apple fritters and two cups of coffee, all compliments of the Patty Cake Bakery.

Patty, the blonde bimbo baker, liked the way Dirk filled out his worn jeans and, apparently, didn't mind the old T-shirt, because she was always generous, dolling out the sugar and caffeine. She was also a major

14

cop groupie, which irked Savannah and pleased Dirk to no end.

Since Dirk was also in his mid-forties — a tad past his "glory days" — he was constantly starving for attention from the opposite sex, wherever he could get it. He wallowed in every bit that came his way, even from a moderately desperate, blatantly oversexed donut clerk.

Long ago, Savannah had gotten sick of the goo-goo eyes and the silly tittering and the deliberately deep bending over the counter while Patty was waiting on them. But Savannah kept her mouth shut. Patty was as well known for her generously frosted maple bars as she was for her appetite for the boys in blue, and Savannah was a woman with her priorities in order . . . having a healthy appetite of her own.

She glanced down at her ample figure and wondered briefly how many of Patty's maple bars and apple fritters she was toting around with her on any given day. Several pounds' worth, to be sure. But Savannah liked to think that most of her "extra poundage" was well placed. And the admiring glances she got from quite a few guys told her that Patty's pastries were being put to good use.

The guy sitting beside her was one of those. Frequently, she caught him giving

15

her a sideways look that wasn't very different from the ones Patty gave him when she was sacking up the goods. And, considering how long Savannah and Dirk had worked together — first as partners on the San Carmelita Police Department and then as investigators of numerous homicide cases — she found it most complimentary that he still noticed and enjoyed her curves.

But then he sped up a bit too much and hit a pothole, jarring every bone in her body.

"Dangnation, Dirk," she snapped. "If I had dentures, they'd be in my lap. Would you take it easy?"

He loved it when she criticized his driving. "Hey, I didn't do nothin' wrong! You know they never fix the roads out here. Besides, I can't drive like an old lady if you wanna nail this guy."

He had her there.

Savannah was just as eager as he was to slap a fresh pair of handcuffs on Norbert "Stumpy" Weyerhauser. And just because Stumpy's mom, Myrtle, had told them he was home an hour ago, didn't mean he would hang around. If he smelled a rat — or a cop sting operation — he'd be making tracks out of town.

"Do you think she bought it?" Dirk asked for the fourth time.

"Who? Myrtle?"

He nodded.

"Oh, yeah." Savannah chuckled at the memory of the telephone call her assistant had made on Dirk's behalf earlier. "You should have heard Tammy laying it on thick." Savannah dropped her southern accent and donned Tammy's valley-girl tone. " 'Yes, Mrs. Weyerhauser, it's true! Your son, Norbert, has won a forty-one-inch, high-definition, flat-screen television! If you can assure me that he'll be home to sign for it personally this afternoon, your entire family will be able to watch TV in style this weekend!' "

Dirk frowned. "She said forty-one-inch?"

"Yeah, I think so. Why?"

"I don't think they make a forty-one-inch. I told her to say it was a forty-two."

Savannah shrugged. "Oh well. So, Stumpy gets shorted an inch. He's probably used to it."

"What?"

Grinning, she said, "Didn't you ever notice that Stumpy and his limbs are normal height and length?"

"Uh . . . yeah . . . I guess."

"So, where did he get that nickname? I'm thinking from a former wife or girlfriend, someone who knew him intimately."

Dirk smirked. "You're a nasty, evil woman, Van. I like the way you think."

"Well, you know me." She shrugged. "I have a soft spot in my heart for nimrods who break into elderly ladies' houses, steal from them, and smack them around. I think about Granny Reid, and then I have this overwhelming need to beat them to death with a brick of week-old cornbread."

"Yeah, me, too. I can't tell you how happy I was to hear that this dude had violated his parole. I begged the captain to let me be the one to bring him in."

As they neared the street where Stumpy, robber and senior-citizen abuser, lived, they both dropped the casual banter and assumed an all-business demeanor. Stump wasn't known for carrying deadly weapons or assaulting anybody who was actually big enough or strong enough to fight back, but he was still a convicted felon. And they were pretty sure he'd have pretty strong objections to going back to prison. So, they couldn't exactly sleepwalk through the act of nabbing him.

"When we get there, you go to the front door," Savannah said. "I get to cover the back."

"No way!"

"That's the price I charge for going along."

"But he always runs out the back door!"

"I know. I read his sheet. Why do you think I want to cover the rear?"

"Hey, I'm the cop and —"

"Don't you even go there, buddy. If I wanted to *watch* cops doing their thing, I'd be home with my feet up, eating Godiva chocolate, and staring at the TV."

"Damn," Dirk grumbled. "I should have had Jake McMurtry or Mike Farnon come along instead of you. They take orders a lot better."

"Yeah, but they wouldn't have come. They don't like you."

Actually, nobody in the SCPD liked Dirk. Most respected him, even envied him; he was a gifted detective. But he never received invitations to hang out at the local bar after hours or drop by for a tri-tip sandwich when somebody in the department threw a barbecue.

Normally, Savannah wouldn't have mentioned that to a person. She wasn't cruel, as a rule. But she knew Dirk didn't care. He didn't have a people-pleasing bone in his body. And long ago she had decided to be Dirk when she grew up. He saved so much energy . . . not giving a flying fig what anybody thought of him.

"But *you* like me," he said with more than a touch of little-boy vulnerability in his voice.

Okay, he cared a little what a few people thought — the people he loved. And he could count those on one hand.

She gave him a dimpled grin. "Oh, I'm plumb crazy about you, but I still get the rear of the house. End of discussion."

Dirk pulled the truck over to the curb. "Then get out here. The house is up there on the right. The yellow one."

As she started to climb out of the truck, he added, "Watch yourself. He's got a pit bull in the backyard."

She froze, one foot on the ground, staring at him, mouth half-open. "Are you yanking my chain?"

He grinned broadly. "Yeah."

"You lyin' sack!" She got out, slammed the door, and said through the open window, "I'll get you back. See if I don't."

She strolled along the street, picking her path among chunks of broken concrete that had once been a sidewalk, tree roots, weeds, and the leavings of dogs whose owners didn't carry pooper-scoopers.

Glancing up and down the block on both sides of the street, she didn't see anyone

20

looking out the window, sitting on the porch, chatting with the neighbors, or trimming any hedges. Not a lot of hedges got trimmed regularly in this neighborhood.

As she got closer to the yellow house, she eyed the blue one next to it. There were no cars in the driveway. Instead of curtains, faded, flowered sheets covered the windows. The backyard was accessible and, from what she could see, there were no signs of a watchdog.

Looking back, she saw that Dirk was still waiting, watching her through the pickup's dirty windshield, grinning at her. He shot her a peace sign. She shook her head and chuckled. *Some old hippies never grow up,* she thought. But she wouldn't have him any other way.

After one more glance around to make sure she wasn't being watched, she darted down the side of the blue house. It was a small, shotgun affair, long and narrow, with rooms arranged end to end — not unlike the one she had been raised in.

Less than five seconds later, she was in the backyard. From there, she could see the rear of their suspect's house.

She reached into her pocket and retrieved her cell phone. She punched a couple of buttons, and Dirk answered.

"I'm here," she said as she walked through the tangle of weeds, past a collapsed, rusty swing set, and through a broken chain-link fence.

"I'm driving up to the front," he said.

She could hear the truck approaching as she scrambled up to the yellow house and positioned herself at the corner. From here, she couldn't be seen from any of the windows, and she had a clear view of the side of the house and the rear. "I can't see the right side of the house," she whispered into the phone.

"My right or your right?" he asked.

"Your right."

Knowing Dirk, she had already done the "math." Why confuse the poor guy? He confused so easily.

"The right if you're in the house looking out, or . . ."

"Dirk! Are you still in the truck, on the street, looking at the house?"

"Yeah."

"Then I'm at the left back corner of the house. I can't see the right of the house, so you'll have to keep an eye on it. *Your* right. You know, like your right hand. That's the hand you scratch your ass with."

"Jeez . . . you really *are* irritable today."

She heard him cut off the engine and open

22

the truck door.

"I'll keep my phone on," he said, "and put it in my pocket, so you can hear what's going on."

"Thanks," she said. "Good luck."

"You, too."

Her ear to the phone, her eyes on the back door and the side windows, she listened as Dirk walked up to the front door and knocked. It took longer than usual — or at least, it seemed like a long time as her adrenaline levels soared and her heart raced — before the door finally opened.

She heard Dirk say, "Hi, are you Myrtle Weyerhauser?"

"Yeah," was the reply.

"I've got a delivery, a wide-screen television, on the truck there. It's for a Mr. Norbert Weyerhauser. Is he your husband, ma'am?"

"No, Stu— I mean . . . Norbert is my son."

"Well, if he can sign this form, I'd be happy to —"

"He ain't here."

"But you told our office on the phone that he is. I'm afraid I can't deliver it unless Mr. Weyerhauser signs for it."

"Gimme that paper. I'll sign for it."

"No, ma'am. Can't do that. And besides,

I'll need Mr. Weyerhauser to help me unload it. See, my partner was sick today — out with the flu — and I can't carry it in by myself."

"Are you a cop?"

"A cop? Me? Why would you say that? Do I look like a cop?"

"Yeah, actually, you kinda do. What's in that box in the truck? Is it really a TV?"

Savannah went from "vigilant" to "high alert" in an instant.

The voices on the phone faded as she lowered the phone and listened intently to a new sound . . . a scraping noise . . . coming from the other side of the house.

Ducking, so that her head would be below the windows, she hurried across the back of the house. She paused at the opposite corner, then took a quick peek around.

At first, she wasn't sure what she was seeing — a flash of silver in the sunlight. Some sort of metal was sticking out of the upstairs window.

Then more of it protruded . . . and more . . . tilting down toward the ground.

A ladder.

She grinned, closed her cell phone, and stuck it in her pocket. She unsnapped her side holster, freeing her Beretta . . . and waited.

She didn't have to wait long. No sooner had the end of the ladder reached the ground than a hairy leg popped out of the window, and then another followed.

Dressed in baggy shorts that hung low on his hips, flip-flops, and a T-shirt large enough to use as a tent for a backyard campout, Stumpy Weyerhauser was making his getaway.

Or at least, Stumpy thought so.

She waited until he was halfway down the ladder before she sauntered around the corner of the house and over to the foot of it.

He was huffing, puffing, and unsteady as he descended. The flip-flops didn't help as he tried to get solid footing and kept sliding off the backs of the sandals.

So intent was he, hanging on tightly to the sides of the ladder and casting furtive glances toward the front of the house, that he didn't even notice Savannah as she walked up behind him.

He didn't realize she was there until she reached up, grabbed the hems of his shorts, and jerked them down around his ankles.

Instantly, she regretted the action, because his underwear came down, too, and she found herself "face-to-face" with one of the least attractive features of an unattractive man.

"Hey! What the hell!" he yelled as he whipped his head around and nearly fell.

He tried to grab at his shorts with first one hand, then the other, while clinging to the ladder, and again, it was nearly his undoing. The side rails bent and the entire contraption wobbled as he tried to maintain his balance and re-dress his backside.

Her hand on her still-holstered pistol, Savannah laughed at him and said, "Careful there, Stump. You don't wanna take a tumble with those britches down; you could skin something important."

"You stupid bitch!" he shouted. "What's the matter with you?"

"Whoa, Norbert! Watch who you're calling names there, good buddy. You're in no position to make enemies."

She reached over and nudged the side of the ladder. Not enough to knock it down, but definitely enough to get a rise out of the already stressed Stumpy.

"Hey! Knock it off! You're gonna make me fall and —"

Again, he reached for his shorts, while trying to step down one more rung. Apparently, multitasking wasn't Norbert Weyerhauser's strong suit.

He tumbled off the ladder and landed on his face in a particularly muddy area of a flower bed. Adding injury to insult, the ladder slid sideways with him and landed on him, smacking him soundly on the head.

A small, inch-long gash opened in his scalp, and bright red blood began to ooze out.

"Hey, Stump . . . you've sprung a leak, boy," Savannah said as she stepped across him, straddling his body, then sat down on his back.

The wind went out of him in a whoosh.

He struggled only a moment as she pulled his arms behind him. Taking some handcuffs from her slacks' waistband, she called out, "Hey, Dirk! Back here!"

"What . . . are you?" Stumpy asked, struggling to breathe with her weight pinning him. "A . . . cop?"

"Close enough," she replied as she saw Dirk come running around the corner.

He looked infinitely alert, ready for action, body taut with tension . . . until he saw her sitting on the facedown Stumpy. Stumpy with mud on his face, his shorts still pulled down to his ankles, his butt bare as the day he was born — only hairy and not half as cute.

Dirk froze, staring at them, his mouth

open, taking in the scene.

Then his eyes locked with Savannah's.

"What the hell are you doing?" he asked her.

"Apprehending your suspect for you. And you're welcome," she replied with a grin.

"She . . . she . . . sexually assaulted me!" Stumpy whined, thrashing around. "And she's . . . squashing . . . me." Dirk considered the words for a moment, shook his head as though he simply couldn't process the information, and walked over to them.

Savannah stood and pointed to the cuffs. "After you're done with him, I want those back," she said.

Instantly, Dirk was indignant. "Hey, I gave you a pair to replace the ones I —"

"Don't get all huffy with me! You gave me one pair for my birthday after ripping off three pair from me over the years. So, by my calculations, I'm short two sets and a birthday present."

Dirk reached down, grabbed Stumpy, and hauled him to his feet. In another quick move, he hoisted his prisoner's shorts back up to their original position. "There you go, Norbert," he said. "I just improved your appearance tenfold."

"I'm telling you," Stumpy whimpered, "that crazy woman sexually assaulted me!"

28

"No, she didn't." Dirk took him by the arm, leading him toward the front of the house. "I've known her for twenty years," he said, "and in all that time, I couldn't convince her to sexually assault me."

Dirk glanced back over his shoulder at Savannah, who was following close behind. "And . . ." he added, ". . . as we've all seen, I have way more to offer her in that respect than you do."

A woman with pink, foam hair curlers, a lavender chenille robe, and a cigarette hanging from the corner of her mouth, came running up to them. "Norbert!" she yelled around the cigarette, "I told you it was a scam. There's ain't nothing in that box they brung. I checked it! It's empty as your head. You ain't never been lucky enough to win nothin'!"

"Ah, shut up, Ma," Norbert replied, shuffling along as Dirk led him toward the pickup.

Savannah wondered where the woman had found antique, pink, foam hair curlers. She wondered how old that chenille robe was. She wondered if every time Norbert had abused one of his elderly female victims he had been thinking of his mommy.

But there was something else that piqued her curiosity even more.

29

She had to ask.

Turning to Mother Weyerhauser, she said, "I have to know . . . who was the first person to call him 'Stumpy'? Was it you?"

"Hell no." The cigarette, stuck to her lower lip, bobbed up and down a couple of times. "It was that idiot bimbo that he dropped out of high school to marry. She started calling him that right before she divorced him. I've always called him 'Norbert.' "

Savannah gave Dirk a big smirk as she opened the truck door and helped him tuck the bloody, grumpy Stumpy inside. "Told ya so."

# CHAPTER 2

By the time Dirk delivered Savannah back to her house, she could feel her tummy rumbling. The morning's donuts had long worn off, along with the coffee caffeine buzz. She was in serious need of nutrition, and she figured Dirk was, too.

As he pulled the pickup into her driveway, she made the generous decision to, once again, feed the bottomless human abyss.

"Wanna come in and have some lunch?" she asked him. "I made chicken and dumplings for Granny Reid."

She waited for the ecstatic response that she knew was coming. Her chicken and dumplings were world renowned — both her grandmother's and Dirk's all-time favorite. Granny had been heard to say, "Savannah's gotta put a brick bat on top of the lid on that pot, or her dumplin's will just go floatin' up and out the kitchen winder."

"Uh . . . no . . . not now," Dirk replied, avoiding her eyes. "I'm not hungry."

"What? *You* not hungry? Since when?"

"I shouldn't have eaten that apple fritter earlier. I'm on a diet."

His last sentence had been mumbled, barely audible, but she had heard it. Heard, but not believed it.

"You? On a diet? Lord, help us all. First global warming and now *this?*"

Instantly, Dirk donned his sullen face. "I don't want to talk about it."

"Oh, we're going to talk about it. We are *so* going to talk about it. Since when did you ever —"

"Shut up, woman," he said, but he was grinning. It was the only thing that kept him from getting his jaws smacked. "Or I'll fly into a blind rage."

"You in a blind rage? Now *that* I believe. But you denying yourself food . . . free food . . . no way."

"This discussion's over. Hop out. I've got places to go."

"Oh, you do not." She sniffed. "You have no life. You have to have a life before you have places to go."

He shot her another mischievous grin, leaned over, and gave her a quick peck on the cheek. "Thanks for the help with

Stumpy. I'll call you later."

"Yeah . . . okay," she said, one eyebrow raised, as she grabbed her purse and climbed out of the pickup.

"Tell Granny, 'hi' for me," he shouted through the open window as he pulled out of the driveway. "I'll come see her tomorrow."

"Uh-huh."

Savannah watched, her arms folded over her chest, as he drove away.

She was still mulling over the mystery of a dieting Dirk as she walked up the sidewalk to the quaint, Spanish-style house that had been her home for years.

The stucco could use some fresh paint, and a couple of the red, clay roof tiles had been loosened during the spring storms, but she loved her home and usually felt a twinge of satisfaction every time she walked up the path to her front door.

But today she didn't notice the sun shining on the marigolds and nasturtiums in their beds or the bougainvillea that arched across her porch. Even her adrenaline rush from catching a bad guy was squelched.

Although she was reluctant to admit it, she was basically a nosy person who liked to know what was going on with the people around her. And having someone in her inner circle behaving unpredictably was particularly irksome for her.

And a non-eating Dirk was as unpredictable and irksome as it got.

She opened the front door, walked inside, and tossed her purse and keys onto a piecrust table in the foyer. And after placing her gun on an upper closet shelf and hanging up her jacket, she walked into the living room.

Instantly, she was greeted by her entourage . . . more of her inner circle.

Two enormous black cats bounded off the windowsills and began to twine themselves around her ankles, rubbing their faces against her legs and purring.

"Hi, Cleopatra, Diamante," she said, stroking first one silky head and then the other. "Did you miss Momma?"

"Hi! How did it go?" asked a beautiful, young blonde woman who was sitting at a rolltop desk on the other side of the room. "Did you catch him? Did he try to run away? Hey, you've got mud on your slacks. Did you have to tackle him, take him down? Was it fun?"

Savannah smiled at her — as always, just enjoying the pure, golden sunlight that was her friend and assistant, Tammy Hart.

"Yes, sweet pea," she said, scooping Cleopatra into her arms and nuzzling her, "to all of the above."

Long ago, Savannah had made a conscious decision to stop being envious of Tammy's youth, her effervescence, her svelte figure and teeny-weeny hiney. After all, having such a bundle of positive energy in her life was a blessing. Savannah knew that it was Tammy who kept her young and infused with boundless joy.

The kid's size-zero butt — the decision not to envy *that* took daily reaffirming.

"Anything new?" Savannah asked, setting Cleo on the floor and picking up Diamante. "Any messages?"

"Just your granny. Her plane left a couple of hours late. She's due to arrive at seven fifteen."

"Tarnation. I was hoping I could get her back here in time for supper."

Tammy looked confused. "But you can make it back from LAX by eight thirty or nine if traffic's good."

"Gran has supper at four thirty and is in bed, reading her Bible and her *True Informer* by seven."

"Oh, right." Tammy looked down at the mud on Savannah's slacks. "Did Stumpy run very far before you caught him?"

Savannah smiled as she set Di onto the

35

floor beside her sister. "No, not far at all. His shorts were around his ankles. You can't exactly make tracks very fast that way."

Tammy was amazed. "They fell down?"

"With a little help." Savannah thought of Norbert Weyerhauser in all his glory and shuddered. "I think I'll go take a long, hot bubble bath. You know . . . wash the 'Stumpiness' off me."

As Savannah headed up the stairs, it occurred to her that maybe she should do a bit of extra housecleaning before her grandmother arrived. But the sheets on the bed in the guestroom were fresh, and she'd be sure to place a cut rose in the bud vase on the nightstand and some Godiva truffles in the candy dish on the dresser.

It didn't take much to make Gran feel at home.

Besides, although Granny Reid was an immaculate housekeeper herself, she was far too kind a soul to notice anybody else's dust. And if she did, being a genteel southern lady, she would never mention it.

"I'm comin' to see you, Savannah girl, not your dirt," had been the mantra, years ago when apologies were made and housecleaning was higher on Savannah's list of life priorities. Now "basically sanitary" and "moderately tidy" were her only standards.

Savannah's heart warmed at the thought of seeing her beloved Gran, the woman who had always been grandmother, mother, mentor, and best friend to her.

And as Savannah drew herself a hot bath in the Victorian, clawfoot tub and added a generous amount of jasmine essential oil to it, she checked the rose bubble bath to make sure there was enough to last for Gran's two-week visit.

Floral scented baths were imprinted on the Reid girls' DNA, along with a love of chocolate, romance novels, and silky, feminine undies.

But no sooner had Savannah lit the votive candles, pulled the shade down on the window, and settled into the blissful, fragrant warmth of the bath than her cell phone rang.

She glanced at the slacks she had left hanging on a hook on the back of the door and scowled. They continued to play an irritating, frenetic version of "La Cucharacha" — a tune she had chosen for Dirk.

No particular reason. But the song annoyed her and so did he, so it had seemed appropriate.

"Dadgummit!" she said, hauling herself out of the tub and splashing jasmine-scented water onto the floor as she slipped and slid her way on the wet tile over to the door.

She snatched the phone out of her pants' pocket, flipped it open, and said, "You know, I never really liked you all that much."

"You do, too."

"I'll have you know I'd just gotten into a nice, hot bath and —"

"So, you're naked?"

She snapped the cell phone closed and returned to the tub. But she kept the phone in her hand.

Dirk never gave up that easily.

The moment she was settled back in the tub, the phone rang again.

"Would you leave me alone?" she said. "I have to drive to LAX and pick up Gran in a few hours, and this is the only time I can relax and —"

"Then you don't want a piece of this?"

"A piece of what? You've got nothing good to offer me. You're dieting, remember?"

"A piece of a homicide case."

She sat up so abruptly that her bath water nearly splashed over the edge of the tub.

"Really?"

"Yeah, and not your usual gang or drug shooting, either. This one's up on Lincoln Ridge."

"No way!"

Savannah closed her eyes for a moment and mentally scanned the row of mansions that were perched atop the seaside cliff. Lincoln Ridge overlooked not only the ocean, but the picturesque Pacific coastline stretching for miles in both directions.

At least three famous actors, one rock star, and a dot-com mogul lived there, along with other assorted celebrities and high-society darlings.

"Who's dead?" she asked.

"Maria Wellman."

"That quack, diet-doctor dude's wife?"

"Who said he's a quack?"

"Anybody who says that all you have to do is listen to his CD one time and the fat will just melt right off you . . . that's a quack."

There was a long silence on the other end. Then: "Well . . . he might not be a quack. It might work."

"Holy cow, you bought one of his CDs."

"Did not."

"Did, too. There's no way you'd sound that disappointed unless you plunked down hard cash for that crap."

"You wanna go out to the scene with me? Or do you want to sit there, soaking in your bathtub, and feel superior to everybody else?"

"Just the people who bought that stupid CD." She chuckled. "All right. I'll drive myself, in case I have to leave before you do and go pick up Gran."

He told her the address.

"I'll be there in ten minutes," she said. "I have to get dressed."

"Don't go to all that trouble just for me."

She snapped the phone closed.

"I want to live on Lincoln Ridge," Savannah muttered to herself as she guided her '65 Mustang up the steep, narrow road toward the top of the cliff. "I want a view like this, and a mansion like one of those, and plenty of staff to keep it clean. And I want to lie on a satin chaise lounge in a peignoir and eat bon-bons all the live long day."

Although she wasn't certain whether bon-bons were pieces of chocolate or ice cream, she was pretty sure she wouldn't mind taking up bon-bon eating as an occupation.

But then, she reconsidered and decided she liked her own little house and didn't mind sitting in her comfy chair, wearing a T-shirt and jeans and eating Hershey Kisses, either.

Life was pretty good, if you decided it

was . . . even without a mansion and bon-bons.

And when she rounded a curve and saw an array of police cruisers, their lights flashing, parked in front of the Wellmans' mansion, she decided she didn't envy everybody in this neighborhood. Not at all. Having eight cop cars and a dozen policemen outside your door was never a good thing.

As she parked the Mustang and got out, several of the patrolmen gave her nods, waves, and other greetings. Savannah had always been well liked by her fellow law enforcement officers. The San Carmelita PD brass . . . not so much. Before they had fired her years ago, she'd had a love-hate relationship with them. After the canning, it was pure hate-hate.

Solving a murder case, exposing the dark, dirty secrets of your town's top officials, and ruining their lives — it could wreck your career every time.

As she approached the imposing, contemporary house with its odd, sharp angles and strangely pitched roof, she squinted and wished she were wearing her sunglasses. The exterior of the mansion was a blinding white, reflecting the late afternoon sunlight. And, although many of the homes in this area were surrounded by mature, lush plant-

41

ings, this house had hardly any foliage to soften its stark appearance.

Savannah thought of her giant, twin bougainvilleas that framed her doorway — named Bogey and Ilsa — and decided again that, humble as it might be, she did prefer her own home.

Near the door, she spotted Dirk. He was haranguing a couple of subordinates and, therefore, never looked happier. When he glanced her way, she gave him a finger-waggling wave and a flirty grin, and in return she got a curt nod.

Dirk wasn't one to be mushy in front of the guys.

As he turned his back on them and walked toward her, she saw the poisoned-dart looks they gave him and cringed. She would have been crestfallen to be on the receiving end of those looks.

Dirk didn't give a dang. He only needed to hold up two fingers to count the people he deigned to impress. No doubt, Granny Reid would be his pointing finger . . . Savannah the middle.

And Savannah considered that most appropriate.

Glancing at his watch, he said, "Hey, you really did make it in ten." He looked her up and down with lasciviousness that was

42

minimized due to the close proximity of other "manly men." "Did you take time to dry off?"

"Dried off and put on fresh undies. I don't do that for just anybody, you know."

He grinned. Sometimes he couldn't help himself.

"Lucky me," he said. Turning toward the house, he added, "Wanna see the body?"

Just to irritate him, she laced her arm through his and half-cuddled up to him. Ten pairs of eyes shifted their way and a few of the fellows snickered. "Of course I want to see the body," she murmured, leaning her head close to his, as though whispering sweet nothings. "You don't think I rushed over here to see *your* body, do you?"

She expected him to squirm and maybe even blush a little as, one by one, every cop on the scene turned to watch them. All were wide-eyed, and a couple had their mouths hanging open. But instead, he laughed, a big, hearty, deep-throated laugh that — on a day when she wasn't mad at him about something — she had to admit was pretty darned sexy.

"I know what you're trying to do," he whispered as they walked toward the front of the house. "You're trying to ruin my reputation as a hard ass."

"Don't you worry, darlin'," she said. "These boys know you, through and through. They'll always think of you as an ass."

"Gee. Thanks." He thought it over for a moment. "But a *hard* ass?"

She shrugged. "Eh."


When Dirk led her into the Wellman mansion, Savannah stepped three feet into the foyer and stood quietly for a moment as she looked around her and reevaluated her Life-contentment Level.

"Okay," she said. "Never mind."

"What?" Dirk asked.

"I've reconsidered. I *do* want to be rich when I grow up. This is awesome."

Here, too, everything was painted a stark white, but the beveled glass in the double doors and sidelights cast rainbow prisms around the walls, giving the massive entry life and color. Some giant palms grew from a red mahogany vase in the center of the room, a container that was at least five feet tall.

Savannah decided that she needed a five-foot vase in the middle of her living room. What a conversation piece that would be!

The vaulted ceiling soared three stories high. And to the right, a graceful, floating staircase with clear, Lucite treads, wound upward, looking like an immense DNA molecule.

And straight ahead, Savannah could see through the house and its floor-to-ceiling windows to the ocean.

With the afternoon sunlight glittering on the water and the rows of lacy white foam lining up to wash ashore, the Pacific was a living postcard, advertising the glory of sunny Southern California.

The house had been designed to create a sense of being one with that grandeur.

"I love this," she told Dirk. "You'd feel like a mermaid, living here."

He gave the house a dismissive wave and grunted. "Too big," he said. "Too much to clean."

She shot him a sideways look. "Oh, right. It would just plum wear you to a frazzle, scrubbing this place the way you do that trailer of yours . . . once every year or two."

He grinned. "Whether it needs it or not."

When they walked into the living room, Savannah saw more mahogany vases filled with palms, and cubist leather furniture in white, black, and red — but no occupants.

"Where's the family?" she asked.

"It's just the husband. He wanted to go upstairs and make some phone calls. I told him he could."

"How did he seem?"

Dirk shrugged. "Shaking like a cold, wet dog. Seemed more scared than sad."

"He did it. Woman gets murdered . . . you look at the intimate partner."

"You always say that."

"And I'm usually right."

He opened his mouth to reply, then closed it.

Savannah chuckled. Dirk wasn't one to argue when he knew he couldn't win, and the statistics were on her side.

"Through here," he said as he led her to a set of glass doors that opened onto a patio area.

When they walked outside, the smell of the salt air and the warmth of the sunlight washed over her. Normally, Savannah would have closed her eyes, at least for a moment, and soaked in the healing peace of it all. But today, in this place, the peace had been broken. Even the sea's essential tranquility couldn't counteract the sense that something nearby was terribly wrong.

"She's down there," he said, pointing to a set of stone stairs that started at the cliff's edge and descended to the beach.

Savannah headed down the steps, taking her time, because they were fairly steep, and

46

there was no handrail. Dirk followed close behind.

She could feel him tensing, but she knew better than to say anything. Dirk had a pronounced fear of heights. Even a stepladder presented a challenge to his phobic psyche. These stairs had to be a nightmare for him.

"This cliff's gotta be seventy feet high," he said, sounding slightly breathless.

She thought it was probably more like forty or fifty, but she could understand why it seemed a lot higher to him. And she was relieved for him when they finally reached the bottom and stepped onto the sand.

She looked to her left and braced herself, as she always did at times like these. The Grim Reaper's handiwork was seldom pretty and always unsettling, even when the passing was the result of natural causes. But a death under unnatural circumstances was the most unsettling of all. And something told her that Mrs. Wellman probably didn't suffer a stroke or heart attack and tumble down the cliff.

Instinctively Savannah knew that, at the very least, this was a tragic accident. Maybe worse.

But, looking northward, she saw nothing but the beach, more cliffs, and more luxury homes stretching into the misty distance.

"Over here," Dirk said, heading toward the right and a rocky area, where the sea washed among the stones and receded, leaving tide pools filled with anemones and seaweed.

Savannah took a moment to reach down and roll up the hems of her linen slacks. Her loafers would be soaked, but her pants didn't have to be.

She also paused to note the tracks in the sand where she stood. One set of prints, made by bare feet, led from the water's edge toward the rocks. Another matching set headed from the rocks back to the beach. She wasn't surprised to see that the return prints were deeper and not as cleanly defined. It looked like their maker had been running.

The other two sets, stretching from the stairs to the stones, she would recognize anywhere. They were Dirk's running sneakers.

He did more sneaking than running in them, but they had a distinctive tread that she had seen many times at crime scenes throughout the years.

"I see you've been down here a couple of times, already," she said as she caught up to him.

"Yeah." He glanced back at the sand, at his prints. "If I ever commit any sort of felony, I'll have to buy some new shoes, or you'll nail me."

He stretched out his hand to her, to help her balance as she stepped onto the rocks.

"Naw," she said, grabbing his hand. "I'd give you a pass."

"You would not."

"That would depend on whether you cut me in on the deal or not."

"Interesting that you assume it'd have to do with money. What if it was a crime of passion?"

"Oh, please. What . . . ripping off a donut shop?"

He looked genuinely sad. "Don't talk about food." He pointed toward a particularly large rock. "She's over there. Behind that one."

They walked in that direction, and Savannah could smell the body before she saw it.

While decomposition might be a perfectly natural and altogether necessary function of nature, Savannah didn't have to even pretend to like it. And it was the memory of the stench, rather than the visuals, that haunted her when she thought back over the bodies she had viewed.

She couldn't help being just a bit relieved

when she saw that Dirk had covered the corpse with a yellow tarp. It was nice to see a bit at a time, as you chose to, rather than getting hit with the whole effect at once.

She walked up to the tarp and pulled back one corner to find she was looking at a leg, and a foot wearing a jeweled, designer high heel with an ankle strap. Flipping the tarp back a bit more, she saw the dead woman was wearing its mate on the other foot.

Glancing at the imposing cliff above them, Savannah said, "Wow, that long fall and she managed to keep both shoes on."

"How do you know for sure that she fell off the cliff?"

"Her shoes have four-inch heels. It would have been really hard to walk down those stairs wearing them. Besides, they cost a fortune, even for her budget. No woman wears her best heels to the beach to get all gritty and wet. She's a beach girl, living here on the water. She would have changed her shoes or come down here barefoot."

"Hm-m-m . . . that's what I figured, too."

*Yeah, sure you did,* Savannah thought, *Mr. Expert on Women's High-Fashion Footwear.* But she kept her mouth shut. She had to limit how many times she pissed him off in the course of a day. A pissy Dirk was not a thing of beauty.

"What's the body like?" she asked.

"Actually," Dirk said, pulling back the rest of the tarp, "she's in pretty good shape, considering she's outside and it's the beach. No crabs yet."

"Good. I might sleep tonight after all."

As he uncovered the face, she realized she had spoken too fast. The crabs might not have found the body yet, but the insects had. And while the coroner, Dr. Jennifer Liu, would find the degree and phases of infestation all quite fascinating and helpful in her investigation, Savannah could do without it.

But, as always, she pushed the horror to the back of her mind and switched into an analytical, professional mode.

She squatted beside the body and studied what she could see without touching or moving anything.

Even with the smears of blood on her face, it was obvious the dead woman was wearing heavy evening makeup. And her blonde hair was styled in a formal updo, which was slightly askew, but still in place, thanks to copious amounts of hair spray.

"She's got a head wound," Savannah said, staring at a nasty gash on the side of her forehead.

"Yeah, I saw that." He knelt on one knee

next to her. "In the temple area like that, it could have been a fatal blow."

"It's clean, no dirt in it." She looked up at the cliff that was more sand than rock, and added, "It doesn't really look like a scrape . . . or like she smacked it coming down. She might have gotten it before she fell."

"Yeah, that's what I was thinking."

She resisted the urge to give him a smack of his own. "Did you notice that the sun's shining today, too?" she asked.

"What?"

She sighed. "Never mind."

He uncovered the rest of the body, revealing a beautiful, full-length evening gown made of black, shantung silk. A thousand hand-sewn beads accented the front and the waistband.

The woman would have blended in nicely on the red carpet at the Academy Awards.

"Wow," Savannah said. "She was dressed . . . uh . . . fit to kill."

"Yeah, the husband said they went to a charity ball last night."

"There's just one thing."

"What's that?"

"She isn't wearing any jewelry. No earrings. A woman doesn't dress up like that and go out without even a pair of earrings in her pierced ears."

"Okay, if you say so. Maybe it was a robbery."

"We'll have to ask the husband about the jewelry. What time does he say they left the party?"

"He said they came home separately. She had a headache and left early, around nine thirty. He stayed until nearly midnight."

"How did she get home?"

"She drove their car. He took a cab."

"And was she here when he got home?"

"No. He says the car was here, but he couldn't find her in the house or the yard."

"When did he report her missing?"

"He didn't. A jogger on the beach found her about noon today and called it in."

Savannah glanced over at the barefoot prints leading from the water to the body, then back in the direction they came.

"And you were the first to respond?"

"Yeah. And it's a good thing, too, or those morons up there would have come down here and trampled all over the scene."

"Oh, come on. Not all of those handsome young patrolmen are dummies."

He bristled.

So she said, "You've taught them how to respect a crime scene."

He unbristled.

Grinning, she added, "By yelling obsceni-ties, verbally abusing them, and threatening them with great bodily harm."

He snorted. "Somebody's gotta do it."

Dirk's cell phone rang. He dug it out of his jacket pocket and answered it in his usual gracious, loquacious manner. "Yeah, what?"

She considered nominating him for poet laureate.

"All right. Come through the house to the backyard and down the stairs. We're with the body here on the beach."

He hung up. "Dr. Liu," he explained. "They're here."

Savannah looked down at the body on the rocks and felt a little sense of relief, as she always did, that the coroner and Crime Scene Unit had arrived to take over.

No matter how many times she did it, dealing with a corpse at the scene was always difficult. It was the hardest part of any investigation. Except for one other thing.

She took a deep, steadying breath. "You think the husband's finished with his phone calls?"

"Whether he is or not, I gotta talk to him again," Dirk said, his face reflecting the dread she felt.

Because, the only thing worse than dealing with the remains of a person who had passed on . . . was dealing with the loved ones who had been left behind.

# CHAPTER 3

As Savannah and Dirk left the beach and started to climb the stone steps, Savannah looked up and saw a beautiful Asian woman descending the stairs. Her long, glossy black hair spilled around her shoulders, and the snug, black miniskirt she was wearing seemed strangely at odds with her boxy, white, lab coat.

She had exquisitely shaped, long legs, and she was wearing what appeared to be stainless steel, four-inch-high stilettos.

"Okay, I stand corrected," Savannah said over her shoulder to Dirk. "You *can* walk down these stairs wearing super-high heels."

But when she glanced backward, she saw that Dirk had barely heard what she'd said. He was transfixed on the sight above him, and she couldn't summon even an ounce of indignation about his ill-mannered ogling.

Dr. Jennifer Liu, San Carmelita's first female coroner, was simply stunning.

"Hey, Dr. Jen," Savannah greeted her as they met halfway up the stairs. "You're lookin' perky today."

"Hi, Savannah," Dr. Liu returned warmly. "Haven't seen you lately. You haven't dropped by with a box of Godivas in a long time."

Savannah chuckled. It was true. More than once, when she was anxious to get autopsy results, she had taken a box of truffles to the morgue under the pretext of "PMS bonding."

Dr. Liu was far too sharp to believe that the offerings were anything more than an excuse to drop by and finagle information before the coroner's report was complete. But she was also smart enough not to admit she was being bribed.

Savannah would do anything to learn the official cause and manner of death three hours before the murder was even committed. And if five pounds of chocolate enabled her to make a pest out of herself and get the jump on a case, she wasn't above it.

Besides, Dr. Liu usually shared the goodies, and that was endearing.

"Sergeant Coulter," the coroner said, giving Dirk a cursory nod.

Dirk was as much of a nuisance at the morgue as Savannah, even worse. And he never brought chocolate, so he was low on Dr. Liu's list of favorite people.

They never brought out the best in each other.

"The DB's down there," Dirk told her, pointing down the stairs and to the right. "You need me to go with you and help you find it?"

She gave him a withering look. "I can find one stray blond hair on a brunette victim or a single carpet fiber and match it to a killer's car trunk. I think I can find a dead woman on a beach."

"Then she's all yours," Dirk said, brushing by her and continuing on up the stairs.

He passed a couple of young men, also wearing white lab coats with the coroner's seal printed on the pockets, who were on their way down. He grunted a half greeting to them as he hurried by. They nearly fell off the steps trying to get out of his way.

"Mr. Sunshine and Light," Dr. Liu grumbled as she watched him go. "I don't know how you stand him."

"Ah, Dirk's all right," Savannah said, thinking that, sometimes, it felt like she spent her life trying to convince people that Dirk really *was* a good person. After all, any guy who liked dogs, cats, and Elvis couldn't be all bad. "You just have to get to know him," she added for good measure.

"No, thanks." Dr. Liu gave Savannah a smile. "Putting up with him, that's *your* job. And mine is waiting on the beach, so . . . I'll see you later."

"How long you figure it'll take you to process her?" Savannah asked as Dr. Liu continued down the stairs.

"We're a little backed up. I should be done with the autopsy by tomorrow around lunch time." When she reached the bottom step, she leaned over and took her high heels off.

Too bad Dirk had missed it, Savannah thought. He was a major hiney man.

"So, if you'll be done by noon," Savannah said, "I'll show up at ten . . . and bring chocolates?"

"Exactly." Dr. Liu stuffed the stilettos into her bag and stepped onto the sand with bare feet, her toenails painted bright red. "And this time, don't eat any of the raspberry creams. Those are my favorites."

When Savannah reached the top of the stairs, she looked around for Dirk. He was standing at the edge of the yard, where the lawn ended abruptly, giving way to the sharp cliff.

He was staring down at a flower bed that was overflowing with yellow marigolds and

59

orange nasturtiums.

"See something?" she asked as she walked up to stand beside him.

So lost in thought was he that he jumped a little when he noticed her. "What?"

"You're looking at something. What is it?"

"Why doesn't she like me?" he asked, looking a little hurt.

"Why doesn't who . . . what?"

"Why doesn't Dr. Liu like me? I've always been nice to her."

"You've never been nice to her. Not once."

"Never? Ever?" He looked completely flummoxed. "Really?"

"Really. You snap at her. You're surly with her. You demand that she come up with results in the blink of an eye and solve your cases for you. You —"

"So do you."

"Yeah, but I genuinely like her."

"So do I."

"You like her legs."

"I never noticed her legs." He grinned broadly. "I'm always too busy looking at her rear."

Savannah sighed and pointed to the flower bed. "What's here? What were you looking at?"

But before he could even answer, she saw it . . . the area where the marigolds and nasturtiums were crushed, the soil trampled with numerous footprints.

She stepped closer and squatted, studying the dirt and flowers. "There was a struggle here. And those are fresh," she said. "The broken plants are barely even withered. And the footprints are clear, nice and deep."

"Yeah, I'll have to tell Dr. Liu to have her lazy-ass assistants get up here and get some castings of those to —"

Savannah cleared her throat.

"Um . . ." He donned a saccharine smile. ". . . I mean, ask the CSU if they would be so kind as to get their lazy butts up here and take some castings of those prints, and then get the results to me whenever they damned well feel like it."

"Oh, much better." She rolled her eyes. "It's a beautiful thing — watching personal growth in progress."

"What?"

"Never mind." Leaning down, until her face was nearly touching the flowers, she saw something strange sticking out of the loose soil. It was about six inches wide and looked like a gray butterfly's wing.

With one finger she pushed some of the nasturtiums aside and saw that it was attached to a fairy . . . or rather, a broken fairy statue, about a foot long, that was half-buried in the dirt.

"You'll want to tell the team about this," she said, pointing it out to him. "That thing looks heavy enough that it might even be your murder weapon."

He studied it with interest and nodded. "Yeap, that would be a first in my career. 'Cause of Death: Bludgeoned by a Tinkerbell.' "

She stood up and shook her legs to restore circulation.

Squatting in your forties wasn't what it was in your twenties.

"And, by the way," she said. "Those are high-heel prints . . . the little holes there in the dirt."

"Yeah, I noticed that already."

"And Mrs. Wellman had dark soil like that on the heels of her shoes."

"Yeap. Saw it."

She bit her bottom lip and stared at him long and hard. "And the blood? You also saw the blood stain on her left heel?"

She had him. He glared at her, slack-jawed for several long moments. She watched the mental battle register in his eyes. Lie? Or tell the truth?

Finally, with his best poker face and most even, noncommittal tone, he said, "Blood. Blood on her left heel."

"Yeap."

More tense silence.

He broke. "You saw blood on her left heel?"

"Naw." She turned to walk back toward the house. "I was just messin' with you."

"I hate you."

She laughed. "No, you don't. I'm the best friend you've got."

"And what a sorry commentary *that* is on my social life."

By the time they walked into the house, Dirk had stopped complaining, and Savannah had put aside all thoughts of teasing him.

Few things were more important than tormenting Dirk, but talking to the deceased person's family — who also just happened to be your primary suspect — was one of those things.

Neither of them wanted to have to draw Dr. Wellman out of his bedroom seclusion at a time like this, but it had to be done.

After examining the body and the edge of the cliff, they were both pretty certain that Mrs. Wellman hadn't simply taken one step too many while strolling around her backyard in the dark. She had fought for her life before being pushed to her death.

And that meant they were looking for a killer.

But as they entered the living room, they heard voices. Angry voices. A man's and a woman's.

The two were arguing in an adjoining room, so loudly that Savannah and Dirk could hear everything they were saying.

"I want my money," the female was saying, "and if I don't get it, I'm going to make a lot of trouble for you."

"You've already made trouble for me," he replied. "You're nothing *but* trouble."

"When am I getting it? When?"

"I can't believe you're hassling me at a time like this."

"Oh, yeah, you're just heartbroken. I'm sure. Give me a break. Like you give a damn that she's dead. You're probably happy. You probably did it yourself, just to —"

"Shut up! Shut your mouth! You say something like that with the cops right outside my door? What's wrong with you?"

"I'll say a hell of a lot more than that if you don't have my money to me by this time tomorrow. I mean it. If you don't believe me, you just wait and see."

They heard quick, heavy footsteps as someone stomped through the house, away from them and toward the front door.

Savannah rushed past Dirk, heading for the foyer, trying to step as quietly as possible.

She was just in time to see an extremely thin young woman with lots of curly blonde hair, rush to the front door, jerk it open, and leave the house.

Mostly, Savannah had seen her backside, but she was fairly sure she'd know her if she saw her again. Even in a culture where being stick skinny was the primary measure of a female's worth, this one was exceptionally scrawny. Her tight jeans had displayed thighs that weren't much thicker than Savannah's forearm.

Savannah hurried to the beveled glass sidelight and looked through it to the front yard. The blonde darted back and forth among the patrolmen, making her way to a little blue compact parked on the side of the road.

As she sped away, Savannah caught the first three letters of the license plate. PLW. She pulled a notebook and ballpoint from her jacket pocket and scribbled down the letters.

Replacing the pad and pen, she turned, intending to rejoin Dirk in the living room. But, instead, she found herself face-to-face with the man of the house.

And Dr. Wellman didn't look happy to see her.

He was red haired with a ruddy complexion and a thin, auburn mustache, dressed in a violet polo shirt and sharply creased, beige slacks. His cheeks were brightly flushed, and he was sweating profusely, considering that the house was a comfortable temperature.

*That must have been a heck of an argument,* Savannah thought. Or was it all because his wife's dead body had been found at the foot of his cliff?

She thought it over for a moment, then decided that he looked more mad than sad. And that little bit of info she would scribble in her mental notepad, to be considered later.

"Who the hell are you?" he asked her. His eyes were narrowed and intense, but his tone was slightly shaky.

"Her name is Savannah Reid," said a deep, authoritative voice behind them . . . without a bit of shakiness. "And she's with me."

Dirk walked into the room and stood beside Savannah, hands on his hips, his best Clint Eastwood scowl on his face. And it was a pretty good face, because he practiced it regularly in his rearview mirror when he was supposed to be driving — much to

Savannah's consternation as his frequent passenger.

She chuckled inwardly. She didn't exactly need his protection from the good doctor in his purple shirt, but she appreciated the thought.

"Did you find . . . um . . . the body?" Wellman asked Dirk. "Was it where the jogger said it was?"

"Yes, it was," Dirk replied.

"And is she . . . I mean . . . is it for sure that she's . . . ?"

"Yes." Dirk softened his tone a bit and added, "I'm sorry."

Savannah watched closely as something that truly looked like grief flitted across Wellman's face. But it was gone in a heartbeat, replaced by the stony stare that was giving her the creeps.

In some ways, it was more disconcerting, this lack of emotion, than the more common outpouring of sorrow.

"How did she die?" the doctor asked. "Did she fall off the cliff?"

"She definitely fell off the cliff," Savannah said. "We don't know yet exactly *why* she fell."

Dirk cleared his throat. "Doctor, the last time you saw your wife, was she intoxicated?"

Wellman shrugged. "She'd had a glass of wine during dinner. And maybe a couple more between dances."

"How many people would you say attended the ball last night?" Savannah asked.

"Oh, a hundred. Maybe more."

"Did your wife spend her time talking to any one person in particular?"

"Not really. She was quite comfortable in social settings. She liked to flit around the room, visiting with first one, then the other. I didn't notice her talking to anybody special . . . other than me, of course."

"Of course," Dirk said.

"I know this is a difficult question," Savannah said, "but, to your knowledge, was anyone upset with your wife? Did she have any enemies that might wish her harm?"

He hesitated and glanced away, looking through the house to the rear windows and beyond that, to the cliff edge. "No, not really. Maria had a temper and spoke her mind, and that didn't exactly endear her to some people. But nobody hated her enough to do something like that."

"I beg to differ with you," Dirk said, watching the man closely, studying every nuance of the doctor's facial expression, tone of voice, and body language. "It takes a lot of hate to push somebody off a cliff to

68

their death."

Dr. Wellman stared at Dirk for a long moment, then at Savannah, his eyes searching theirs. And Savannah could feel a deep, gut-shaking fear radiating out of him.

"And that's what you think happened?" he asked.

Savannah nodded. "Yes. I'm sorry."

"It couldn't have been an accident?"

"We don't think so."

Savannah waited for him to adjust to the news before she asked, "Dr. Wellman, your wife was dressed beautifully for the party. Can you tell me if she was wearing any jewelry?"

"Yes! She was wearing a sapphire and diamond necklace and earrings that she'd rented from a jewelry shop on Rodeo Drive. Don't tell me they're gone!"

"I'm afraid so."

"And her wedding ring? She had a beautiful princess cut stone. I paid a fortune for it."

Savannah shook her head. "I'm sorry, but she wasn't wearing any jewelry at all."

"Oh, man, that store's going to come after me for that stuff. I can't afford to pay for it. You'd better find it!"

"We'll do what we can," Dirk told him. "I'll inform all the local pawn shops and jewelry stores to be on the lookout for it."

Savannah noted that Wellman seemed even more perturbed by the loss of the jewels than by the loss of his wife. But then, you could never really tell. Some people displayed their emotions quite differently from others.

A lengthy, tense silence was broken by the jingling of a merry tune, coming from the vicinity of the front of Wellman's slacks. He stiffened, started to reach into his pocket, then stopped himself.

Again, he wouldn't meet their eyes but fixated on the ocean view, as he shifted from one foot to the other.

The song became louder and louder.

"You can get that if you want," Dirk said with a grin that was half a challenge. "We don't mind waiting."

"It's okay," Wellman snapped.

Discreetly, Savannah glanced down at her watch and noted the time: 5:46 P.M.

No sooner had the phone stopped ringing than it started again, the same ringtone.

"Somebody really wants to talk to you," Dirk said. "You might want to pick it up. Could be important."

This time Wellman dug his hand into his pocket and took out the phone. But instead of answering it, he turned it off.

"I'm a doctor," he said, clearly annoyed and more than a little nervous. "I get nuisance calls all the time."

"And what sort of doctor are you?" Savannah asked. Of course, she knew, but she was hoping to irritate him further.

One of her favorite theories was that an irritated person was more likely to show you who they really were. So, long ago, she had decided to irritate people as quickly and as often as possible.

As Granny had frequently told her: "You don't really know a person till you've had 'em mad at ya."

And the doctor was getting madder by the second. His already ruddy face flushed a few shades brighter. She could have sworn his mustache turned a bit redder. "I'm surprised you don't know who I am," he said, lifting his shoulders and puffing out his chest. "I've been on several national talk shows lately."

Savannah shrugged. "Sorry. I don't watch a lot of daytime television. What's your specialty?"

He gave her a pointed and lingering look up and down her figure. Then, in a voice thick with contempt, he said, "I specialize in weight loss."

Giving him a bright smile, she quickly

replied, "Ah, no wonder you can afford a house like this. The world's just full of folks who worry themselves sick over nonsense like that."

"But apparently not *all* people," he replied, again looking her up and down.

She continued to give him a broad, wooden smile. But her blue eyes had a cold fire in them. "Some of us are just lucky that way, I suppose."

"Lucky?"

"Yes. Lucky. Self love is a rare commodity in this day and age. What with everybody telling us we're not worth a tinker's dam unless we're all a certain size, shape, or color."

"How about you?" Dirk said, stepping a little closer to Wellman. "You got any personal enemies who'd wish you harm? Anybody who might hurt your wife to get even with you?"

"Yes."

Savannah's eyebrows rose a notch. An investigator seldom got an affirmative to that question. Most people who had true honest-to-goodness enemies — not just your average pissed off relatives, friends, and neighbors — had done something to deserve them. And they usually didn't welcome the chance to talk about it.

"I have one guy in particular who's been threatening me lately," he continued.

"And who is that?" Dirk got out his own notebook and started to scribble in it.

"His name is Terry Somers. He was one of my patients."

"He bought some of your CDs online, or he actually came into your office?" Savannah asked.

Wellman smiled . . . an unpleasant little smirk. "Ah, so you *do* know who I am."

Savannah returned the smile with an equal amount of unpleasantness. "Was he a patient or a customer?"

"I treated him in my office."

"Did he lose a hundred pounds instantly after the first visit?"

"I was treating him for a gambling problem. Addiction comes in all forms, you know."

"That's so true. Some people are genuinely addicted to all sorts of stuff. And they suffer because of it. I feel for them something awful." She stopped smiling. "Then there are some others who call their bad habits 'addictions' so that people won't expect them to get rid of them."

"And which are you?" the doctor asked, his jaw clenching. "Are you addicted to food, or is overeating simply one of your

73

bad habits?"

"Neither. I just like food. And, apparently, it likes me, too, or it wouldn't stick around like it does." She tossed her head, stuck out her right hip in a Mae West pose, and gave it a pat.

"So, Doctor," Dirk said, a little too eagerly, "tell me more about this Somers. What's he got against you?"

"Well, I'm really not supposed to tell you . . . doctor-patient confidentiality and all that . . ."

"Ah, spill it," Savannah said. "It's not like the people watching your infomercials are gonna lose faith in your integrity and stop buying your CDs or whatever."

Wellman's eyes flashed with anger, but he turned to Dirk and said, "Terry Somers is a degenerate gambler who's in debt to some really bad guys. He came to see me for treatment, but had a slip a week later and lost a fortune in a high-stakes poker game. He didn't pay, they broke his leg, and he's blaming *me* for it!"

Savannah gave a little half-gasp. "How *dare* him!"

"Yeah, well, you may think it's funny, but when somebody's telling you that he's going to kill you because you ruined his life, it's pretty scary stuff."

"And did Somers actually threaten to kill you?" Dirk asked. "Did he use those words?"

"No, he was a little more graphic. Told me he'd blow my brains out of my head and stomp on them. That paints quite a picture . . . made a bit of an impression on me."

Dirk scribbled away. "When did he say that?"

"Last Wednesday."

"Where?"

"In my office . . . in front of my receptionist and three other patients who were sitting in my waiting room."

"And your receptionist's name is . . . ?"

"Um . . . her name is Roxanne Rosen."

"And the names of those other three patients?"

"I can't tell you. You know, doctor-patient —"

"Yeah, yeah." Dirk closed his book and tucked it back into his pocket. "Just so you know . . . the Crime Scene Unit is processing your wife's body, the beach, your yard, and they may even want to do some work here inside the house."

"Inside my house? But why? She died out there and —"

"I'm asking you to be as cooperative as

75

possible, Dr. Wellman," Dirk replied.

Savannah could tell he was trying not to sound irked. But Dirk would never win an Oscar . . . unless it was for playing the role of a curmudgeon.

She said, "All we want is to find out what happened to your wife and who's responsible. I'm sure that's what you want, too."

"Yeah, well, you check out Terry Somers . . . find out where he was last night . . . and then you'll have her killer."

Wellman sounded so sure that Savannah nearly believed him. Nearly, but not completely.

As she and Dirk ended the interview, said good-bye to Wellman, and left the house, she decided that — degenerate, broken-legged gambler or not — the doctor was still her number one suspect. At least for the moment.

As they walked to their cars, she glanced down at her watch. "I have to go get Granny from the airport," she told him. "Her plane was late, but even at that, I have to allow for Santa Monica traffic."

"Yeah, sure. Get going. You can't keep my favorite lady waiting," he said with a sweet smile that warmed her heart.

Dirk truly loved her grandmother, and Savannah considered that one of his greatest virtues. On a bad day, it was his only virtue.

"I thought *I* was your favorite lady," she said.

"Nope." He gave her a slap on the back as he opened her car door and pushed her inside. "But you're a solid runner-up."

# CHAPTER 4

By the time Savannah battled the aggressive, harried drivers who navigated the maze that was Los Angeles International Airport, she was cranky. And by the time she fought her way through the frenetic crowds inside the terminal — getting smacked on the knee by a guitar case, wielded by a multi-tattooed, heavily pierced musician, who was running for a plane — she was crankier . . . and limping.

But the moment she saw her grandmother coming down the hallway toward her, all traces of irritation vanished.

Savannah loved her brothers and sisters, Dirk, Tammy, and her friends, Ryan and John. But she adored Gran.

And the sight of that shining bouffant of silver hair, the bright, colorful muumuu, and big, garish, matching earrings, always lifted her spirits to heaven and back.

She had no qualms about pushing businessmen aside, along with women and children, to get to her favorite person on earth.

Savannah grabbed the carry-on from Granny's hand, slung the strap over her shoulder, and then gathered her grandmother into her arms.

They hugged, laughed, and kissed as tears welled up in both women's eyes.

Savannah savored the warmth of the embrace, breathing in Granny's unique scent, a fragrance Savannah had cherished since childhood. It was a blend of a rose-based perfume, Ivory soap, and talcum powder. And for a little girl who, along with eight younger siblings, had been abandoned by her father and abused by her mother, Granny's sweet fragrance had always represented love, safety, and stability.

"Now, don't go squeezing me too tight, Savannah girl," Gran said, pulling back slightly to look up into her granddaughter's eyes — deep blue and so like her own. "I ate a big bowl of fruit salad before I got on that plane this morning, and I'll never do that again."

"What?" Savannah searched her mind but didn't get the reference.

"Let's just say . . . when you're in your eighties, you shouldn't overdo the roughage

79

when you're gonna be sittin' in close quarters with a bunch of strangers for hours."

"Ah, gotcha." Savannah laughed. "I'll roll the Mustang's windows down on the way home." She put her arm around her grandmother's shoulders and walked her slowly through the terminal, following the BAGGAGE CLAIM signs. "How was your flight?"

"I was jammed between two fellas in suits who weren't the least bit interested in making conversation."

Savannah grinned. She wasn't at all surprised. Gran could talk the hind leg off a donkey, and most airline passengers weren't fascinated by her tips on growing prize-winning roses or her life philosophy.

"Their loss," Savannah said with heartfelt sincerity.

"They was both messin' with their computers. One was playing solitaire and the other was watchin' a dirty movie. My neck's plum sore from having to turn my head for two hours."

"Didn't want to miss a minute of it, huh?" Savannah nudged her.

She poked back. "Darn tootin'."

They walked a little farther.

Savannah cleared her throat. "So . . . learn any new tricks, watching that movie?"

"Nope. Pretty much same-ol', same-ol'."

80

"Savannah, sugar, this dinner of yours was well worth the wait. If it was any tastier, I don't think I could stand it," Granny said as she popped another dumpling into her mouth, closed her eyes, and chewed, savoring the moment.

Looking around her table, Savannah counted her own blessings in the form of family and friends who had become family.

To her right was Dirk — a blessing most of the time. Or, at least, enough of the time for her not to murder him in cold blood and dispose of his body in a landfill.

Next to Dirk was Tammy, the sunlight in Savannah's life, bosom friend, and office assistant who answered her phone and paid her bills — without whom she would have no electricity or running water.

On the other side of the table sat Ryan Stone and his life partner, John Gibson.

Whenever Savannah needed a little something to "make her eyes happy," she would just look at either of them and bask in their magnificence. Ryan was the epitome of tall, suave, and handsome, with thick dark hair, muscles that showed even through his stylish clothes, and a wicked twinkle in his eyes.

A bit older, but no less gorgeous, John had hair as lush and silver as Gran's, a rich British accent, a debonair mustache, and the manner of a country gentleman. He would have looked perfectly at home riding the moors of Cornwall on a white stallion in a tweed jacket with a brace of hunting hounds.

At the other end of the table was Granny, happy and contented with her lot in life, as always — even more so, considering the chicken, dumplings, gravy, and biscuits.

And making figure eights between Savannah's ankles were Diamante and Cleopatra, purring in anticipation that someone would either drop a bite of something tasty on the floor or maybe even pass some tidbit down to them.

When Savannah's dining room was filled with her favorite people and critters, and their bellies were full of her good Southern cooking, she was a happy gal.

"Pass me that bowl of pickled cucumbers and onions," she told Dirk, "and help yourself to some more mashed potatoes and cream gravy."

He handed her the bowl, brimming with its vinegar brine and sliced cucumbers fresh from her garden, but he shook his head slightly when she offered him the gravy boat.

"No, thanks," he mumbled. "I've had enough."

"What?" Tammy nearly dropped her celery stick.

Tammy sat at the table with them frequently, but she always brought along her own stash of "real food," as she called it. She wouldn't be caught dead eating a dumpling or Savannah's chocolate-dipped, peanut butter cheesecake.

Savannah loved her dearly but would never understand her ways. The girl was just . . . well . . . strange.

*"You* have had *enough?"* Tammy said, incredulous, staring at Dirk. "You aren't groaning about how miserable you are! You haven't unsnapped your jeans yet! How can you say you've had enough?"

"Just drop it, okay?" Dirk grumbled, avoiding everybody's eyes as he gazed unhappily down at his barely used plate.

"Are you sick?" Savannah said, waving a basket of biscuits under his nose.

"I'm just trying to . . . you know . . . watch what I eat these days."

"Watch what you eat?" Savannah was as bewildered as Tammy. "You still on this diet kick? Since when do you watch what you eat? Watch it disappear off your plate maybe . . ."

"Leave the man alone," Granny said, "and if he's foolhardy enough to turn down those biscuits, sail one down the table to me! I ain't bashful."

The biscuit basket was passed down to Granny, getting lighter and lighter as it made its way from person to person along the way.

Peach preserves and butter followed in its wake.

Soon the conversation drifted toward everyone's favorite topic. And that included Gran.

As she frequently reminded them, being over eighty didn't mean a lady lost her ghoulishness.

"I can't believe Maria Wellman is dead," Ryan said. "We just saw her the other night at the ball, and she was bright-eyed and bushy-tailed."

"Bushy-eyed and bright-tailed would be more like it," John replied with a grin. "She was a lass in her cups if ever I saw one."

"Hm-m-m." Dirk thought that one over. "Wellman told us today that she hadn't drank that much."

"He let her drive home," Savannah said. "Probably didn't want you to know that she was DUI."

Dirk shrugged. "It doesn't matter now.

It's not like I'm going to arrest her."

"Still," Ryan said, "he has a bit of a reputation to uphold in the community, a medical professional and all."

"His reputation isn't all that sterling." John took a sip of his Earl Grey tea. "I met that man a year ago at the playhouse fundraiser, and I thought something was amiss with him then."

"In what way?" Dirk wanted to know.

"First of all, he was quite evasive about where he received his schooling. I wouldn't be the least bit surprised if his doctorate is in a field completely unrelated to medicine . . . assuming he has one."

"Plus," Ryan said, "his whole schtick is highly suspect, to say the least."

"Absolutely," John agreed. "He was chattering away about this spectacular weight loss program of his, telling a group of us about how listening to his CD and engaging in some sort of self-hypnosis could enable one to drop all excess weight in a matter of days."

"Without following a nutritious diet and strength-training exercise?" Tammy was scandalized.

Savannah sniffed. "The only way to lose a bunch of unwanted, excess weight without starving to death is to get a divorce. And even that takes six months here in California."

"People worry far too much about a number on a scale," John said.

Granny nodded, buttering her biscuit. "You'd think that one number was all there was to 'em. There's a gal there in McGill who's got a voice like an angel . . . fills up the church every Sunday with the pure beauty of it. But boy, she gains a pound, she's miserable. Loses a pound, she's shoutin' 'glory!' Up and down, all the time."

"And, lucky for Wellman," Dirk said, "there are lots of people out there willing to plunk down a couple hundred dollars for a quick fix. You oughta see that joint of his on the beach."

Savannah nodded. "Beautiful place. Spacious, nicely decorated, chic but comfortable. A gorgeous view." She sighed and put down her fork, suddenly a little less hungry. "All except for the dead body on the beach."

"Yeap," Granny said. "A corpse in front of your house, that'll put a damper on a party ever' last time."

After everyone had finished eating, Savannah and her guests retired to the living room for coffee and Death by Chocolate cake. It took nearly two hours for Granny to get them caught up on McGill gossip. The rural, north Georgia community had surprisingly juicy scandals for such a tiny town.

Granny was in fine form, regaling them with tales of how the mayor had been caught sneaking out the back door of the mortician's house at daybreak, when the undertaker was out of town. The librarian had been accused of dipping into the moneys collected from the annual book drive. And the chief of police had run his cruiser into a tree and totaled it — his second major accident in six months. "Hear tell he had something he shouldn't have in his coffee thermos . . . somethin' a mite stronger than coffee, if you know what I mean," Granny had said in a conspiratorial tone that made Savannah stifle a snicker.

But once the tales were told, and the coffee and cake devoured, Savannah noticed that Gran's eyelids were getting a bit heavy.

Ryan and John noticed, too.

Standing and smoothing his cream-colored wool slacks, Ryan smiled at Savannah — causing her pulse rate to go up at least twenty-five percent — and said, "We have to get going. Thank you for a lovely evening, as always."

John rose and picked up his cashmere sweater from a nearby chair. "Yes, this was positively delightful." He gave Gran a courtly kiss on the back of her hand. "As always, beautiful lady, it was a pure joy to see you."

Granny giggled, blushed, and ducked her head. "Ah, stop messin' with my heart, boy. I'm old enough to be your mother."

He leaned over and gave her a mustache-tickling peck on her cheek. "Perhaps," he said, his voice velvety, his eyes twinkling, "but you *aren't* my mother."

"Take him and those blue eyes of his home," she said to Ryan, "before I forget I'm a lady."

"Yeah," Savannah said, "this ain't McGill, Georgia. We've got ourselves moral standards here in Southern California!"

As Savannah was walking them to the front door, Dirk jumped up from his chair and followed close behind.

After she had kissed them both good-bye on the front porch and thanked them for coming, she watched as Dirk walked with them out to their car.

Nosy, as always, she watched and listened closely as he asked Ryan something. And the fact that he glanced her way and then lowered his voice made her all the more curious.

She heard something about "hair" and

"ocean," but beyond that, she drew a blank.

And when he walked back to the house, a half-sheepish look on his face, she knew she had to pry it out of him or burst.

Waving good-bye to Ryan and John as they drove away, she asked, "So, what was all that rigmarole about?"

With exaggerated pseudo-innocence, he said, "What? What are you talking about? I was just asking them something about the case."

She studied his face by the light of the porch light — the too-wide eyes, the fake half smile, the tight jaw.

"Were not! Don't you lie to me, boy."

He bristled. "Hey, can't a guy have a little privacy? Do I have to tell you every damned thought I have? You have to hear every word I say?"

"No, just the ones you don't want me to hear, because there's no good reason for you to hide something from me. And that means you're up to no good." She took a deep breath and fixed him with her best indignant glare. "Now, what was that about?"

He stared at her, breathing hard, leaning forward until they were almost nose-to-nose. "I am *not* going to tell you. It's none of your business."

89

He started to walk around her to go back inside the house, but she stepped between him and the door.

"I don't want to hurt you," she said. "Not with Gran and Tammy here as witnesses. But I will."

There were a few more moments of tense silence; then he sighed, shoulders slumped — a defeated man. "All right. If you must know . . . I asked Ryan where he gets his hair cut. And he told me it's a place on Ocean Avenue, down by the marina. There. You happy now?"

"Why would you give a hoot where Ryan gets his hair cut? Like the day's ever gonna dawn that you pay more than ten bucks for a haircut."

His eyes narrowed. "Stand aside, woman. I've got to say good night to your grandma and then go talk to Wellman's receptionist."

He meant it. She could tell by the way his nostrils were twitching.

Besides, if she didn't piss him off too badly, and if Granny was as ready for bed as she appeared to be . . . she might be able to tag along on the interview with the receptionist.

"Okay," she said with a quick, bright smile. "Wanna take a piece of cake with you to go?"

He gave her a deeply suspicious look as he walked past her and said, "No, thank you. Like I said before, I'm watching how much I eat."

But the look wasn't half as distrustful as the one she shot at his back as he went inside.

Dirk watching what he ate?

Looking for a new barber? An *expensive* barber?

What in tarnation was this world coming to?

"So, why are you going to talk to Wellman's receptionist first?" Savannah asked as they cruised down Main Street in his Buick, heading for one of the town's least upstanding bars down on the waterfront.

"You don't approve?" he snapped. "Who do you figure I'd talk to before her?"

"Maybe Terry Somers? He seems your most likely suspect at the moment. What with that ugly threat he made in the doctor's office."

Dirk pulled onto one of the largest streets, one of the few in town that were well lit. The orange streetlights flickered on his face as they passed by, and his scowl told Savannah he was still quite irked from their little exchange on the porch.

He had let her come with him, but she suspected it was because he hadn't wanted to fight with her in front of Gran. Granny Reid was one of the few people on earth he deigned to at least try to impress.

"When I talk to Somers, I'm gonna lean hard on him," he said. "And I want to know exactly what I've got on him before I start leanin'."

"Gotcha," she said, nodding thoughtfully. "That's smart."

"Uh-huh."

He flipped on his left blinker — with at least twice as much force as was necessary. "I'm going to turn here . . . if that's quite all right with you?"

"Sure."

"Good."

She sighed. It was going to be a long night.

# CHAPTER 5

The disco era was over . . . at least in San Carmelita. It had died a natural death, along with giant shoulder pads, grown men singing in falsetto and sounding like ten-year-olds, and massively big hair.

But nobody had told Rick.

On the outskirts of town, Rick's Disco sat just off the road, with a junkyard on one side and an empty lot that was being used as a neighborhood dump on the other.

In 1978, Rick had been married to a gal named Charmaine, and Charmaine had thought it would be fun to paint the outside of the club with turquoise and purple stripes. Later, Rick had divorced Charmaine — not because of her lack of decorating taste, but because she'd been fooling around with the bartender.

So, Charmaine was long gone, but her legacy remained. Rick's Disco was still an eyesore, even in a neighborhood filled with smelly garbage and rusted Plymouths.

Dirk had a working relationship with Rick. Rick ratted out bad guys whenever Dirk asked him to, and in return, Dirk didn't close him down for his numerous license violations.

When Savannah and Dirk walked through the front door of the disco, they saw that Rick was tending bar . . . again. It seemed he was always firing or beating up his help. They couldn't seem to keep their hands off his women.

"Pouring your own beer?" Dirk asked as they sidled up to the bar. "Where's the Irish dude you had in here last month? Was it . . . Sean . . . or Michael?"

"Kelly," Rick said, wiping the sweat off his brow with the dishrag thrown over his shoulder. "His name was Kelly, and he ran off with Juanita."

"Oh, sorry," Dirk said.

"Hi, Savannah." Rick looked genuinely happy to see her. He reached across the bar and shook her hand. His fist was as big as one of Gran's Sunday afternoon pot roasts, and the rest of him was proportionally as large.

Rick had drank a few too many of his own drafts.

Savannah glanced around, taking in the

94

purple and turquoise walls — Charmaine had been nothing if not consistent — the dance floor with its colored, backlit squares and the obligatory disco ball.

The ball was no longer spinning, at least half of the squares on the floor were dark, and no one was dancing.

Rick's Disco was just not a "happening" place.

Other than the three young women who sat in the far corner booth, drinking tropical drinks from plastic pineapples adorned with paper umbrellas, the joint was dead.

"Who're you after tonight?" Rick asked Dirk. "Or are you here to take Savannah for a few spins around the floor?"

"I'm no John Travolta," Dirk told him.

"No," Savannah added. "He's more of a ballroom dancer . . . Viennese waltz, foxtrot, hot 'n' heavy tangos. Stuff like that."

"Yeah, right." Dirk grinned, but just a little. "She's Ginger, and I'm Fred, and we're looking for a Roxanne Rosen. Her roommate said she'd probably be here."

"Sure. Roxie comes in here every night to blow off steam with those gals over in the corner. She usually comes in about ten."

Savannah glanced at her watch. It was 9:45. They'd have to wait a few minutes, but then . . . five minutes of waiting anywhere for anything with Dirk was like serving hard time in the state pen.

Dirk did some things well. Waiting wasn't one of them.

"Damn it," he muttered. "I've got better things to do than hang around this lousy —"

"No, you don't," Savannah said brightly as she dug a twenty dollar bill out of her purse. "We'll keep our man Rick here company and have a couple of sodas while we hang."

Slapping the bill on the bar, she said, "Rick, darlin', pour us a couple of colas, shove in your *Saturday Night Fever* CD, and play us some 'Disco Inferno.' This is the closest thing to a date I've had in weeks."

Roxanne Rosen didn't show up at ten. And at 10:06, Dirk had enjoyed as much of the Bee Gees as he could stand.

"Those dudes sound like chicks," he mumbled into his soda. "I like a man to sound like a man. Like Elvis or Johnny Cash."

"They're both dead," Savannah replied sadly.

"But they both still sound great."

"True."

"If she doesn't show up soon, we're leaving," he said, twisting on the bar stool and rubbing the small of his back. "I'd rather just sit in the Buick outside her house till she shows up. At least we'd have comfortable seats and good music."

"No," Savannah said. "This place has a ladies' room. I've peed in way too many bushes over the years just so that you could listen to 'Hound Dog' and 'Folsom Prison Blues.' We're waiting here."

He started to protest but shut up when the front door opened and a young woman with copious, long blonde hair walked in.

She was wearing a snug-fitting, long-sleeved, black T-shirt and skin-tight jeans. And something about her extremely thin thighs rang a bell in Savannah's memory.

"Ah-ha," she said to Dirk. "That's gotta be our girl. She's the one I saw leaving Wellman's house today."

"The one he was arguing with?"

"Yeap. The one who demanded money and then stormed out."

Dirk smiled a broad "gotcha" grin, set his glass down, and pushed it away from him.

Farther down the bar, Rick gave them a knowing look and a nod toward the blonde.

Savannah took the last drink from her glass, then got up with Dirk and walked over to the woman, who had joined the others in the corner booth.

"Roxanne Rosen?" Dirk asked her.

She looked up at him with eyes that were a strangely intense and unnatural shade of aqua, which Savannah figured had to be the result of contact lenses.

She seemed to be having a problem focusing on Dirk. And even from several feet away, Savannah could smell the alcohol on her breath. She'd gotten a head start on the evening's festivities.

"We need to talk to you," he said.

"I'm busy," she replied.

"Get un-busy." He took out his badge and passed it under her nose. "I'm a cop."

"Woo-hoo," said one of the blonde's girlfriends.

"Boy, Roxie, you're in trouble now!" said another.

"Let's go over there." Dirk nodded toward some tables on the other side of the room.

"You gonna arrest her?" Roxie's buddy asked.

"Maybe he's going to cuff her," one said, giggling.

"And frisk her!"

"Can we watch?"

"Will you frisk me, too, Mr. Policeman?"

Savannah walked beside Dirk as the three of them made their way across the half-lit floor with its stationary mirror ball.

"You get the nicest invitations," she said, nudging him in the ribs with her elbow.

"Yeah, just what I want . . ." he grumbled, ". . . frisking nitwit bimbos who reek of booze. Like I haven't had way too much of *that* over the years."

Once they were settled around a table, Dirk caught Rick's attention and motioned for him to lower the music volume a bit.

"Good," he said. "Now I can hear myself think." He turned to Roxanne, who was giving him a suspicious and increasingly hostile look. "I have to ask you a few questions about the death of Maria Wellman."

Savannah watched her carefully, and she was pretty sure the woman turned a couple of shades whiter underneath her generously applied bronzer.

Roxanne struggled for her next statement, her mental gymnastics showing on her face.

Having interviewed countless individuals over the years — both guilty and innocent — Savannah could almost tell what the woman was thinking.

*Should I admit that I know Maria is dead, or pretend to be shocked?*

But, apparently, Roxie couldn't decide, because she just sat there with a blank look on her face and said nothing.

Savannah wasn't inclined to let her get away with it.

"You *do* know that your boss's wife is dead, right?" she asked her.

"Uh . . ." Her eyes cut back and forth between Savannah and Dirk. ". . . Yeah. I guess so."

"I didn't ask you if it's going to rain two months from today," Savannah said, her tone only a little softer than her words. "This is something you'd be pretty darned sure about. People remember it when they hear that somebody they know just fell off a cliff and died."

"Yeah, okay. I know it." Roxanne ran her fingers through her carefully mussed locks. "But I didn't have anything to do with it."

"Nobody said you did," Dirk told her. "But now that you're getting all hinky on us here, I'm starting to wonder."

"Who told you she was dead?" Savannah asked.

"Um-m-m . . . well . . ."

"That's another one of those answers that shouldn't require a lot of thought." Savannah leaned across the table and gave the blonde her most intimidating interrogation stare — the one she usually used for drive-by-shooting, pit bull–fighting, hardcore gangbangers. "Listen to me," she said. "A

100

woman is dead, probably murdered. And you could get yourself in a helluva lot of trouble in a heartbeat if you hold anything back."

"Yeah," Dirk added. "I could take you in right now for obstruction of justice if you don't start talking."

This time, when Roxanne ran her fingers through her hair, her fingers were trembling. "Uh . . . can I have a lawyer?"

"Do you need a lawyer?" Savannah asked. "Sergeant Coulter's just asking you some simple questions here. You want legal representation for that?"

Roxie shrugged. "No, I don't guess so." She paused, then said, "Dr. Wellman told me."

"When?" Dirk wanted to know.

"Today. I stopped by there . . . on an errand. But he was all upset, and he told me she was dead."

"What were his exact words when he said it?" Savannah asked.

"I think he said, 'Maria's dead. A jogger found her down on the beach. I can't mess with you right now.' "

"Mess with you?" Savannah said. "What did he mean by that? What were you there for?"

Again, Roxanne hesitated, considering her

answer carefully. Finally, she said, "I was there to pick up something."

"What?" Dirk asked.

"Some money that they owe me."

"For what?" Savannah said.

"My paycheck. They owe me one."

Savannah thought about the conversation they had overheard earlier at the house. It made sense, but still, it seemed like a big hullabaloo to be making over one late paycheck.

"Were they in the habit of withholding your wages?" she asked.

"No. But I need it to pay my rent and stuff."

"Any particular reason why they were late with this one?"

Again, the suspicious pause. "Um . . . not really."

"Okay." Savannah turned to Dirk. "This is like pulling hen's teeth here. Why don't you have a go at it?"

He took over. "I actually came here to ask you about Terry Somers."

A look of fear washed over Roxanne. "Oh, I don't like him. He's a bad guy, for sure . . . but please don't tell him I said that. He's not somebody I want for an enemy, if you know what I mean."

"No, I don't know what you mean." Dirk

leaned back in his chair. "Tell me."

"He's, like, in the mob or something. He's big and mean-looking, and I'm pretty sure I saw a gun stuck in the back of his pants one day in the waiting room when he leaned over to get a new magazine."

"We hear," Dirk said, "that there's bad blood between him and your boss."

"Oh, *big* time. He hates Dr. Wellman! Right there in the office he threatened to kill him!"

"Because . . . ?"

"Because the doctor told him he could cure his gambling problem, but when it didn't work — like, duh, he really thought it would? — he blamed Dr. Wellman for it."

"Do you think Terry Somers would hurt Mrs. Wellman?" Savannah said.

"I don't know if he even knew her . . . had ever met her. But if he came out to the house to hurt the doctor, and he found her there alone, and she did her usual routine on him, he might have. *Anybody* might have."

"Her usual routine?" Dirk asked.

"Yeah, you know, the raving lunatic routine."

Savannah and Dirk both stared at her for several seconds; then Savannah said, "Maria Wellman was a raving lunatic?"

"Oh," Roxanne nodded vigorously, "everybody who knew Maria knew that. It's not like it was a secret. That gal was a maniac bitch on wheels. It's really no wonder somebody killed her."

Savannah had already unfastened the retention snap on her holster and had her hand on her Beretta's grip before Dirk even knocked on Terry Somers's front door.

Anyone who had been described as big, mean, armed, and as having at least an association with organized crime, wasn't somebody who you wanted to mess with. And knocking on their door at 11:30 at night, when they had recently been assaulted by mob debt collectors — some people might construe that as being "messed with."

Feeling Dirk tense beside her, she knew he was thinking the same thing.

When Somers didn't answer, she said, "Maybe we should've waited till morning when he'd be less irritable."

"I'm *more* irritable in the morning."

"That's true."

"And he's awake. I can hear the TV."

"Me, too." She listened more closely and heard a familiar theme song. "Hey," she said, "he's watching *Cops*. Good one."

"Yeah. Really. You'd be surprised how many times —"

The front door opened about a foot, and Savannah's hand tightened around her gun.

But the guy on the other side of the screened door peeking through the narrow opening didn't look all that menacing. He was several inches shorter than Savannah and would have to run around in a rainstorm to get wet.

And, even though the door was less than half open, she could see that his right leg was in a cast, and he was holding a fluffy, orange tabby cat in his arms.

"Are you Terry Somers?" Dirk asked.

Savannah could tell by his tone that he was as surprised as she was.

"Yeah, who are you?" He peered at them through thick-lensed glasses.

Dirk presented his badge. "Sergeant Dirk Coulter, San Carmelita Police Department. This is Savannah Reid. Could we come in and talk with you?"

When Somers hesitated, Dirk added, "I realize it's late, but it's very important."

"I was just getting ready to go to bed, but . . . yeah . . . okay. I guess so." He stepped back and opened the door wider.

Savannah wasn't even over the threshold before it hit her, the stench of an uncleaned cat litter box.

Actually, she was giving him the benefit of the doubt that somewhere in the house there was, indeed, a litter box for the poor animal to use. And the thought also occurred to her that if her own two cats, Diamante and Cleopatra, were treated to these sorts of accommodations, they would probably attack her and kill her as she slept.

Once inside, Savannah shuddered again, looking around the room at the avalanche of empty pizza boxes, drained beer bottles, flat potato chip bags, and assorted trash that covered nearly every horizontal surface.

The dark brown sofa was coated with a layer of light-colored animal hair. *Tabby's no doubt,* she thought. Yes, the poor thing definitely needed to run away from home.

"You wanna sit down?" their host asked, brushing some of the garbage off one end of the sofa and onto the floor.

"Uh, no, thanks," Dirk said, glancing around. "We won't be that long."

"The housekeeper's on vacation." Somers then reached behind him and pulled out a revolver.

In an instant, both Savannah and Dirk had their own weapons in their hands and pointed at him.

"Holy shit! Don't shoot!" Somers said,

laying it on the coffee table, on top of a stack of porn magazines. "Damn. I was just taking it out of my pants because I didn't want to sit down on it. It's uncomfortable, okay?"

Savannah could feel the adrenaline hit her system, and when it got to her knees, they nearly buckled under her. She could hear her pulse pounding in her ears.

"Oh, man, what the hell's wrong with you?" Dirk said, picking up the discarded revolver. "You pull a gun around cops? You wanna die?"

Dirk holstered his weapon, then emptied Somers's revolver and stuck the bullets into his pocket.

Savannah took her finger off her Beretta's trigger and lowered her own weapon, but she decided to hold on to it, just in case.

"I've had some problems lately," Somers replied sheepishly. "That's how I got this. . . ." He pointed to his cast. "I was mugged by some punks in Hollywood, and I've been a little jumpy ever since. I didn't know who you were when I answered the door."

"We look a lot like muggers to you?" Dirk's face was flushed, and he was breathing hard. She could feel the rage rolling off him in waves.

Savannah knew exactly how he felt. Her heart was still racing.

Somers was lucky to be alive. If either she or Dirk had been ten years younger and a little less experienced, he'd be well on his way to keeping Maria Wellman company in Dr. Liu's morgue.

She had killed in the line of duty before, and it wasn't an experience she wanted to repeat in this lifetime.

"I don't like somebody pulling a gun in my presence," Dirk continued, "and I don't like being lied to, either. So far, buddy, you're O for two."

This time it was Terry Somers's face that turned a shade redder as anger flashed in his eyes. For just a moment there, Savannah caught a glimpse of a guy who could have made an ugly threat in a doctor's office without caring that there were witnesses.

"I don't know what you're talking about," Somers said, his jaw tight, fists clenched at his sides. "You talk to all victims of violent crimes like this?"

"Only the ones who get themselves in trouble by not paying their gambling debts to connected guys."

"Who told you that?" Somers practically screamed at Dirk, his eyes bugging out in an extremely unsettling, creepy way.

Savannah was glad that Dirk had emptied the weapon. She was equally glad she hadn't holstered her own yet, just in case he had another one stashed in the cat hair–coated sofa or hidden in a moldy pizza box.

She could understand why Roxanne Rosen had been afraid of him. And since he was at least five inches taller than the petite Roxie, Savannah could even see why she considered him big.

But Dirk was a lot bigger, and as Savannah could attest, plenty mean. And still armed.

"It doesn't matter who told me," Dirk told him, leaning toward him, quite deliberately invading his personal space. "Word gets around, you know? And that's not all I've heard. I understand you've got a major beef with Dr. Robert Wellman."

Now Terry Somers was spitting mad. Literally. When he spoke, spittle flew out of his mouth. Savannah half-expected to see his head start spinning around.

"Yeah, I've got something against that snake oil–selling son of a bitch," he said, loud enough for the neighbors to hear. "I paid him a fortune to help me stop gambling. If you already know how I got this busted leg, then you know how well his shit works."

"You threatened his life," Dirk said.

"I might have."

"In front of witnesses," Savannah added.

"Okay, I did."

"Where were you last night?" Dirk asked.

"Right here, watching TV with my cat and trying to drink enough that my leg wouldn't hurt. Why?"

When neither Dirk nor Savannah answered him right away, he was suddenly highly interested, excited. "Wait a minute. Why are you asking me about Wellman and where I was? Did something happen to him? Did he get beat up?"

Again they didn't reply.

"He got offed?" The sheer delight on his face at the mere prospect was telling. He looked like a kid who had just been told that Santa might come for a second visit sometime in July.

"Did he?" he insisted. "Did he? Is he dead? That's why you're here, isn't it?"

"No," Dirk said.

Somers's face fell. "Oh."

"His wife was killed." Savannah watched his expression closely to see the effect her words would have on him.

He gasped. "Killed, like murdered?"

"We think so."

"Damn! Really? Oh, man! That's wild!"

Somers sat down suddenly on the couch. And when his cat tried to jump up onto his lap, he brushed her aside, shaking his head. "I can't believe it. I mean, I believe it, considering . . . but, wow!"

"You believe it, considering what?" Dirk wanted to know.

"Considering the kind of person she was. She was in his office the first time I came by to ask for my money back. She told me off, using words I never even heard a woman use before. No wonder somebody killed her. I gotta tell you, that woman was a major bitch!"

Savannah nodded somberly. "So we've heard."

"Yeap," Dirk added. "That seems to be the general consensus."

Later, they left Somers and walked to the Buick parked at the curb, neither of them speaking until they were well on their way.

"Tired?" Dirk said.

"Very. You?"

"Yeah. And I have a feeling this is going to be a tough case."

"Trying to find somebody who *didn't* want Maria Wellman dead?"

"Exactly."

# CHAPTER 6

When Savannah opened her eyes the next morning, for just a moment, she thought she was a little girl again back in Georgia.

Like thousands of other mornings, the incomparable aroma of fresh coffee brewing, bacon frying, and biscuits baking beckoned her from the far reaches of the house.

"Oh, my Lord," she whispered. "If heaven doesn't smell exactly like that, let me just come back to earth."

She jumped out of bed, threw a robe over her nightgown, and rushed downstairs with a vim and vigor she seldom displayed before noon.

"Granny! What are you doing cooking?" she asked as she ran into the room and found her grandmother standing in front of the stove, frying eggs. On the back burner, a pan full of grits bubbled, and a plate of crispy bacon sat on the counter nearby.

"I heard you come in late last night, so I figured you'd be tuckered out," Gran said, expertly flipping the eggs. "I'll have to give that young man of yours a serious talkin' to, keeping you out till the wee hours of the morning thataway."

"We weren't up to nothin' naughty," Savannah said with a chuckle as she leaned over and kissed Gran's cheek.

"Hmmph. That's what you used to say when you was a teenager and you and Tommy Stafford were keeping company. And we both know that was a bald-faced lie."

Savannah pulled the half-and-half from the refrigerator and put a generous dollop into her Minnie Mouse mug. "I reckon it depends on your definition of 'naughty.'"

"I can understand the temptation there." Gran opened the oven door a crack and peeked at the biscuits. "Tommy was a pretty boy. Still is, for that matter. He looks especially fetching in that policeman's uniform."

"I know. Remember, I saw him and his uniform last time I was home."

"Course, your Dirk looks pretty fine, even in that old beat-up leather coat of his."

Savannah sniffed. "Since when is he 'my' Dirk? He's just Dirk."

Granny gave her a knowing, sideways look and grinned. "Okay. Whatever you say, sweet cheeks."

Savannah took a long drink from her mug, then closed her eyes and savored the moment. How was it that Granny could use the same coffee from her own canister, the water from her tap, and her coffeepot, and yet brew something so much better than her own?

"If I didn't know better," Granny said, "I'd think that you and your Dirk — who's not yours, according to you — had a little tiff last night when Ryan and John were leaving."

"A little one. But we got over it."

"Well, that's good. You have to make up before the day's over. 'Don't let the sun set on your wrath,' the Bible says."

"Yeah, there's nothing like having somebody you're interviewing pull a gun out of his britches to put things into perspective."

Savannah put her mug on the counter and started to set the table for two. Then she glanced at the cat clock on the wall with its switching tail and rhinestone eyes and decided to set it for three.

"Dirk'll probably be by any time now," she said as she laid out the plates.

"Does he come by every morning?"

"Not every morning, but most." She paused, silverware in hand. "Now that I think about it, he's been coming by a bit less lately."

"Oh?"

"In fact, he's been acting mighty strange . . . stranger than usual, even for him. He's not been dropping by as often, watching his diet, not answering his phone sometimes in the middle of the afternoon, and last night, I overheard him asking Ryan about a place to get a decent haircut."

"Has he bought new boxer shorts lately?"

"New *boxer shorts*? Now, how the heck would I know a thing like that?"

Granny grinned at her, and Savannah realized she'd just been questioned by someone who was a much better interrogator than she was.

"That's always a sign that a man's up to no good," Granny said, dishing up the eggs. "All of a sudden he's watching his weight, frettin' over his hair, and gets new underwear — especially if he ain't a dietin', fashionable, new-underwear kinda guy."

Savannah mulled that over and didn't like the feeling that was welling up inside her.

It felt a lot like petty jealousy.

Only not all that petty.

"And the other day," she said, "when I

called him at three thirty in the afternoon, he avoided telling me where he was . . . and . . . he sounded all out of breath."

"Hmmm . . ." Gran walked past her, a plate of bacon in one hand and one of eggs in the other. "Then I'd say it's a darned good thing he ain't 'your' Dirk, or you'd have good reason to get your bloomers in a kink."

Dirk didn't show up for breakfast. And when she hadn't heard from him by 10:30, Savannah couldn't stand it anymore.

"That does it. By crackie, I'm calling him," she told Granny and Tammy, who were spending a far more peaceful morning than she was, in spite of her pacing and fretting.

Tammy was at the desk, staring at the computer screen and reading them everything she could find on the Internet regarding Maria Wellman's death.

Granny sat in Savannah's comfy chair, the cats keeping her feet warm on the ottoman, a crocheted afghan over her lap. She was reading the *True Informer,* her favorite tabloid, keeping abreast of all the latest news about UFOs and which starlet had most recently flashed her crotch for the paparazzi.

"So, if you want to call Dirko, call him," Tammy said. "Tell him that the Associated Press even picked up the story. That Dr. Wellman is a big shot, what with all those talk shows he did. There's an article here by one of his biggest critics, Dr. Bonnie Saperstein. She's a weight loss doctor in Twin Oaks who says he's a charlatan. Says he got his papermill doctorate from some Russian Web site."

Savannah didn't reply, but kept pacing.

Finally, she stomped to the foyer and grabbed her purse off the table next to the door. "Okay. I'm gonna call him," she said, fishing out her cell phone. "If I don't, he might go over to Dr. Liu's without me, and he'll get snippy with her for not getting that autopsy done as quick as he wants her to, and then we won't have anything to go on for hours, and . . ."

Her voice faded away as she walked into the kitchen, punching buttons on her cell phone.

Tammy clicked away for a moment or two, then said to Gran, "Has she always been like that?"

"Like what?" Gran asked without looking up from her paper.

"Getting in a tizzy over nothing."

Gran sighed and turned the page. "Savannah was born tizzied."

Tammy giggled. "But we love her anyway."

"Yeap. You gotta take a body however you find 'em."


"So, what were you going to do, just go to the morgue without me?" Savannah asked Dirk when she got into the Buick.

"No," he said. "I was gonna call you. I got busy. I had some things to do this morning."

He pulled away from the curb, reaching over and grabbing a chocolate sucker from the dash. Handing it to her, he said, "Unwrap that for me, wouldcha?" And after a moment's pause, he added, "And get another one out of the glove box if you want one for yourself."

She gave him a thorough once-over.

He hadn't gotten his hair cut. He didn't seem to be sweaty or out of breath.

She wondered if he was wearing new boxers . . . and felt the overwhelming urge to slap him naked and find out.

But instead, she opened the glove compartment and found at least two dozen of the chocolate suckers stuffed inside.

"What's all this?" she asked. "Since when do you eat lollipops instead of real food?"

"They satisfy my chocolate cravings and

only have fifty calories each. They're a good bang for your junk-food-calorie buck."

"Okay, that's it!" She slammed the glove box closed. "You are going to tell me, once and for all, why you're dieting. And don't give me some song and dance about recapturing your girlish figure, because you look just fine and dandy right now."

"I do?" He looked far too pleased to suit her, considering how aggravated she was with him.

"Yes, you do. So, what's going on here?"

He thought a moment, and then his grin faded. "But you're only saying that 'cause you haven't seen me with my clothes off."

"Not for ages. Not since that time when we had to stay in the same motel room, and you went traipsin' off to the bathroom in the middle of the night without telling me to close my eyes first."

"Hey, I'd warned you . . . I'm just not a pajama sorta guy."

"You could've left your boxers on."

"Briefs. Not a boxer sorta guy, either."

"More information than I need, thank you."

They traveled along in silence until they were almost to the morgue.

That was as long as Savannah could hold back. "So, what's the big deal?" she said.

"Who cares if you lose weight or whatever. *Nobody* ever sees *you* with your clothes off."

He grinned. It was a half-hearted, sheepish sort of a grin that she couldn't, for the life of her, interpret.

"Oh," he said. "You'd be surprised."

Savannah steeled herself as they walked up the sidewalk to the morgue. She didn't like the place; it creeped her out.

It wasn't the fact that there were dead bodies inside. Dead people usually caused a heck of a lot less trouble than the live ones.

But she had too many bad memories of the place. Too many instances of taking victims' family members there to make identifications. Too many times when she'd walked through those doors and learned new and horrible things that human beings could do to each other.

It never failed to amaze and horrify her how creative bad guys could be.

And then . . . there was Kenny Bates.

Savannah liked most people unless they gave her good reason not to. Her list of folks she truly hated was a short one, and she believed that everyone on it had worked quite hard to get there.

But she loathed Kenny Bates.

Kenny worked the morgue's front desk —

if you considered eating nacho cheese chips, swilling sodas, pretending to look busy while looking at porn on his computer, and hitting on every female who walked through the door, work. If those activities had been part of his job description, the taxpayers would have gotten way more than their money's worth out of Officer Kenny Bates.

Dirk held the door as she walked inside. She could see Bates sitting behind his desk.

As usual, he quickly exited the screen he was ogling on his desktop monitor and adjusted his toupee.

He didn't bother to brush the chip dust off the front of his uniform that was far too small for his extremely rotund body. Kenny's grooming standards had their limitations.

When he stood to greet the new arrivals and saw who they were, Savannah got the first inkling that maybe their rocky relationship had changed for the better since the last time she had visited here.

He gave her a dirty look, then abruptly sat back down and spun around in his chair, turning his back on her.

"Still carrying a grudge, I see," Dirk said as he walked over to the counter and picked up the clipboard with its sign-in sheet.

Bates said nothing.

Dirk turned to Savannah, "I hate to tell you, Van, but I think the romance is over between you and Kenny here."

"Appears so," Savannah said. "Boy, you beat a guy half to death with his own porn magazine, and he gets all huffy on you. Go figure."

Still no reaction from Bates.

Dirk scribbled his name and the time on the sheet, then chuckled. "You know, Savannah," he said, "ol' Kenny here still gets ribbed about that. Sorta ruins a dude's rep, getting beat up by a girl . . . even you. And with his own property no less. You tore that magazine to shreds. And it was all caught on tape."

He motioned to the camera in the upper corner of the room. "You have any idea how many times us guys have watched that?" he continued. "I heard somebody even posted it on the Internet."

Bates was breathing hard, his extremely wide back going in and out like a blacksmith's bellows. But he didn't break his silence.

They passed by him and started down the long corridor leading to the medical examiner's autopsy suite.

"Refresh my memory," Dirk said. "Why was it exactly that you attacked him with that rolled-up magazine?"

"He told me I looked like the center-fold . . . and then he showed me the center-fold. She was ugly. And she was in a remarkably unladylike position. As a genteel belle of the South, I took offense."

"It's a wonder you didn't kill him."

"Damn tootin'."

At the end of the depressing hallway with its gray walls, charcoal-colored tiles, dingy ceiling, and flickering fluorescent lights was a set of large double doors.

Dirk stopped in the middle of the hallway and slapped his forehead. "Shoot, I forgot to bring the chocolate. I thought about what you said about how I'm never nice to her, and I was gonna take some money out of petty cash and buy her some."

Savannah grinned, reached into her purse, and pulled out a small box of Godiva's chocolates. "Like these?"

"Oh, girl. You rule!"

"I do. And don't you forget it." She glanced at her watch. "Eleven forty-five. She said she'd be done by noon. You'll only be fifteen minutes early. That's gotta be some sort of record for you. Normally, you'd be camped out on her doorstep, making a nuisance of yourself."

"You're civilizing me."

"That'll be the day."

"Lemme have that box of chocolates."

"Why?"

" 'Cause I wanna be the one to give 'em to her."

"No! I bought them. I brought them. I'm getting the credit for it."

"But I need to score the points. She already likes you."

"That's true." She shoved the box into his outstretched hand. "You owe me fifty bucks."

"Fifty dollars! These things cost fifty dollars?"

"No, but I figure I should make a profit on the deal."

He growled.

She had already opened the door on the right and was sticking her head inside.

"Yoo-hoo," she called. "Dr. Jen? Anybody home?"

"Yeah, come on in."

Savannah went inside, followed closely by Dirk.

Dr. Liu looked quite different from the woman on the beach the night before. Her miniskirt and hooker heels were gone. She was dressed in green scrubs and sneakers with paper booties over them. Her pretty face was covered with a mask, and her long hair was tucked into a surgical cap.

On the stainless steel table in front of her lay the earthly remains of Maria Wellman. And, apparently, the doctor had already done her work, because the large "Y" incision that reached from the pubic bone up to the sternum, and then branched up to the front of each shoulder, had already been closed with sutures.

"Wow, you're all done! That's great!" Dirk said, a bit too cheerfully. "Fast service there."

"Yeah, okay," the doctor replied, far less enthusiastically.

He shoved the box of chocolates under her nose. "Here you go, Doc. Just a little something to show you how much we appreciate all you do around here."

She stared at the box for a moment, then held up her hands, covered with bloodied surgical gloves, in his face. "Thanks, but now's not really the time, if you know what I mean."

"Oh, sure. Got it." Dirk looked around, spotted a clear area on the stainless steel counter nearby and hurried over to it. He placed the box there, setting it down with the gentle care of an explosives specialist handling a live bomb. "There you go . . . a little treat for after you get the blood and guts off your hands there."

"Oh, yum." Dr. Liu looked at Savannah, and even through the protective face shield, Savannah could see a twinkle in her eyes. "Thanks . . . uh . . . Dirk," she said. "Bringing me chocolate is usually something that *Savannah* does."

Dirk looked a little guilty. "Well, yeah, but she's sorta wearing off on me. I'm picking up on all the Southern hospitality junk."

"Yes, I'm sure that Southern hospitality had everything to do with me receiving that gift, and I'm very grateful."

She walked over to a biohazard waste disposal can and opened it with the foot pedal. As she peeled off her gloves and tossed them inside, she said, "Your lady wasn't very healthy. Considering what she was doing to her body, she wasn't going to live a normal life span."

"She died of natural causes?" Dirk said, sounding both a little disappointed and relieved.

"No, she was murdered." Dr. Liu removed her surgical greens — top, trousers, and cap — and threw them into a laundry bin. Underneath, she was wearing a spaghetti-strap T-shirt and tiny, snuggly fitted shorts that Savannah wasn't at all sure weren't underwear.

She glanced over at Dirk and found him totally mesmerized by the sight that had just been revealed to him. He stared, slack-jawed, obviously in a fantasy world all his own.

Briefly, Savannah wondered if Dr. Liu realized the effect she had on her audience. She decided that, if she was aware that she was a raging sexpot, the fact wasn't high on the doctor's list of priorities. Anyone as beautiful as she was was probably accustomed to seeing men with drool on the fronts of their shirts on a regular basis.

Liu took off her mask and hung it on a hook on the wall. Then she walked over to a sink, took off her goggles, and began to wash them with plenty of disinfectant soap.

"What do you mean she wasn't healthy?" Savannah asked.

"For one thing, she was a big drinker. The liver showed the sort of damage consistent with chronic alcoholism. And not just your usual hepatocyte injury, either. There was a lot of inflammation, the kind you'd find in a heavy binge drinker."

Savannah felt a wash of sadness as she thought of her own mother, whose home was a bar stool in McGill's trashiest saloon, with only a picture of Elvis on the wall above her head to keep her company. "Try to drown your sorrows in a beer mug, and they just keep bobbing back to the surface," she said sadly.

"Every time," Liu agreed. "And there was substantial damage to her esophagus . . . also alcohol related. She was well on her way to a massive gastrointestinal hemorrhage. It wouldn't have been pretty."

"But what about the cause of death?" Dirk asked as he watched, still fascinated by the sight of a coroner washing her hands . . . and looking like page seven of a Victoria's Secret catalogue.

"Cause of death was blunt force trauma to the head. Manner of death — homicide."

"If she fell off a cliff," Dirk said, "how can you be sure the blow was delivered by a murderer? Maybe she just smacked her head on a rock on the way down."

"It was the broken fairy statue, wasn't it?" Savannah said. "The one in the flower bed at the top of the cliff."

"We're pretty sure it was. I heard from Eileen over at the lab. It tested positive for human blood. Also, the injury on Wellman's head was the same size and shape as the edge of the statue's base. I'm prepared to say it's your murder weapon."

"I knew it," Dirk said. "Tinkerbell did it."

"Hey, I'm a major Tinkerbell fan; watch

what you say," Dr. Liu said as she dried off her hands. "And for your information, that statue isn't a Tink. It's just your garden-variety woodsprite, not to be confused with a true pixie."

"O-o-okay." Dirk shot Savannah a sideways glance.

"But even if it was a statue of one of the lower faery folk," she said, "I'm offended that anyone would use an artistic representation of any fey being as a murder weapon. Talk about inviting bad fortune from the spirit world!"

Dr. Liu walked over to a locker, opened the door, and kicked her sneakers off. She tossed them inside. "And that's not all. Your victim had been in a fight."

Dirk nodded. "We could tell that, what with all the churned-up dirt there in the flower bed. Did you get some good footprint casts?"

"Only of high heels, and you'll have to ask Eileen to be sure, but we're pretty sure they're all Wellman's."

She reached for her miniskirt, hanging inside the locker on a hook. "The fight I'm talking about happened before the night she fell. She had fingertip bruises and a couple of slight scratches on her right upper arm. Somebody grabbed her there hard, I'd say.

The bruises and scratches weren't perimortem, like all the other ones she got on her way down the cliff. These were maybe a couple of days old. And . . . I'd say she defended herself pretty well in her squabble. Four of her ten fingernails had been broken."

"*Had* been?" Savannah asked.

"Yes. She'd had them professionally repaired during a manicure that was fresh — probably done the day she died."

"And you took scrapings from under her nails?" Dirk asked.

Dr. Liu shot him a dirty look. "Uh, duh, Dirk. I *did* take Autopsy 101 in med school."

"Just asking."

"Well, don't."

"Get snippy with me . . ." he grumbled, ". . . I could take back my chocolate."

"You could try." She slipped on the miniskirt, which barely reached to the bottom of her short shorts; then she took the stilettos from the top shelf.

"Wow, that's interesting, that business about the fight," Savannah said. "Dr. Wellman didn't say anything about his wife getting into an altercation a day or two before she died. If she broke her fingernails on her opponent, she had to leave some marks. We'll have to check *him* for scratches."

Savannah gave Dirk a sideways glance to see if he was as fascinated as she was by all they'd just heard.

But Dr. Liu was bent over — way over — facing away from them, while she fastened the ankle strap on her high heel. And Dirk was far beyond hearing anything.

He had fascinations of his own.

# CHAPTER 7

Savannah decided that any woman who had raised nine children and cooked enough mashed potatoes in her lifetime to fill the Grand Canyon, deserved the best lunch that San Carmelita had to offer. And that was especially true if the woman had waited patiently until 2:30 in the afternoon to get that lunch.

"I'm sorry we kept you waiting so long," Savannah said as she, Gran, and Dirk filed into the cozy café that had not only the best BLT with avocado in town, but also the finest view.

Situated on the town pier, the Sundowner Café had provided peaceful ocean panoramas for its patrons for years. Not to mention copious snacks for the seagulls who loitered on the tops of dock pilings outside, waiting for gullible, softhearted diners to toss them their leftover french fries.

"You must be starved half to death," Dirk

said, as he graciously seated Granny in the chair with the best view.

"My stomach thinks my throat's cut," Gran replied, tucking herself and her new lavender floral-print muumuu into the chair. "And you know, we don't eat 'lunch' back where I'm from. We call this 'dinner.' And your 'dinner' is our 'supper.' So, I don't know if I'm comin' or goin'."

"You're fixin' to have a nice dinner in the middle of the afternoon," Savannah told her. "So, just relax, sit a spell, kick your sandals off there under the table — 'cause nobody's gonna see your feet anyhow with these long tablecloths — and enjoy yourself."

A pretty little waitress with sun-bleached hair and a deep tan hurried over to their table, an eager-to-please smile on her face. "May I get you something to drink?" she asked Gran.

"Ice tea," Gran replied, draping her napkin over her lap, pinkies extended — her best "Sunday dinner company" manners.

"Sweetened or unsweetened?"

*"Unsweetened?"* Gran frowned up at her. "Now what the blazes would be the point in drinkin' *that?*"

"Sweetened it is."

The waitress took the rest of the order and

scurried away.

Gran shook her head, incredulous. "This California really is a foreign country . . ." she said, ". . . asking a body if they want sugar in their iced tea. What sorta malarkey is that! Next thing you know, they'll be wantin' to know if you'll drink nonfat milk in your coffee instead of cream, like the good Lord intended."

Savannah made a mental note to speak to any waitress beforehand who might be serving them breakfast during this visit.

Granny smoothed a wayward lock of silver hair into place, adjusted her right earring, and folded her hands demurely on the table in front of her. The perfect Southern lady.

"So," she said, "fill me in on this murder case of yours. I wanna know all about it, and don't spare me any of the gory details. I watch those forensic shows on TV, you know. I can handle it."

Dirk chuckled and gave her a warm smile, his eyes shining with affection. "Granny, I wish I'd had you for a grandma when I was growing up. Mine were both sourpusses. I don't think either one of them cracked a smile in their whole lives."

"Well, you got me for a granny now. Ain't that enough?"

He leaned over and kissed her on the

cheek. "It is enough. I'm a lucky man."

"Ain't no such thing as luck. *Blessed* is more like it."

"We're all blessed just to be sitting here together today," Savannah said as she watched Dirk lift his glass of root beer, take a long drink, and hide a grimace. Dirk had ordered the soft drink because Granny Reid was dining with them. Otherwise, he'd be having a beer.

Savannah was grateful that he honored her grandmother, and was equally glad that they'd be spared Gran's "demon rum" sermon.

Gran made no differentiation between beer, a fine Chardonnay, or rot-gut whiskey. It was all "demon rum" in her book . . . and led to iniquity.

"You never know what folks have been through," Gran was telling Dirk. "Life can be hard. Maybe your grandmas had just run dry on smiles by the time you came along. Some people do. That's why you gotta give 'em one of your own."

Later, over ice cream sundaes, Granny weighed in on all she had heard throughout lunch regarding their case. "Sounds to me like it's either the husband or that Somers guy. Why don't you just go tell 'em to peel off their shirts and drop their drawers . . . see who's got scratches on him and then arrest his sorry rear end?"

"I wish I could legally do that," Dirk told her. "And I probably will, whether I can or not. But, unfortunately, it's not that easy. I really doubt that either guy'll submit to a strip search without me serving him with a warrant first."

"And he doesn't have enough on either of them to get a judge to issue one," Savannah added.

"But Somers threatened the doctor with bodily harm," Gran said, playing with the cherry on top of her sundae. "Ain't that a crime around here?"

"It's not something I could put him away for, if that's what you mean," Dirk replied.

Granny shrugged. "Don't matter. The husband probably did it. There's just evil run amuck in this world, what with so many men layin' hands on their women in anger. It's a sad thing, I tell you. Time was when women were treated with love and respect by their menfolk."

Savannah held her tongue, deciding not to mention that domestic violence had to be one of the oldest crimes known to the human race.

But, remembering how kind and loving

her grandfather had been to Granny, Savannah could certainly see how Gran felt the way she did.

A buzzing sound came from inside Dirk's jacket. He took out his cell phone and answered it.

"Coulter. Yeah. Oh, yeah?"

Seeing him perk up, instantly alert, Savannah felt her own adrenaline level rise a bit. A break maybe?

"When did they call this in?" He listened, nodding. "Where are they now?"

He grabbed his notepad and scribbled down an address on Palm Street that Savannah recognized. It was a large office complex on the other side of town, a prestigious professional building where the town's best doctors and a few attorneys practiced.

"Okay," Dirk said. "Call them back for me, and tell them I'll be there in about fifteen minutes. Tell them 'do not leave.' I want to talk to them for sure. Yeah, thanks."

He hung up.

Savannah couldn't help being excited. Dirk hardly ever told anybody "Thanks."

"What's up?" she asked him.

"A road crew, the street maintenance guys, are working there behind that big, fancy office building on the corner of Palm and Lester," he told her. "They're filling

137

potholes or whatever . . . have been for a couple of days now. Anyway, they saw the story on the news last night — Maria Wellman's picture and what happened to her. And they remembered seeing her fighting in the parking lot with somebody four or five days ago. And not just arguing, either. It was a real, honest-to-goodness, hands-on tussle."

"Who was she fighting with?" Savannah asked. "Terry Somers? Her old man?"

"I don't know. That dumb new receptionist we've got at the station house didn't think to ask them. Hopefully, I can get out there to question them before they have a change of heart and decide it's not a good idea to speak to the police."

He caught the waitress's attention and motioned for the check.

"Lunch is on you?" Savannah asked, trying not to sound too surprised in front of Gran.

"Of course. How often does a guy get to take *two* beautiful women out to lunch? I'm happy to do it."

"That's one of the things I like about you, boy," Gran said, beaming at him across the table. "You're just so generous."

Savannah nearly choked on her drink. "Yeap, that's our Dirk," she said with a big

138

grin. "He just gives and gives till it hurts."

She saw the slight grimace that crossed his face when he opened the folder and read the total on the check — the grimace he tried so hard to hide.

Leaning over the table, she patted him on the arm. "Now see there," she said. "Hurts somethin' awful, don't it?"

As Savannah walked along the pier, her arm around her grandmother's waist, seagulls circling overhead, the waves crashing onto the giant pilings below, she took a momentary mental break and counted her blessings.

"I wouldn't want to be anywhere in the world right now," she said, "but right here with you, Gran."

Granny nodded, her silver hair glistening in the bright sunlight. Her blue eyes were full of life and joy as she gazed out at the ocean, the islands floating above the distant haze, the water churning itself into row after row of lacy foam.

"Who would have thought it, Savannah girl," she said. "All those years ago, you and me, struggling just to keep those kids' bellies full, clothes on their backs, and a roof over our heads . . . one that didn't leak ever' blamed time it rained . . . Who would have thought we'd be here, walking in the sunshine on a dock in California?"

"I thought it," Savannah said softly. "I dreamed it."

"And you worked hard and made your dream come true. Here you are, doing what you always wanted — chasin' down bad guys — and in the place you dreamed about. I'm proud of you, sugar."

"And I'm proud you finally got all nine of us out of the house and on our own."

" 'Twasn't easy. And what with rents so high these days, they keep trying to sneak back in."

"The electric fence and pack of pit bulls don't keep them out?"

Granny chuckled. "No, but they slow 'em down a mite."

They had reached the end of the pier, where a number of fishermen were working at catching a free dinner — cutting bait, tending their lines, and occasionally adding a catch to their coolers.

One father was showing his preschool-aged son how to put a worm on a hook, and Granny gave them both a sweet smile.

"When are you and Dirk gonna tie the knot and have a couple of those?" she asked Savannah.

"Tie the . . . what?" Savannah suddenly

lost the ability to think or speak.

Granny laughed as she leaned her elbows on the rail and took in a deep breath of the moist ocean air. "You heard me. You two've been beatin' around the bush way too long. You might as well take the leap."

"Please, I'd rather take a leap off here," Savannah said, pointing to the cold, swirling water below that was crashing against the barnacle-encrusted supports.

"Yeah, right."

Granny gave her "the look" — the look that said she knew you had taken the last drink out of the refrigerator water jug and hadn't refilled it.

"We could never get married," Savannah said. "It wouldn't work. We'd fight all the time and drive each other crazy."

"Unlike now."

"We'd have to see each other every single day."

"Instead of . . . say . . . six days a week, the way you do?"

"Even the good Lord took the seventh day off. I'd have to get a break from him once in a while, or I'd murder him." She nudged Gran with her elbow. "And there aren't any cotton fields around here like there are back home."

Gran looked surprised. "You remember that?"

"You disappearing off into the cotton fields after you and Pa had a row? Sure I do."

Shaking her head and laughing, Gran said, "There were times when I danged near stomped that cotton flat. That man could make me madder than a wet hen, but I loved him dearly. And I miss him every single day of my life."

They stared out into the infinite blue, both taking a moment to remember a man they had adored and respected, honoring him with a rare, Reid-woman silence.

"You know," Gran finally said, her voice heavy with emotion, "you can't judge a union by the amount of disagreements that goes on in it. The happiest married people on earth fight from time to time. You show me a couple who never gets into it, I'll show you one where somebody's a doormat."

Savannah smiled. "And neither you nor Pa could be called doormats."

"Neither are you or that Dirk of yours. You're both strong, opinionated people, so the sparks are gonna fly from time to time. Ain't nothing wrong with that, as long as the fightin's fair."

"Yeah, we fight fair. Nobody bleeds. Not

past what a tourniquet can control."

"Then you might as well be married. At least then, you could really enjoy yourselves when you make up."

"Does that mean I'd have to do his laundry?"

"You could, or make him do it hisself, like he's been doing all these years. But even if you did, he'd be low maintenance. You wouldn't have to iron that Harley T-shirt of his. And you might get your lawn mowed and your oil changed once in awhile."

"I wouldn't let him touch my Mustang. I've seen how he abuses that poor Buick of his."

"Then there's the nicest part . . ." Gran continued, ". . . hearing a deep, sexy voice in the dark telling you that even though you had an awful day, tomorrow's bound to be better."

Savannah could feel a buzzing inside her purse. "Ah," she said, "saved by the bell."

She saw her own name on the caller ID. "It's Tammy," she told Granny. "I guess she got those errands done and is back at the office. I'm not sure why. There's not much to do there."

"I think she likes hanging out at your house because she loves you."

"I think you're right." Into the phone she

said, "Hi, babycakes. What's shakin'?"

"Ryan and John are here," Tammy told her, sounding very pleased about it.

"Oh?"

"Yeah, they came by to pick up their ramekins."

"Their what?"

"Those little dishes you borrowed to serve chocolate pudding in when you had that backyard barbecue."

"Ah, right . . . ramekins. Tell them I'm so sorry. I should have returned those before now."

"Naw, they don't care. Said they were in the neighborhood anyway. But that's not why I called you. I was doing some stuff here on the computer, and then they came, and we've all been sitting here doing research on that Wellman guy and his wife."

"Oh, really?"

"You gotta see this! We've found something really, really cool! Can you come home and see it?"

Savannah knew she could just ask Tammy what she'd found and continue to enjoy her time with Gran on the pier. But poor Tammy worked so hard for the pittance Savannah could afford to throw her way whenever a paying job came along.

And Gran was right about one thing:

Tammy loved Savannah and the work they did together. She thrived on whatever meager praise she received and, of course, the pleasure of playing Nancy Drew and solving cases.

Savannah figured the least she could do was play along with her.

She covered her phone with her hand and said to Gran, "She's dancing in her bloomers over there about something she's found on the Internet. Do you mind if we go home and see what it is before she pops?"

"Let's see . . . go back to your house, put my feet up, pet those pretty kitties of yours, and eat whatever goodies you put in front of me. Hm-m-m."

"Ryan and John are there."

"And feast my eyes upon the likes of Ryan Stone and John Gibson." She placed the back of her hand to her forehead, fluttered her eyelashes, and did her best Scarlet O'Hara almost-swoon. " 'Twill be a hardship, but I'll bear up."

When Savannah and Gran arrived back at her house, they found Tammy sitting at the rolltop desk in the corner, staring at the computer screen. Ryan and John had arranged a couple of Savannah's dining room chairs on either side of her, and they, too, were absorbed in what she was doing.

Cleo was curled up asleep on Ryan's lap, and Di was on John's, savoring a prolonged scratch behind the ear.

Diamante and Cleopatra firmly believed that if anybody sat down, creating a lap, it should be immediately occupied by a feline who was either napping or getting petted or both.

"So," Gran said, "what's all the ruckus about?"

"Yeah, it better be good," Savannah added. "That beach was mighty pretty today." She glanced at Gran. "And the company was nice, too."

"I'm sorry to interrupt your day," Tammy told them. "But this couldn't wait. And we had to actually show it to you . . . couldn't just tell you about it."

Ryan stood, cradling the cat in his arms. "Here, Granny," he said, indicating his chair with a nod. "Sit down and look at what we've got."

"I don't go in much for computers and the like," Granny said, but she gladly took the seat.

"Come over here, dear," John told Savannah as he, too, rose and offered his chair. He set a disgruntled Diamante on the floor. With a switching tail, she strutted away into

146

the kitchen.

Savannah sat down and gave Tammy a nudge. "Okay, I'm all eyes and ears. Lay it on me."

"Well . . ." Tammy said, milking the drama, ". . . before Ryan and John dropped by, I was finding all sorts of stuff on here about Wellman and his wife. They'd really only become rich and famous last year. Before that, nobody had heard of them. And boy, does he have some quacky ideas about weight loss."

"Like what?" Savannah asked.

"His hypnosis, reprogramming-the-mind stuff. I mean, hypnosis can be a valuable tool to help a person eat the right things and exercise regularly. And I'm sure it helps someone who's trying to lose weight to understand why they overeat . . . you know . . . unresolved emotions and all that."

Savannah reined in her impatience and said as calmly as she could, "Okay . . . and you found . . . ?"

"All this stuff about how he thinks that fat is just stored emotions, and if you listen to his CDs or watch his DVDs, even *one* time, you can stir up all those repressed emotions and release them and all your fat into the universe."

"Well, a bunch of people have bought his

stuff, and I haven't seen big blobs of fat floating up into the sky . . . so, I guess it's safe to assume it doesn't work that way." Savannah drew a deep, steadying breath. "So, he's a schmuck. Anything that might help us solve the murder?"

"When Ryan and John got here, I told them what I was doing, and how I wasn't finding any information about them, except this recent stuff. Robert and Maria Wellman both just sort of appeared out of nowhere. I couldn't even find out where they had lived before moving to San Carmelita a couple of years ago."

"And that," Ryan said, "was when John suggested we check out the family tree and ancestry sites."

John nodded. "I thought perhaps if we knew where their families lived — parents and siblings — we could start from there."

"And we found something very interesting." Ryan pointed to the screen. "Show them, Tammy."

"I found a number of Wellman family trees. One in particular seems to be centered in the Las Vegas area." A few entries and clicks of the mouse and Tammy was on the site. She pointed to the diagrams on the screen that showed the various branches of the family.

"As you can see," she continued, "this is a particularly well-developed site. They have little paragraphs telling something about each family member, and most of them even have a picture of the person."

"This is good," Granny said, squinting at the monitor. "We need one of these for the Reid bunch. Although we'd need a heap bigger screen than that one when we got to our nine younguns."

"I found Maria and Robert Wellman here on the family tree," Tammy said. Again, she entered her search data and clicked. "There they are."

She pointed to the screen, where the photo of a couple — possibly taken on their wedding day — was displayed with a caption beneath that read: ROBERT AND MARIA WELLMAN.

Savannah only had to look at the faded picture to know it was taken about fifty years ago. The lady's pillbox hat with a half veil and the man's bow tie and sharkskin suit with tiny, narrow lapels, spoke of a yesteryear's fashions.

The smiling lady in the photograph, holding a bouquet of roses, bore no resemblance at all to their victim. But, although the man wasn't the same Robert Wellman she and Dirk had interviewed earlier, he did have similar facial features.

"That might be Wellman's parents," Savannah said. "They're around the right age, and this guy looks a little like the doctor."

"Maybe Robert's a junior," Gran suggested. "I don't know if they go in for that in Nevada, but we got us a mess o' juniors down South."

"That's what we thought at first, too." Ryan was grinning like a magician with a great trick somewhere up his sleeve.

"But we kept looking," John said. He patted Tammy's shoulder. "Show them, love."

Tammy moved her cursor around on the screen, made a few selections, and brought up new images.

"We saw plenty of pictures, even some videos, of Dr. Wellman and his wife on other Web sites, plus seeing him on TV," she said. "So we were searching, looking for similar names or people who looked like them. Imagine how surprised we were to see this. . . ."

Savannah watched the new frame pop up on the monitor. There was no doubt about it; the face looking back at her was Robert Wellman. And it wasn't the Robert Wellman wearing the bow tie, either. This was the man she had spoken to in his seaside mansion . . . the guy whose wife had just been found murdered.

Tammy pointed to the caption beneath the picture.

Savannah stared at it, uncomprehendingly, for a moment. Then she said, "Who the heck is Bobby Martini?"

"Exactly." Tammy giggled.

"Maybe they got it wrong . . . the people who made up the Web site. Maybe it was an accident, putting 'Bobby Martini' under Robert Wellman's picture."

"That's no mistake," John said. "His name and picture are on a number of this site's pages. We studied the family tree, branch by branch. Your so-called Dr. Wellman is the real Robert Wellman's nephew. And his name is Martini."

"So, Bobby Martini assumed his uncle's identity?" Savannah's head was spinning, processing this new information and thinking how much fun it was going to be to tell Dirk.

"According to the social security death index," Tammy said, "Robert Wellman, the uncle, died five years ago. How much do you want to bet that Martini is using his uncle's social security number?"

"But how about his wife, Maria?" Granny said. "If Robert Wellman is really Bobby

151

Martini, then Maria's name isn't . . . I mean, wasn't . . . Wellman, either."

Tammy started jiggling around in her seat, like a kindergartner who desperately needed to go to the little girls' room. "Oh, oh, that's the best part! Here, look at *this*."

Again, more clicking, typing, searching. And another picture appeared on the screen.

It was Maria Wellman, all right. She was about ten years younger and had black hair, but there was no doubt in Savannah's mind this was the same person. "That's her, but . . . the name . . . Gina? Who's Gina Martini?"

Granny shook her head and sighed. "I'm all bum-fuzzled now. People oughta have to keep the name the good Lord gave 'em. And the hair color, too. Otherwise it's just all too confusing."

"So, Gina ripped off Bobby Martini's aunt's identity, too?" Savannah asked. "Robert and Maria Wellman are really Bobby and Gina Martini. Wow."

"Hold on to your hat," Ryan said. "It gets better."

Savannah wasn't sure she could handle "better." But she said, "Okay, lemme have it."

Tammy brought up yet another page, which was a picture of an enormous oak tree. On the limbs and branches of the tree were text boxes, containing names, dates, and the relationships between those remembered there.

"The family tree," Savannah said. "In all its glory."

Tammy tapped on the screen with her fingernail. "Check it out. Right there."

Savannah read what it said. Then she read it again. And then once more.

"Holy shit," she whispered, forgetting for the moment that her grandmother was sitting nearby.

"Yeah," Tammy said, terribly pleased with herself.

"Am I seeing what I think I'm seeing?" Gran asked breathlessly.

"Yeap," Ryan replied. "Bobby Martini and Gina Martini weren't husband and wife. They were brother and sister."

Granny did a tsk-tsk and shook her head. "I thought I'd seen some nasty cow-pucky back where I come from, but that there . . . that's one mighty messed-up family."

# CHAPTER 8

Savannah waited as long as she could stand it to call Dirk — one minute and thirty seconds. And it only took her that long because someone had left the phone off the charger, and she couldn't find it.

She finally hit the "Pager" button on the base and located it in the cupboard with the cat food.

Reluctantly, she admitted that things around her house were getting misplaced more and more frequently the older she got. Her reading glasses had wound up in the freezer a couple of days ago, and that couldn't be a good sign.

"It's a good thing my butt's well attached," she muttered as she leaned back against the kitchen counter and punched in his number on the phone, "or I'd probably find it in the crisper drawer of the refrigerator."

He answered after the second ring. "Coulter."

" 'Coulter,' my butt. Don't act like you don't know it's me. I know you've got caller ID. Listen . . . you aren't going to believe the news I've got," she started to tell him.

But he cut her off. "Me, too," he said. "I just left those road maintenance workers over there where they're working by Wellman's office building, and boy, they had a story and a half to tell me! Wait'll you hear it!"

"Like I said . . . I've got news of my own! Tammy found out that —"

"Naw, I'd rather tell you in person. You've gotta go with me on another interview anyway. I'll swing by and pick you up in ten minutes." He hung up.

She stood there, staring at the silent phone in her hand, wondering if this was what it felt like to be ignored and taken for granted.

"Yes," she muttered to herself. "This is exactly what it feels like. That boy needs a good skillet whack upside the head. That'd cross his eyes and set him straight."

When she walked back into the living room, where Tammy, Ryan, John, and Gran were still gathered around the computer, Tammy said, "Well, was he impressed with what we found out?"

"I didn't tell him."

"You what?"

"He irked me, so I held out on him. That'll teach him." She walked over to her favorite chair, sat down, scooped Cleo into her lap, and kicked her shoes off. "Actually, he's on his way here to pick me up in a few minutes. Said he wanted to take me on some interview. I'll tell him the news when he gets here."

Savannah looked across the room at her grandmother sitting there next to Tammy, a twinkle in her eyes, a broad grin lighting her face. She enjoyed "sleuthing" — as Tammy called it — as much as any of them. In fact, Savannah was pretty sure she had inherited her nosiness from Granny, along with the famous Reid blue eyes, curvaceous, bodacious figure, and occasional bouts of pure cussedness.

"Don't worry, Gran," she said. "I'm not going out with him again today. I'm staying home and visiting with you. We'll bake some brownies and watch a Cary Grant movie together. Sound good?"

"Sounds ridiculous," Gran replied. "If Dirk wants you to go on an interview with him, you hightail it outta here. You're not going to sit around the house keeping an old lady company when you could be catching a cold-blooded, good-for-nothing-but-fertilizer killer."

"She certainly isn't," John said. "Savannah's going with Dirk, and you, dear lady, are coming out to dinner with us at Chez Antoine."

Granny lifted her hands in heavenly surrender. "Oh, if I have to. But you tell that Antoine, 'no snails or frog legs.' "

"Oh, I'm pretty sure he remembers how you feel about those delicacies from the last time we took you there," Ryan said.

"Indeed," John added. "I believe everyone who was dining at Antoine's that evening remembers that you don't eat . . . how did you put it? Ah yes — reptiles, amphibians, or critters that slither around in their own slime."

As Ryan passed by Savannah on his way to the kitchen for a glass of water, she caught him by the arm and whispered in his ear, "Do you think Antoine will let her back in the place, you know, considering?"

"All taken care of. When I heard Gran was coming to town, I called him and asked him to cater John's next birthday party."

"But that isn't for eleven months. Don't you think he'll find your motives a little suspect when you walk in there with Gran on your arm tonight?"

"Sure he will. But Antoine's far too gentle-manly to throw a dear, silver-haired lady out of his restaurant . . . in front of his other customers."

Savannah looked back at her grand-mother, who was still sitting next to Tammy, both of them studying the images on the computer monitor with rapt attention. "I'd like to see anybody try to throw my granny anywhere she didn't want to go. They might accomplish it, but oh . . . the scratching, the biting, the kicking and gouging. All that blood and gore."

Ryan thought it over and shook his head. Somberly, he said, "It wouldn't be worth the price they'd pay."

"Not even close."

Savannah had expected a pretty spectacular reaction from Dirk when she told him the news about Robert and Maria Wellman — specifically, that they weren't Robert and Maria Wellman.

And she wasn't disappointed.

He nearly ran the Buick off the road and into a lemon grove.

"Are you kidding me?" he asked, slightly bug-eyed.

"I kid you not. Brother and sister."

"That's so gross." He shuddered. "You

don't think they . . . you know . . . yuck."

She shivered along with him. "You're so typically male. Your brain automatically gravitates toward 'nasty.' I hadn't even thought of that."

"Oh, you did, too."

"Well, I thought about it for a minute. Then I decided that they're just living in the same house, posing as husband and wife, for some other bad — but not icky — reason. Something that has absolutely nothing whatsoever to do with creepy stuff."

"Like incest."

"Yeah, yeah, whatever."

"Maybe they're serial killers on the run. Maybe they ran a brothel outside Las Vegas and robbed and murdered all their johns, left 'em hanging on meat hooks in a trailer in the backyard . . . something like that?"

She shot him an alarmed sideways look. "You scare me sometimes, boy."

"Live in fear, woman. Live in fear."

"Yeah . . . whatever."

They drove along in silence for a while down the narrow, two-lane road that wound among the citrus groves that bordered the town on the east side. The dark green leaves of the trees contrasted beautifully with the snowy blossoms, and the sunwarmed, ripening fruit scented the moist, late afternoon air with an intoxicating perfume. Once in awhile, they passed a stand of eucalyptus trees, planted to function as windbreaks, and that fragrance mingled with the others.

Situated high on the foothills, the road also afforded an occasional view of the ocean in all its splendor.

After living here so long, Savannah thought she might have grown accustomed to the breathtaking beauty of the glittering, turquoise sea. But she hadn't. And she was sure she never would.

"Oh yeah," she said, snapping out of her commune with nature and back to business. "You didn't tell me your news."

He looked a little pouty when he said, "Well, now that you told me that thing of yours, it doesn't seem so important."

"Took the wind out of your sails a bit, did I?"

"Sorta. And I'm not sure what it might have to do with what you guys uncovered."

"So, lay it on me and maybe I can figure that out, too."

He sniffed. "Get over yourself."

She laughed and punched him on the bicep. "You haven't even told me where we're going, who we're going to interview."

"You haven't given me a chance to talk since you got in the car."

"The floor's all yours, puddin' cat." She glanced down at the floorboard, littered with newspapers, boxing magazines, and mostly empty fast-food containers. "Garbage and all."

He turned left, leaving the picturesque foothill road and heading down into town . . . the bad part of town . . . Stumpy's part of town.

*But not anymore,* Savannah thought with a self-satisfied grin.

"So, give me your news, boy," she said. "Lay it on me. What did the street maintenance guys have to say?"

"A couple of them were gals. Women's lib's brought you girls a long way. Now you can fill potholes with the good ol' boys."

Savannah shrugged. "It had to happen. A woman's got a right to do roadwork and anything else she wants to do. And, of course, being female, she'll do it better."

"You're just feelin' cocky because you got better news than me today."

"Is mine better?"

"Yeah, but mine's pretty good."

"Are you going to tell me what it is, or just keep me guessing?"

He gave her a mischievous grin.

"I know what that look means," she said. "It means I'm going to be getting mighty irked at you mighty quick."

He pointed to a sign up ahead and a dirt road entrance. "We're already there," he said.

"Canyon Park? Your mysterious interview is in the park?"

"Yeap. Watch and listen."

He drove the Buick down the long, narrow road that stretched from one end of the park to the other, passing the swings and slides, the sandbox and barbecue pits.

Ahead, Savannah saw a yellow minibus in the parking lot. A group of elementary school children stood in a cluster near the bus, listening to a couple of women and a young man.

Savannah recognized one of the females. "Roxanne? You're here to see her?"

"That's right."

"Why?"

"Ask me no questions, I'll tell you no lies."

"Don't irritate the crap outta me, I won't slap your jaws."

He parked near the bus and opened his car door. "Follow me," he said. "This should be fun."

For once, she did as he said and trailed along behind him as he strolled over toward the kids and their chaperones.

When they were about thirty feet away,

Roxanne Rosen glanced their way. The moment she recognized them, a look of anger mixed with apprehension passed over her face. But she quickly covered it with a wooden half smile.

Savannah noticed that she was dressed far more conservatively than before in loose-fitting, dark green slacks and a long-sleeved shirt of the same color. The seal of the city of San Carmelita was embroidered on the shirt's pocket.

"Hello again," Savannah said to her as they walked up to her.

"Uh . . . yeah, hi," she replied, giving a furtive glance to the right, then to the left, as though looking for an escape route.

"Hello, Miss Rosen," Dirk said. "I need to talk to you."

"I'm busy. We've got to get these kids back into the bus and on their way." With a wave of her hand, she indicated the group of kids and other adults, who were all listening intently, sensing something was amiss with one of their attendants.

"I'm busy, too," Dirk replied, considerably less friendly than before. He turned to the other woman in the group. "Can you do without Miss Rosen here for a couple of minutes? I'm a" — he looked down at the innocent, young faces, all aglow with interest — "a law enforcement official . . . if you know what I mean."

"The S-C-P-D?" the woman said, equally cryptic.

"Precisely."

"Okay." She turned to Roxanne. "We can handle them. Do what you have to do."

Reluctantly, Roxanne left the group and joined Savannah and Dirk. As they walked away from the children, Savannah overheard one little girl say, "Boy, when they start spelling stuff, you *know* it's bad."

"You'd better have a good excuse for embarrassing me like that in front of the children and my fellow volunteers," Roxanne said, once they were over by the picnic tables and well out of earshot of the others.

"Volunteers?" Savannah said.

"Yeah. We bring underprivileged kids out here once a month for an all-day field trip. It's part of the Parks and Recreation program." Roxanne plunked herself down on one of the picnic table benches and ran her fingers through her thick, carefully mussed curls. "I'm trying to do a good thing here, and you have to come along and ruin it."

Dirk sat down across the table from her. Savannah did the same.

"There's no reason at all for you to be embarrassed," he told her. "The kids don't

164

know what's up, and as far as the adults . . . Your boss's wife got murdered. That's no secret; it's all over the news. It only stands to reason that you'd be questioned by the cops. So, get over it. You haven't done anything to be ashamed of, right?"

The piercing look he gave her put even Savannah on alert. What was going on here? Savannah knew that about-to-shoot-somebody-at-high-noon squint. And she knew that Dirk reserved it for people who had the dubious honor of ranking number 1 on his suspect list.

"Where were you night before last?" Dirk asked. "And don't lie to me, because I promise you that I'm going to check it out."

She thought it over, then shrugged. "Hanging out with my girlfriends at Rick's Disco."

"What time, exactly?"

She batted her suspiciously turquoise eyes a few times, looked around, as if looking for someone to rescue her, then said, "About eight o'clock."

"No later than that? Rick told me you usually come in around ten."

"I went in early, okay? It was Becky's birthday. We were celebrating."

"What did you do before that?"

"I sat at home and watched TV and drank

165

screwdrivers. And since you're probably going to ask . . . that's what I did when I left there, too, okay? Now that I don't have a job anymore, that's what I do."

Tears flooded her eyes, making the fake aqua blue of her eyes even more intense. She folded her hands in front of her, fingers laced together, and stared down at them. "And I volunteer to help kids with crappy lives have a good time once a month. That's me. That's what I did that night. That's what I do."

Something in the young woman's words and demeanor touched Savannah. And, just for a moment, Savannah could feel herself hoping that Roxanne Rosen wasn't the one who killed Maria Wellman, aka Gina Martini.

"Why don't you have a job anymore?" Savannah asked.

Roxanne wiped her eyes with the back of her hand. "What?"

"You said you don't have a job anymore. What happened?"

"Yeah." Dirk leaned across the table, staring at her with that strange look again. "Tell us all about that, Roxie."

Roxanne tugged at the cuff of her sleeve. "They . . . Dr. Wellman . . . he let me go."

"Why?" Dirk wanted to know.

166

"I guess they needed to make cuts . . . not as much business or whatever," she said.

"And now you're lying to me." He turned to Savannah. "Tell her how much I love being lied to."

"He'd rather have a prostate exam and a root canal . . . at the same time. Don't lie to him. It makes him cranky."

Roxanne tugged on her cuffs again, then sighed and said, "Okay. Maria was actually the one who fired me. She and I had an argument about . . . some stuff and . . ."

"What stuff?" Savannah asked.

"She was always on me about one thing or the other. She was terrified that they weren't going to make every single dollar they possibly could. She watched how much paper I used in the office, how many pens and paper clips I went through. I never met anybody so greedy in all my life."

"You got fired because of an argument over paper clips?" Dirk said. "Is that what you're trying to tell me?"

"Cranky," Savannah whispered, nodding toward Dirk. "Very cranky."

"It started over printer ink. I printed out some invitations to my nephew's birthday party on the office printer, and she got all in a tizzy over it. It was as we were closing the office for the day. She followed me out to the parking lot and . . . well . . . it kinda escalated there."

*Ah,* Savannah thought. *This is what the road crew saw . . . Dirk's big news.*

Dirk gave Roxanne a nasty little grin. "I know what happened in the parking lot. So you'd better tell me your side of it and not leave anything out."

Roxanne looked like she was about to be sick. But Savannah could see the resignation in her eyes as she started to speak. She had a certain look of relief that came from deciding to tell the truth. "Like I said, it started with the business about me using the office's ink and paper. Ten whole sheets! But I'd had a really bad day with some patients yelling at me, telling me they wanted their money back because the CDs were a big rip-off. And I just sort of snapped."

"Is that when you hit her?" Dirk said.

"No, there wasn't anything physical. It was just a verbal thing." Again, she pulled nervously at the edge of her shirt cuff.

Dirk reached across the table and grabbed her around the wrist. "Then you won't mind if I roll up your sleeve and look at your arm, right?"

When she didn't reply, he unbuttoned her cuff and pushed the material up her arm.

Four long, parallel scratches lined the inside of her forearm. They were deep, ugly, and red, as though infected.

"Maria Wellman broke her nails on you," Dirk said. "Several witnesses saw the two of you going at each other, hitting, scratching, and pulling hair, so don't tell me it didn't get physical."

Roxanne hung her head, pulled her sleeve back down and buttoned it.

"So," Dirk continued, "she yelled at you, and that's when you snapped and tied into her."

"No! That's when I told her that she had bigger things to worry about than paper and ink. I told her that her husband was screwing every female patient he could get his hands on, and it was a matter of time before they got sued and he lost his license."

Savannah shot a quick sideways glance at Dirk to see if this was news to him, too. It was. She saw the momentary look of surprise on his face before he squelched it.

"And that's when *she* hit *me,*" Roxanne said.

"She struck you first?" Dirk asked.

"She slapped me across the face, and nobody slaps me and gets away with it." Roxanne's eyes blazed with anger, and it occurred to Savannah that this girl would, indeed, be capable of killing someone if they pushed her too far.

"And you hit her back," Savannah said.

"Oh, absolutely. I slugged her. And then she pulled my hair, and I pulled hers . . . and then we went at it, big time."

"Where was the doctor all this time?" Dirk asked.

"He was still in the office, I guess. But then he came out and broke us up."

"Who would you say won the fight?" Savannah couldn't help asking. Being a Southerner, these things mattered greatly.

"I guess I did. She was on the ground, and I was on top of her. He had to pull me off."

Savannah thought of Stumpy. "Yeap, if you were on top when it ended, you won."

They all sat in quiet thoughtfulness for a moment. Then Savannah said, "Tell me, Roxanne, that thumping that you gave her there in the parking lot . . . did you get it all out of your system? Or did you have to go to her house a few days later for some more?"

Roxanne looked at her with her fake turquoise eyes shining with a sincerity that Savannah thought was probably real. You couldn't always tell for sure, but it seemed genuine to her.

"I've only been to the Wellmans' house once," Roxanne said, "and that was yesterday, after Maria was already dead. I was just trying to get my last paycheck. Needless to say, after I ratted Dr. Wellman out to his wife and then beat her up, he fired me. I think the only reason they didn't press charges against me was because they didn't want it to come out that he fools around with his patients."

"If she hit you first," Savannah said, "why didn't you press charges against her or sue them?"

"It was my word against hers. The cops wouldn't have done anything. And as far as suing them, I couldn't pay an attorney. Hell, I do well to afford electricity for my TV and orange juice for my screwdrivers."

Dirk took his pen and notebook from his pocket. He flipped the pad open. "Listen to me, Roxanne," he said. "Right now I'm looking at you for this killing."

"Why me?"

"Are you kidding? You've still got her scratches on your arm and a dozen people saw you sitting on top of her, pounding her into the asphalt. So, if you want to get off the hook for this, you'd better start naming names."

"Like who?"

"Start with the patients Wellman was banging."

"Several of them have moved out of the area, but two are still around."

"Okay, give me those."

"Who do you want first? The one whose husband said he was going to kill Wellman? He caught her smoking the doctor's cigar. Or the one who was mad that he wasn't leaving his wife to marry her the way he'd promised? She claims she's pregnant with his kid."

Dirk grinned at Savannah, then clicked his pen and got ready to write. "Oh, either one will do just fine. Let 'er rip."

# CHAPTER 9

As Savannah watched the tiny guy struggle to carry the enormous box up the sidewalk to his house, it occurred to her — not for the first time — that perhaps Roxanne Rosen wasn't the best judge of who was large and who was small in this world. She would never recommend that Dirk arrest someone based on one of Roxie's physical descriptions.

"Does that guy look like a 'brute of an Irishman bricklayer' to you?" she asked Dirk, who was sitting in the driver's seat, watching with her from the curb across the street. "Those are the words she used, right?"

"Hey, don't complain," he said. "If I'm gonna have a tussle with a guy, I'd rather he be skinny and five foot one any day."

The guy nearly dropped the box, then did an awkward little dance as he balanced it on one knee and tried to get a better grip.

"He looks more like a Latino jockey than an Irish bricklayer to me," Savannah said, refusing to give it up. "But that's the address Roxie gave you, I'm sure." She pointed to the numbers on the house. "Maybe she was yanking our chain and right now she's on her way to Vancouver or Tijuana."

"She'd better not be!" Dirk jerked the car door open. "If she skips, I'm going after her and dragging her back here, kicking and screaming. And I'll book her for murder one, too, so fast it'll make her big hair and empty head spin. Let's go talk to this bricklaying brute."

Savannah smiled, got out of the car, and walked along with him across the street. She loved to watch Dirk get in a dither over absolutely nothing. He would go insane over things that hadn't even happened yet but maintain his cool in a genuine crisis. A long wait in a line at the grocery store could destroy his week, but he was a great guy to have around if somebody needed CPR at a bad car crash.

As they approached the man with the box, he turned around to look at them and promptly dropped it on the sidewalk. Savannah heard the sound of breaking glass and cringed. "Uh-oh," she told Dirk. "If he's got an old lady, he's in trouble."

"Can I give you a hand with that?" Dirk asked him.

The man glanced toward the house, a look of dread on his face.

"Yeap, there's an old lady," Savannah whispered.

"No, thanks." The guy reached down, pulled up the edge of his T-shirt, and wiped the sweat off his face. "Moving bites."

A little bell chimed in Savannah's head. "Ah," she said, "are you moving in or out?"

"In. Just bought it last week. I was happy in our apartment, but no . . . *she* had to have a house." He gave the box a kick. "But you notice that she's not the one carting all the boxes in and out. And she won't be the one mowing the lawn and weeding the flower beds, either. That's for sure."

Dirk nodded, agreeing, but not too vigorously, considering Savannah's proximity. "Let me guess," he said, "you bought this place from a guy named Brian Mahoney, right?"

"Yeah. How did you know?"

"Thankfully, I'm smarter than I look," Dirk said with a sigh. "Tell me something, buddy . . . do you have any idea where this Mahoney guy moved to?"

"Oh, yeah! Man, he moved up in the world! He bought a place in Spirit Hills."

175

"Do you happen to know where in Spirit Hills?" Savannah asked, thinking that, although the gated, exclusive enclave was small, they couldn't exactly go door-to-door looking for a construction worker who had recently had a windfall.

"Yeah. It's the big, white house with pillars, like in *Gone with the Wind,* on Anacapa Drive. Man, that guy must've won the lottery or something."

"The dude with the box full of broken dishes had a good point," Savannah said as Dirk flashed his badge to get past the guard of the gated community of Spirit Hills. "I know *I'd* have to win the lottery to live here."

The sun was setting into the ocean, its coral light staining the sky, as the hills turned twilight purple.

This was Savannah's favorite time of day, and she had to admit, this was one of her favorite parts of town.

They passed one exquisite home after another as they drove deeper into the residential area for the most economically enhanced of San Carmelitans. A Tudor manor sat next to a Romanesque villa, neighbored by a French chateau, each grander than the next.

Those who lived on Lincoln Ridge, next

to the Wellmans, might have the best ocean views in town, but these estates, with their expansive acreage, sweeping lawns, guest houses, and horse stables, seemed more like the palaces Savannah had dreamed about as a poor child growing up in McGill.

Although, as an adult, she had witnessed some of the tragedies that occurred even here, in this secluded community. Unfortunately, a gatehouse could guard against only a limited amount of life's woes.

Human drama and suffering knew no financial limitations.

"Still," she said, "if I have to suffer, I'd rather it be in one of these places."

"You're talking to yourself again," he told her.

"No, I'm not. I was talking to you."

"What you were saying didn't make any sense."

"That's because you weren't listening when I said the first part."

"There wasn't any first part. You were talking about the guy with the broken dishes and then the fact that you'd have to win the lottery to live here, and then you skipped to something about suffering. I'm telling you, you were talking to yourself again."

She thought it over, took a deep breath, and said, "I picked it up from you. Your bad habits are rubbing off on me."

"I knew it had to be my fault somehow."

She grinned at him. "Do you realize how much time we'd save if you just accepted that at the beginning of an argument?"

He grinned back. "Did I ever tell you I love the fact that you're a feisty broad?"

"Dirk, nobody but old farts say 'broad' anymore. And don't use me and the 'L' word in the same sentence. Certainly don't use it around Gran. You'll get her all excited."

"Granny's rooting for me, huh?"

"Yeah, yeah, yeah. It's only 'cause she thinks we're fooling around, and she wants me to make an honest man of you."

"Now there's a thought."

"No, it's not a thought. Don't think."

They passed a particularly winsome Tuscan-style villa, and she pointed to it. "Win the lottery and buy me that," she said. "Then we'll talk."

"Yeah, right." He shook his head. "So, you're only interested in rich men?"

"Rich has nothing to do with it. I'm only interested in men with houses big enough that, if they irritate the dickens outta me, I can 'retire to the west wing' and be rid of 'em for a while."

"You couldn't give me one of these places,

178

too much grass to mow."

"Sheez. What's with you guys and grass mowing?"

"It's not that we mind doing it all that much. It's just that we don't wanna *have* to do it on our day off."

"You never take a day off."

"Yeah? Well, if I ever do, I don't want to spend it listening to some woman gripe about how I never mow the lawn."

"Then since you work all the time and don't have a wife or a yard, I guess it's not something that should keep you awake all night, frettin' about it."

"That's right. The joys of bachelorhood."

They rounded a curve in the road and she saw it ahead, the antebellum mansion — or at least the Southern California version of a Southern antebellum mansion.

Savannah wasn't terribly impressed, having seen the real thing in Georgia. There were, after all, a few of them that Sherman and the Union army hadn't burned to the ground.

As houses in this area went, this one was a bit less ostentatious, slightly more modest — if, indeed, a house with six Corinthian columns could be considered modest.

In Savannah's part of town, this place would be the shining gem of the neighborhood. But in Spirit Hills, the residents of this home were officially the "poor relations."

"Your heart's just gotta bleed for them," she muttered to herself.

"What?"

"Never mind. You're not listening again."

"Oh. Sorry."

"It's okay."

They pulled into the driveway and up to the house, where an enormous pickup sat. The vehicle was black with yellow, orange, and red flames streaking down the sides and oversized tires.

And Savannah spotted another disturbing feature. "Hey, buddy," she said as they walked past it. "Gun rack on the back window."

"Yeah, I saw that," he said.

"Of course you did."

They both reached under their coats and unsnapped the retention strap on their holsters. And as she went through the motion, the thought occurred to Savannah that she'd been doing that a lot more frequently lately.

It was an unsettling thought.

When she had originally bought the weapon and strapped it onto her body, she had sincerely wished that she would never,

ever have to use it. Never have to even think about using it.

She hadn't been that lucky.

As they walked up to the door and rang the doorbell, Dirk said, "We'll just keep this nice and friendly. Find out what we can and get going. If we need to come back later with backup, we will."

Savannah was a little surprised that Dirk would communicate any degree of concern over the interview. He was one of those "manly" men who hated to admit when he was feeling a little shaky about something.

But she had to admit that she did, too. She already didn't like Brian Mahoney, and she hadn't even met the guy yet.

Her opinion of him wasn't improved when she saw him in the flesh, either.

The front door opened and the term "a mountain of a man" flashed through her mind. He seemed to fill the doorframe with his bulk, and it was all muscle. His dingy-white, skintight T-shirt showed off every defined ripple and bulge.

And while, under different circumstances, that might have been a plus in Savannah's book, his face ruined the effect of the perfect body.

His shoulder-length reddish blond hair looked like it hadn't been combed in a month of Sundays, and his long, scraggly beard was equally unkempt.

While he might have an Irish last name, Savannah was pretty sure that some of his ancestors had been the Viking, rape-pillage-and-plunder sort of guys.

His pale blue eyes did a quick scan of both Savannah and Dirk, pausing momentarily on Savannah's bustline. And while Savannah was the first to admit that she had an impressive bosom — one of the advantages of being less-than-fashionably thin — she still held it against a man just a bit if he leered. It was bad manners.

"Who are you?" he asked, his tone brusque.

Dirk already had his badge in hand. He held it up to Mahoney's face. "Detective Sergeant Dirk Coulter," he barked back. He waved the badge in Savannah's direction. "Savannah Reid. And you are?"

"The owner of this property that you're standing on . . . without any sort of warrant in your hand."

"You're Brian Mahoney?"

"Yeah. What do you want?"

Dirk glared at him, dropping all pretence of niceties. "What I want and what I *intend* is to talk to you about the murder of Maria Wellman. Now what do *you* want? To talk to me *here* . . . on *your* property . . . or down at *my* station house?"

Mahoney thought about it for several long moments. Then he pulled the door open wider and took a couple of steps backward into the house.

"Wipe your feet good," he said. "I don't want you messin' up the floors of my new house."

Savannah made a deliberate show of cleaning the soles of her loafers on the welcome mat as she looked down at Mahoney's feet, at his workman's boots with blobs of paint and lumps of dried cement caked onto them. "No, God knows, we wouldn't want to scuff those tiles of yours," she told him.

"That's some truck you got out there," Dirk said. Then, in a far less friendly tone, he added, "Where are the weapons?"

Mahoney pretended to be confused, then said, "Oh, are you referring to the gun rack?"

"Uh-huh."

Mahoney returned Dirk's pointed stare. "Locked away, safely. All perfectly legal."

"You carry them around with you in the truck on a regular basis?"

Mahoney shrugged and grinned. "Naw. The rack's more of a political statement."

He turned to Savannah. "And you, sugar, with that sexy Southern drawl of yours . . . you know all about good ol' boys and their political statements, right?"

Savannah nodded. "Yeap, I've known a lot of good ol' boys in my day. Some of them were the salt of the earth, some just good, and some not worth takin' behind the barn and shootin'."

"Well, I'm the salt-of-the-earth type myself. So, you don't have to worry about me or anything I've been up to. I'm a law-abiding citizen all the way."

"Hm-m-m . . ." Savannah said. "If you're a good ol' boy, where are your manners? You haven't asked us to 'set a spell' or offered us anything to eat or drink. Where's the hospitality?"

Mahoney's ice blue eyes got even colder. "You're not going to be staying that long." To Dirk he said, "Say what you've got to say or ask whatever you want to and then be on your way."

"Okay." Dirk put his hands on his hips. "Account for your whereabouts the night before last."

"That's when that bitch got killed, huh?"

"Where were you?"

"Here."

"Doing what?"

"Watching TV and having a beer."

Savannah sniffed. "There's been a lot of that going around lately. Were you with anybody who can vouch for you?"

"No. I don't have a lot of company, and I like it that way."

Savannah nodded. "I'm sure everyone's contented with that arrangement."

"How about your wife?" Dirk asked.

Mahoney stiffened all over, his fists clenching at his sides. "What about her? She wasn't here in the house, if that's what you mean."

"Where was she?" Savannah wanted to know.

"Where she is right now. Where she's gonna stay. She's out in the servants' quarters over the garage, and she's damned lucky to be there. If it weren't for me needing my laundry done and somebody to cook and clean, I'd have thrown her out, lock, stock, and barrel."

Dirk smirked. "Yes, we heard there was a bit of trouble in paradise. Something having to do with Dr. Wellman, I believe."

Mahoney's breath came hard and fast, and Savannah could see he was struggling to control his temper. She was wishing Dirk would remember what he'd said about keeping this friendly.

185

"Who told you that?" Mahoney wanted to know. "Who's spreading lies like that?"

"It's not important," Dirk told him.

"It is to me!"

"No. What's important is that a woman's dead. Somebody killed her and we're going to find out who. At the moment, I'm thinking it's somebody who had something against her husband, and from what I understand, that's you."

Mahoney took a step toward Dirk, and Savannah slid her hand under her jacket, taking hold of the Beretta's grip.

"Look, buddy," Mahoney said. "If you know so much about my business, you know what happened between my wife and that two-bit snake. You can't blame me for being pissed at him. In some parts of this country, if I'd shot him and her both between the eyes, nobody would have thought twice about it."

"Oh, I think we're pretty progressive now in all fifty states," Savannah said. "Even where I come from, we figure that divorce is the answer to adultery, not murder."

She turned to Dirk. "I've enjoyed about enough of this gentleman's hospitality," she said. "I'm going to go sit out in the car and wait for you."

Without another word, she turned around

and walked out the front door, leaving the two men to finish their discussion without her.

But she didn't go sit in the car. She had better things to do with her time.

She headed around the side of the house and toward the rear of the property. Somewhere back there was a garage with a servants' apartment over it and a discarded, disgraced, probably unhappy wife inside.

And experience had taught her that most unhappy women had a lot to say about the guy who had discarded them.

# CHAPTER 10

Savannah found Brian Mahoney's wife, as he had said, in the maid's quarters over the three-car garage.

She had answered the door wearing an old nightgown with food stains on the front of it. She looked and smelled like a woman who hadn't recently bathed.

Depression took its toll.

But she had invited Savannah inside, offered her a chair at the kitchen table, and had put a cup of weak, instant coffee in her hand. And she was trying to answer Savannah's questions with as much honesty as possible. Savannah had to give her credit for that, considering that those answers didn't paint a rosy picture of Lydia Mahoney, her marriage, or her life.

"I thought I was in love with Dr. Wellman," she admitted, sucking deeply on the cigarette she held in her hand.

Savannah noticed that both the hand and

the cigarette were shaking.

"He was so nice to me," she continued. "When I'd go to see him, his face would just light up when he saw me. He'd tell me that he looked forward to my appointments all week. I went to him to stop smoking."

Lydia put one hand to her hair and made a feeble gesture as though trying to fluff the flat, greasy strands. "Of course," she said, "I didn't look like this when I went to see him. I'd dress up, fix my hair and makeup. I look pretty good when I clean up."

"I'll bet you do," Savannah said softly.

Lydia smiled, a half smile filled with sadness. "I had this one red dress. It was his favorite. I was wearing it the first time that we . . . well . . . the first time that I . . ." She sighed. "We never actually did . . . it. He wanted to be faithful to his wife, you know. So, I just, you know, took care of him. Not a lot; just a few times. But Brian got wise to us and dropped by during one of my sessions. He got past the receptionist — you can see how big he is — and walked into the office and caught us. It was really bad."

"What did Brian do?"

"He hit the doctor, several times, really hard. I was afraid he was going to kill him. And when he got me home, he hit me, too."

Lydia put her finger to her lip, and Savannah could see what remained of a scar on her bottom lip.

"Why didn't the doctor press charges against Brian?" Savannah asked, although she was pretty sure of the answer she was going to get.

"He didn't want the bad publicity. Brian was counting on that."

"When he hit him? Or afterward . . . when he blackmailed him?"

Lydia looked stunned and couldn't speak for a moment. Finally, she said, "How do you know about that?"

Savannah waved a hand in the direction of the window and the main house. "It's not too hard to figure out. You two go from living in a little house in the middle of town to a place like this in Spirit Hills. There's a new, tricked-out pickup in the driveway. Somebody came into some big money somehow. And I don't buy the BS about the lottery, either."

Lydia rubbed one hand over her eyes and shook her head. "We're not buying this house. We're just renting it for a few months. The owners are in Brazil, and the guy they left in charge of it is making some extra money on the side by letting us stay here."

"Still," Savannah said. "The truck's new,

190

and your rent here can't be cheap."

"Brian's blowing through money like crazy . . . the cash the doctor gave him, the money from selling our house. He's sure he can get Dr. Wellman to keep paying him to keep his mouth shut. But now with Maria getting killed like that, and you guys investigating the doctor, who knows what's going to happen?"

Lydia stubbed her cigarette out in the tray and promptly lit another. "Brian likes living in a place like this. Says he deserves it after all he's been through in his life. But I don't know how he's going to pull it off . . . what he's going to do. I don't know what I'm going to do."

The women sat quietly for a long time, the silence heavy in the room.

Finally, Savannah said, "Did you consider pressing charges against Brian when he hit you?"

She shook her head. "No. I never have."

"Why not?"

"I can't risk it. He told me he'd kill me if I ever called the cops on him, and I'm absolutely sure he would. He also told me that if I ever leave him, he'll hunt me down and kill me. And I'm sure he means that, too. So, see . . . I'm stuck."

Savannah looked around the room at the

cardboard boxes that were stacked against the wall, still unopened. The sink was piled high with dirty dishes, and the cigarette tray on the table was overrun with butts.

She looked at the woman on the other side of the table who had once been pretty enough in her red dress to turn a doctor's head. But now she looked worse than some of San Carmelita's street people who hung around in the poorer areas of town.

And Savannah fully appreciated the dilemma Lydia faced with her abusive husband. While on the police force, Savannah had encountered women like her every single day. And her heart broke for them every single time.

"Don't go telling me to get a restraining order against him," Lydia was saying. "You and I both know all that does is piss these guys off. And then they come after you even worse than before."

Savannah stared down at the cup in her hands. "Sometimes restraining orders work, with some guys."

"Brian's not one of them," Lydia said. "Believe me, I know."

"I won't argue with you. You know your situation better than anyone else." Savannah reached across the table and patted the woman's hand. "But, honey, if he's hit you before, he'll hit you again. And one of these days, he'll hurt you really bad or kill you. So, if there's any way you can get away from him, do it. And get all the help you can from law enforcement or friends or family or any place you can get it."

"I don't have any family or friends," Lydia said. "Over the years, Brian got rid of everybody who ever meant anything to me — pushed them out of our lives. And, one by one, I let him do it. Now he's got me right where he wants me. I don't have anybody."

Savannah reached into her purse and pulled out her business card. Then she took out a pen and scribbled her cell phone number on the back of it.

She pressed it into the woman's hand. "Now you've got somebody," she said. "You're not alone anymore. You've got me."

After Savannah left Lydia, she was on her way back to the car when her cell phone started ringing. She saw from the caller ID that it was Dirk.

"I'm here in the car," he said. "Where are you?"

"Look in your rearview mirror," she told him. "What do you see?"

"A hot, bodacious brunette," he replied.

"You think maybe I could pick her up, get her to take a ride with me?"

"I'd say your chances are good."

He reached across the seat and pushed the passenger door open for her.

They both hung up their phones as she slid in beside him. "Get anything more from Mahoney?" she asked.

"More attitude and mouth. That's about it." He drove the car around the circular driveway and back onto the street. "And you?"

"I went back to the garage apartment and chatted with his wife."

"I figured. How'd that go?"

"Mahoney blackmailed Wellman. That's how they're affording the house. Although, it's rented, so it's not like they shook him down for a king's ransom or whatever."

"Then why do you think Mahoney would murder Maria Wellman . . . or Gina . . . or whatever her name is?"

"What makes you think he did it?" Savannah asked.

"I don't know if he did or not. I just *hope* he did so that I can bust him."

"That makes two of us." Savannah thought about the scar on Lydia's lip. "He beats his wife."

Dirk scowled and shook his head.

One of the things Savannah loved most about him was his general attitude toward woman beaters, child molesters, senior-citizen robbers, and anybody who hurt anything with a furry face.

Basically, he would be happy to tie cement shoes onto their feet and watch as Savannah pushed them off the end of the city pier. And Savannah agreed with his position on those particular crimes, as long as she got to do the off-the-pier pushing.

"So, who's next?" she asked as they passed through the guardhouse gate. "That Karen gal? The one who's supposedly carrying the doctor's baby?"

Dirk glanced at his watch and frowned. "Um-m-m . . . actually, there's someplace I've gotta be in a few minutes. How would you feel about me dropping you back at your house now? That way you can enjoy your dinner with Granny, while I take care of my business, and —"

"Gran's having dinner with Ryan and John. Remember me telling you that they're taking her out to Chez Antoine?"

"Oh, right."

"And I cleared the whole evening for you. I'm missing out on a superb dinner and the company of my beloved grandmother and two of my dearest friends, just to help *you* with this case."

Dirk squirmed in his seat. "Yeah, I remember . . . now that you remind me. But really, there's something I need to do this evening. It's important and I —"

"So, take me along with you. I can hang out, entertain myself. And then, if we've got time after you're done doing whatever it is, we could go find this Karen Burns gal."

Dirk looked absolutely miserable as he stared straight ahead, refusing to meet her eyes. "I sorta need to do this . . . this thing . . . by myself. But I'll find out where she lives, and we can go talk to her tomorrow morning, first thing. I promise."

"Hey, why are *you* promising *me* anything? This ain't a trip to Disneyland, you know. It's your case. I'm doing this for you. And right now, I'm thinking about Antoine's fresh-baked sourdough bread and his goose liver pate, and I'm thinking I did the wrong thing extending myself for you tonight."

"Oh, hell, Van. You don't even like liver. You told me so yourself. So, now you're just griping for the fun of it."

"Fun? Fun? You think this is fun for me, fighting with you?"

"Must be. You're the one yapping and keeping it going."

It was a long, silent trip home — very

long, very silent.

When Dirk pulled into her driveway, Savannah had her seat belt unbuckled and her purse tucked under her arm even before he had the car stopped.

She started to get out without saying anything to him, but he put his hand on her forearm.

"Just so that I don't have to wonder, which are you mad at me about," he said, "the fact that I didn't tell you where I'm going or that 'yapping' comment, or both?"

"I think the question should be, 'Which am I the maddest about?' "

He nodded. "Apparently, it's both."

"You figure?"

"Then, just to clarify here," he said, his tone sarcastic, "because you and I are friends, I can't go somewhere on my own without telling you where I'm going and what I'm doing?"

Savannah stopped and thought it over before answering. "Well, if you put it like that . . ."

"Ah-ha. Then you admit that I've got a right to my own privacy, and you had no reason at all to get mad at me back there."

"You shouldn't have said that 'yapping' thing. I do not *yap*. Pomeranians and Chi-

197

huahuas yap."

"Okay, okay, then I apologize for the 'yap' thing. Friends again?" He leaned toward her and puckered up his lips.

Reluctantly, she moved a notch closer to him and offered her cheek. He gave it a big, noisy smack.

"I'll swing by to pick you up tomorrow morning a little before nine," he said as she climbed out of the car.

"If you make it eight, I'll feed you breakfast."

"Thanks, but no thanks. I'll just grab some black coffee and a lowfat granola bar on my way out."

With that, he put the Buick in reverse and backed out of the driveway. He gave her a wave and a toot on his horn as he took off.

He wasn't even to the corner before she raced to her Mustang, yanked the door open, got in, and fired it up. "A right to your own privacy . . . a lowfat granola bar . . . my ass," she muttered as she sped down the road after him. "Boy, you're up to no good. And I'm gonna find out once and for all what brand of no-good you're up to."

"Well, spill it!" Tammy said, barely able to contain her excitement at the breakfast table the next morning. "Where did ol' Dirko go?"

Even Granny was on the edge of her seat. "Mind you," she said, "I'm not condoning the practice of you spying on a body, especially a friend, even if it is your profession, but . . ."

"But you still want to know where he went?" Savannah said as she scurried around the kitchen, gathering the remainders of their morning feast.

She set a bowl brimming with strawberry jam on the table. Then she ladled a thick helping of grits onto Gran's plate, to keep the sausage patties, bacon, and sunny-side-up eggs company.

"The harm's already been done — you blackening your soul with all that underhanded sneakiness," Gran said, grinning as she laid a pat of butter on top of the grits. "You might as well tell us what you found out."

"He went to Hardbodies," Savannah plopped down on her own chair, coffee cup in hand.

"Hardbodies? Get outta here!" Tammy said.

"Yeap. And he stayed for two hours. Two hours!"

"What's Hardbodies?" Gran asked. "It

sounds nasty . . . like one of them fan-dancer places."

Savannah chuckled. "It's not a strip joint, Gran. And I don't think they dance behind feathered fans in those places anymore."

Gran sniffed. "Well, I don't keep up on what women of ill repute wear or what they don't wear, so you could be right about that."

"Hardbodies is a health club, a gym," Tammy said. "Although it's more like a meat market than a real gym. I took a so-called yoga class there once and it was quite disappointing. They didn't even —"

"A gymnasium that sells meat?" Gran said. "That doesn't sound very sanitary. I wouldn't want to buy my pork chops or Sunday roast in a place where sweaty men hang out."

"The point is, why would Dirk be going there?" Savannah salted and peppered her eggs, then reached for the cream gravy. "Since when is he into bodybuilding?"

"Maybe it's not his own body he's interested in," Tammy suggested as she sipped her drink made of pulverized vegetables and protein powder. "Did you peek inside to see what he was up to?"

Savannah sighed. "I stood on tiptoe to look in the rear window for at least an hour.

200

But then it started to rain, and the water was running off the roof and down on my head and . . . shoot . . . even I have my limits."

She reached down and rubbed her leg. "Man, my calves are so sore today I could hardly get out of bed and walk."

"Well, what was he doing?" Granny asked.

"Working out."

"That's all?" Granny said. "You got wet as a drowned rat, and you liked to've crippled yourself, and all he was doing was what a body normally does in a gym?"

"That was it, the whole kit 'n' caboodle, right there."

Tammy shook her head. "That was hardly worth it."

"Tell me about it."

"I think," Tammy said, "it's wonderful, Dirk taking control of his life this way. He's evolving to a higher consciousness."

"Yeah, right. Whatever." Savannah grabbed another biscuit. "The worst part of the whole sorry mess is that I'm in a world of pain because of him and his foolishness, and I can't even holler at him about it!"

# CHAPTER 11

That afternoon, when Dirk came by Savannah's house to pick her up, his mood wasn't any better than hers. His greeting was lackluster as she climbed into the Buick, and he didn't have much to say on the way to Karen Burns's house.

Most important, he didn't mention why he was late or where he had been all morning. And she found that particularly suspicious, since he was in the habit of telling her details of his life that were far more intimate than she cared to hear.

Long ago, she had decided that, unless a man put a diamond ring on a woman's finger, she really shouldn't have to hear about how well his new fiber cereal bars were working. When it came to stuff like that, she much preferred to be on a need-to-know basis only.

Twice, he reached up with his left hand and massaged his right shoulder. She saw him wince, and if she hadn't been so pre-occupied with the pain in her own muscles, she might have felt sorry for him.

But when she thought about how Hard-bodies Gym had a reputation for being a pick-up joint, all vestiges of her sympathy evaporated.

Of course, that didn't mean her curiosity was satisfied.

"Shoulder sore today?" she asked.

He gave her a quick sideways glance that was filled with what she was pretty sure looked like pure guilt.

"Yeah," he said. "I must've strained some-thing weeding my flower garden."

"The ornamental Japanese garden that surrounds your trailer there at the park?"

"Yeap. The one with all the water lilies and the koi pond . . . between the hedge maze and the grotto with the marble Gre-cian statues."

"Smart aleck."

"I noticed you were limping a little when you came out to the car. What's up with you?"

"Charley horse."

"In both legs?"

"Yeah. Rotten luck, huh?"

"It bites to be you."

"It does."

As he turned into a neighborhood, not far from hers, she said, "Karen Burns lives around here?"

"Yeah, with her mother. They run a day-care center together. G & K Tot Heaven."

"G & K?"

He shrugged. "That new gal at the front desk has her limitations. She was overly impressed with herself that she'd come up with the address at all."

When they approached the corner property with its high, chain-link fence, Savannah looked at the faded toys in the yard and questioned the appropriateness of the establishment's name.

"Heaven?" she said, pointing out the broken swing set and the sliding board that lay on its side on the ground. Dirty toys were strewn about in mud puddles where grass had once grown. "This place is depressing. I wouldn't leave my cats in here, let alone a child."

"That's because you're a good mommy . . . even to your animals," he said, giving her a sweet smile.

For a moment she forgot about Hardbodies. But it was only for a moment. Then she said, "Thanks. How's your shoulder?"

He gave her a funny look. "It's okay now. Comes and goes."

They pulled into the driveway of the supposed toddler paradise and got out of the car. Savannah had to step over rusted tricycle parts on her way up the sidewalk to the front door.

After Dirk buzzed the button, they heard what sounded like a pack of wild coyotes yipping on the other side of the door.

"Holy cow!" she said. "Sounds like they're watching a passel of younguns in there. And not very well-behaved ones at that."

Eventually, the door opened and a big, no-nonsense-looking woman with steel gray hair and glasses with bright red frames stared through the torn screen at them. "Yeah?" she said.

She was a tall, skinny woman — probably in her fifties. Her thin, straight hair was slicked back into a tight bun at the back of her neck. Her dowdy black sweatshirt and matching pants gave her an even more severe appearance. She looked like a scarecrow on its way to a casual funeral . . . except for the gaudy red glasses.

In one arm she was holding a baby who looked to be about a year old. She was holding a toddler by the hand, and the little boy was throwing a total fit, screaming, pulling, trying to get away from her.

Somehow, Savannah just knew this wasn't

Karen Burns, the siren who had seduced a celebrity doctor.

"Hello," Savannah said, "are you Gertrude Burns, Miss Karen Burns's mother?"

"Yes, I am. What do you want?"

"Is Karen at home?" Savannah asked, showing the woman her private investigator's ID.

"She doesn't have time to talk," was the curt reply. "What do you want with her?"

Dirk produced his badge. "We have to have a private word with Miss Burns. Would you please ask her to come to the door?"

"Look, this is the middle of my work day and —" She stopped to yank on the screeching toddler's hand. "You quit that before I give you a smack and set you in the corner, young man!"

He settled down a bit, and she returned her attention to Savannah and Dirk. "Between the six kids I'm watching," she said, "and my stupid daughter's four brats, I've got my hands full."

"I can see that you do," Savannah said, keeping her voice unusually calm for the boy's sake, "and you should be more gentle with that child. You'll dislocate his shoulder, snatching on him like that. And if you do, my buddy here will arrest you so fast it'll make your head spin."

"I'll have you know, I'm a professional child-care provider!"

"Then act like one," Savannah said, her voice soft and even, though her eyes were blazing.

Savannah opened the screen door, squatted down and held out her arms to the little boy. "Come here to Aunt Savannah, sugar plum," she said. "Mrs. Burns has to go get Miss Karen . . . right away."

Gertrude Burns stood there, baby in arm, glaring at Savannah for a long time; then she turned briskly on her heel and stomped away.

"How are you doing, little man?" Savannah asked the cherub with chocolate something smeared all over his mouth and cheeks.

He answered her with a long sentence in nonsensical baby babble, to which she replied, "I know! You're absolutely right, and I couldn't agree more."

Looking up at Dirk, she saw a tender look cross his face . . . not that dissimilar from when he was petting one of her cats.

"Cute kid," he mumbled, a bit embarrassed to be caught being sweet.

"All kids are cute," she replied, "until they grow up and become human." She brushed some of the boy's wayward blond curls back from his eyes. "Don't grow up, babycakes, you hear me? You stay sweet."

The toddler nodded and smiled.

They heard the clicking of high heels coming toward them. And a moment later, a much younger, but equally thin and tall woman came to the door.

Karen Burns resembled her mother in every way, except that her straight, dark hair hung nearly to her waist, and her tight, black, spandex-enriched dress was anything but dowdy. It hugged every curve, and Karen Burns was extremely curvaceous.

Even down to the beginnings of a baby bump on her belly.

So, at least the rumors of a pregnancy appeared to be true. Now whether it was truly Wellman's or not . . . that would be determined later.

"My mother says you want to talk to me?" Karen said.

She gave Savannah a quick glance over, head to toe, as though sizing up her competition.

The impromptu appraisal irritated Savannah. She always wondered about females who felt the need to evaluate every other woman's clothes, hair, makeup, nails . . . and most important, their jewelry, within the first few seconds of meeting them.

Like any of that made you a better person.

She always had to resist pulling back her jacket and showing them her Beretta . . . just for effect.

Not that wearing a 9mm made her any better, either, but, as accessories went, a gun was a good conversation piece — a lot more interesting than whether a gal's nail tips were oval or squared.

"Yes, we do want to talk to you," Dirk said. "Can we come inside?"

"I don't want them in here," Gertrude called out from some unseen location. "Don't you let them come in this house unless they've got a warrant or something."

Karen sashayed over to the screen door, opened it a bit, and took the little boy from Savannah. "Run along, Stevie. Go see Grandma."

"Yeah, yeah, go see Grandma. Like Grandma's not got enough to do around here," complained the distant, but disturbingly audible, Gertrude. "Mommy's too busy to take care of her own kids, as usual."

Karen rolled her eyes and gave Dirk a flirtatious little grin. "Isn't he cute?" she said. "He's my youngest. Well . . . except for this one." She patted her belly. "I've got four boys already. I'm hoping for a girl this time. So is my fiancé. He said he'd love to have a girl that looks just like me."

*Oh really? And has he seen his future mother-in-law yet?* Savannah thought. But she kept it to herself. Instead, she asked, "And your fiancé's name is . . . ?"

"She doesn't have a fiancé!" Gertrude yelled. "You see a ring on her finger? No-o-o."

Gertrude made a brief appearance as she walked up behind Karen and gave her daughter a fairly hard jab in the ribs. "This one," she said, "she got knocked up by some son of a bitch who's married. Or who *was* married. Let's see if he marries her *now.* I'll betcha he won't. That kind never does. Boy, you really know how to pick 'em. Four kids, four daddies, and not one husband."

"Leave me alone, Mom," Karen snapped back. "These people are here to talk to me, not you. Get lost."

"See how she talks to her mother? Some respect, huh? But you notice she's still living under my roof, eating my food, letting *me* take care of her brats."

"I help you, Mom. I contribute."

"Yeah, you and your high heels and lipstick. A lot you can accomplish wearing that crap. You'd make more money standing out there on the street corner in that outfit. Except that you're too fat. Nobody would

210

want you. That's why that doctor won't marry you. Doctors are rich. They can afford to have pretty wives."

Savannah watched as the feeble light in Karen Burns's eyes flickered and went out. Apparently, her mother's vicious words had finally found their mark — the very center of her heart. And that was hardly surprising.

Savannah had found that abusers instinctively have very accurate aim.

Savannah glanced up and down Karen's slender figure, and while the daughter was maybe five or ten pounds heavier than her mother, she could hardly be classified as "fat" by any reasonable measure.

Dirk turned to Savannah and said, "I don't know about you, but I've enjoyed about as much of this as I can stand. Let's wind this up." Then to Karen, he said, "Just tell me two quick things, Ms. Burns. Is that Dr. Wellman's baby that you're carrying there?"

She put her hand to her belly and patted it lovingly. "Of course she's his. The doctor and I have been in love for a long time now. We're going to be married soon." She glanced over her shoulder, but her mother appeared to have left the area. "I just have to lose some weight first, so that I'll look good in a wedding gown. I have one all picked out, but it won't look right unless I drop another twenty pounds. So, I'm going to this other doctor, Bonnie Saperstein, who does the same hypnosis thing. Robert said it would be better if he and I didn't see each other right now, you know . . . what with Maria getting killed and you cops snooping around, and . . ."

She seemed to realize she'd said too much and snapped her mouth closed, a bit like a frog that had just caught a big, juicy fly.

"Okay," Dirk said, "and one more thing. Where were you the night Maria Wellman was killed?"

She grinned and tossed her head. "I was with Robert."

"No," Savannah said. "You weren't. He was attending a charity ball with his wife. Lots of people saw him there with her."

Karen giggled. "Not all night, he wasn't. He left the ball and went to the Island View Hotel, that really nice one on the beach. We have our favorite suite there. He spent most of the night with me, talking about the baby, making plans for our wedding."

"You were making plans for a wedding while he was still married?" Savannah asked, one eyebrow raised.

"He said he was going to lay down the

law to her, demand a divorce that night — just as soon as he got home!"

"And to your knowledge, did he?" Dirk asked.

"I guess not. I called him the next morning, and he said he couldn't find her anywhere. That must have been before that jogger on the beach found her body."

"So, where do things stand now with you and Dr. Wellman?" Savannah said.

For the first time, Karen's cocky smile faltered a bit. "Um . . . not great at the moment."

"Tell them the truth!" yelled a shrill voice from deeper inside the house. "Tell them that, just like those other morons who knocked you up, this one's not going to marry you, either! I'm going to wind up having to take care of you and all five of your bastard brats!"

"Okay, that's it," Dirk said. "I'm outta here." He turned and started to walk briskly down the sidewalk toward the car.

Savannah hesitated, then said to Karen, "You know, you deserve a lot better than you're getting here, and your kids sure as shootin' do."

Karen swallowed hard and blinked her eyes rapidly a couple of times. "How do you get it?"

"You don't sit around and just hope that somebody's going to give you a better life. You *demand* better . . . of yourself and everybody around you. Do it for your children, if not for yourself."

As Savannah turned and walked back to the car to join Dirk, her heart was heavy, her brain in turmoil.

She thought of the difference between her own grandmother and Gertrude Burns and thanked God for the love and care that had been shown to her and her siblings.

As soon as she got into the car with Dirk, she pulled her cell phone out of her purse. "I'm calling Social Services," she told him. "They need to do a thorough inspection of that place. And if they find Gertrude Burns suitable to care for helpless little children, I'll eat my drawers."

# CHAPTER 12

"This meeting of the Moonlight Magnolia Detective Agency is hereby called to order!" Granny Reid declared, lifting her glass of lemonade in a toast. "All members, and us honorary members, too, are present and accounted for!"

"Let the revelries begin!" John shouted, hefting his glass of merlot to the stars. Ryan did the same.

Dirk, who was exhausted, simply grunted and raised a beer bottle. Tammy toasted with a glass of mineral water, and Savannah joined in with a mug of root beer.

Normally, she'd be having a margarita, frozen, with salt. But she never drank alcohol in front of Granny. That way Gran stayed happy and Savannah didn't get her ears boxed.

It worked out well for everyone.

The backyard cookout had been a wild success. Dirk's barbecued ribs and Savannah's potato salad, baked beans, and corn on the cob had been devoured along with Granny's deviled eggs. Eventually, they'd get around to the blackberry cobbler and homemade ice cream. But between dinner and dessert, while everyone waited for their belts to loosen just a bit, the Moonlight Magnolia gang had decided to do a little work.

They sat in a loose circle around Savannah's patio on her comfortable chairs and chaises, enjoying the ambient light of her colorful Chinese lanterns, some well-placed candles, and the glow of a full moon.

Appropriately, the magnolia tree was in full bloom.

"So, lay out your suspects for us," John said.

"Yes," added Ryan, "we have to know what we're working with here."

"Okay." Savannah took a deep breath. "Thanks to the fact that Dr. Wellman — or Bobby Martini, whichever you choose to call him — couldn't keep his slacks zipped, we have more than our share of possible bad guys . . . and girls."

Gran nodded, a sage look on her face, her silver hair glowing in the moonlight. "Yeap, them sexual sins, they tend to be the ones that pay the biggest dividends. It'd be better for a fella to rob another man, even smack him in the jaw with his fist, than to step out with the man's wife."

"That's true," Dirk said. "Five minutes of fun'll get you a lifetime of troubles."

"And a lot of times, the *fun* ain't even all that fun, if you know what I mean," Savannah said.

Everyone but Gran nodded in agreement.

Gran just looked at Savannah with deep suspicion.

"Or so I've heard. I wouldn't know personally." Savannah cleared her throat. "That's the word on the street, you know?"

Along with Gran believing that Savannah was a teetotaler, she also chose to think that her granddaughter was a virgin. That, too, worked well for Savannah. She was pretty sure she was too big at this point to get a "whuppin' " from Gran, but there was no point in taking chances.

"So, here are our suspects," Savannah said, eager to guide the conversation away from fleshly sins . . . at least, personal knowledge of fleshly sins.

She started the countdown on her forefinger. "First, the killer could be an unknown suspect, a simple robber who followed Maria Wellman home in order to snatch the jewels off her. She had rented a diamond and sapphire necklace and earring set from a Rodeo Drive jewelry store for the ball. And those items and her wedding ring weren't on her body."

"Could the jogger have taken them . . . the one who discovered her?" Tammy asked.

"Doubt it," Dirk replied. "We checked him out thoroughly. He's a simple hippie-type guy who's antimaterialism. He doesn't even have a bank account. Lives in his mom's basement and smokes a lot of pot. Doesn't strike me at all as the violent type."

"No alerts from any pawn shops or jewelry stores about the missing gems?" John asked.

"No, nothing at all," Dirk said.

"As far as our known suspects," Savannah continued, "we have Terry Somers. Terry's a compulsive gambler, in deep to loan sharks. They've roughed him up, even broken his leg, which he blames on Dr. Wellman. He threatened to kill Wellman in front of witnesses. He makes no bones about the fact that he despises him. He wasn't big on Maria Wellman, either."

"On the other hand," Dirk said, "Somers's leg is in a cast and has been since before Maria's murder. It's his left leg, so he could drive if he wanted to, and he was walking around on it okay when we talked to him."

218

"A guy in a cast would leave a pretty distinctive print," Ryan said. "Did you find anything like that at the scene?"

"No, not at all," Dirk replied. "The only footprints they found were some in a flower bed at the edge of the cliff, made by the victim herself."

"How nimble would a guy be with his leg in a cast?" Tammy said. "That would be a bit of a handicap if you were trying to murder somebody."

"Don't forget, Ted Bundy put his arm in a cast as a ruse," Savannah reminded her.

"That's true," Tammy agreed. "Does Somers have an alibi?"

"No, he was home alone watching TV," Dirk told her, "but as it turns out, so were most of our other suspects."

"Like Roxanne Rosen," Savannah said. "She had a fight with Maria Wellman a few days before the killing. A real fight. Dr. Liu found broken and repaired fingernails and old bruises on the victim. Plus we had witnesses to the altercation, some public road workers who came forward with what they'd seen."

"But the witnesses back up Rosen's version of the story that it was Maria who struck first." Dirk set his empty beer bottle on a nearby table and reached into the cooler for a cola. "And we got the idea that Roxanne won the fight and was happy enough with that. I don't know if she had enough anger left over to drive her to murder somebody."

"And no alibi but the telly?" John said.

Savannah nodded. "That's right."

"I think she might be trying to blackmail Wellman," Dirk said. "There at the house on the beach, we overheard her demanding money from him or else she'll go to the authorities. She claims she just wants the wages he owes her, but I wouldn't be surprised if it's more than that."

"Maybe," Tammy suggested, "she knows that his name isn't really Wellman. She may even know why Bobby and Gina Martini changed their names to Robert and Maria Wellman, and why they were pretending to be husband and wife."

"Most folks don't go changing identities like that without a good . . . or should I say, bad . . . reason," Granny said. "They had some wickedness to cover up, or they wouldn't have done such a thing."

"Maybe they were part of a witness protection program," Ryan suggested. "Do you want John and me to check with our friends at the Bureau and find out?"

"That'd be great." Dirk took a swig from

his soda can. "I've got a call in to the FBI, but as usual, they're ignoring me. It's nice to have buddies who used to be feds."

Savannah smiled and thought how far her friends had come in the past few years. The love of solving crimes created a strong bond among people who didn't have much else in common. Ryan and John drank fine wines, ate gourmet food, went to the theater, and supported the local symphony.

Dirk was a beer and hotdogs, Dodger stadium, and boxing on Pay-Per-View sort of dude.

But they all loved to nail a bad guy . . . especially if the bad guy, or girl, was a cold-blooded killer.

"Then we have Brian Mahoney," Dirk said. "He's a big, nasty husband of one of Wellman's patients . . . a patient the doctor seduced. Mahoney actually caught his wife and Wellman in a compromising position — actually, it was his wife who was compromised — and he blackmailed Wellman."

"You know that for a fact?" Ryan asked.

Savannah nodded. "His wife admitted it to me. She also admitted that her husband is violent with her. He even smacked Wellman around when he caught them together."

"But if Wellman has been paying this Mahoney fellow," John said, "why would Mahoney kill Mrs. Wellman? He was angry at Wellman, not her. And by doing something so drastic as murdering Wellman's wife — or sister, as it turns out — he could risk killing the goose that lays the golden egg."

"Mahoney doesn't strike me as a guy who really thinks things through," Savannah told him. "And who knows, Wellman might have decided to cut him off. Mahoney may have come back for more, and Wellman told him to forget it."

"For all we know," Dirk said, "the killer went to the house that night intending to murder Wellman, not Maria, and then things went wrong."

"Then we have Karen Burns, who we interviewed today." Savannah reached down and massaged her sore calf. "She says she's pregnant with Wellman's kid."

"If that's true, she'd have a pretty powerful motive to kill off the wife," Granny said. "It's not like it ain't been done before. Many a man's put his wife in danger by fooling around with an unstable woman."

Tammy spoke up. "What if Karen found out that Robert and Maria were brother and sister? I'd think that would make Karen pretty mad, having him tell her that he can't leave his wife for her, and then to find out he's not even married."

Savannah shook her head. "I don't think so. She's really gaga over him. And she's giving him an alibi. She says he was with her after the ball. Not at home the way he claims he was."

"Yeah," Dirk said. "I'm going to have to talk to Wellman about that."

"When are you going to tell him that you know who he really is?" Tammy wanted to know.

"As soon as I find out why he's living under an alias," Dirk replied. "If he was able to disappear once before and then establish a new identity in another area, he might do it again. I don't want to show him my hand until I'm sure what all my cards are."

"Well, I'm sure of one thing," Gran said. "Mighty sure. That blackberry cobbler is calling out to me from inside the kitchen. And I figure that homemade ice cream has seasoned just enough. I need a few scoops of each."

"How true." Savannah got up and tried not to limp as she headed for the back door. "Man . . . and woman . . . do not live by crime solving alone. We need empty calories to keep us going!"

"Here, here!"

"Now you're talking!"

"Go get it, girl!"

"Don't bring me much," Dirk said. "Remember I'm on a diet."

"Good," replied Gran. "I'll have his, too."

"Are you going out with your young man again this morning?" Gran asked as she and Savannah sat in the living room with their morning coffee and enormous glazed cinnamon buns on Savannah's best Royal Albert Old Country Roses china.

"I thought I'd tell him no today," Savannah said. "I've been neglecting you awfully bad and —"

"Oh, stop it! That's just flat dab silly. I'm staying a long time this visit — probably till you kick me out. . . ."

"It'll never happen."

"And you've got work to do, and I understand that. Besides, Tammy's driving me to Santa Monica. I want to go walking on that pier."

"We've got a pier right here in San Carmelita."

"Yeah, but it ain't got a carousel like that 'un."

"True."

Gran licked some icing off her thumb. "Go call that sweet boy and tell him that you've got better things to do than babysit an old lady."

Savannah laughed, got up, and walked over to the sofa where Gran was sitting. She leaned down and kissed her soft cheek. "I would never have anything better to do than hang out with you."

"Well, I do! I got a carousel horse with my name on it. I was a little girl the last time I climbed onto a merry-go-round, and that's way too long in between rides. So, you scram, girl. Skedaddle."

When Savannah got into the car with Dirk, she was already in a pissy mood. He had told her on the phone earlier that he was going to be a little later than usual picking her up. And he gave the same non-reason as he had before.

"I've got something I've gotta do first."

That was all he had said. And that tidbit of non-information had been just meager and intriguing enough to stir her curiosity.

Savannah wasn't someone who needed her curiosity stirred. It was far too overactive already with no encouragement from anybody.

But as she settled into the Buick, her former irritation disappeared as new concerns flooded her mind. Or more specifically, her nostrils.

"What the heck stinks in here?" she exclaimed, rolling down the side window. "Did you leave old pizza on your floorboard again? Or Mexican food? Nothing smells worse than rotten refried beans!"

"I don't smell anything," he snapped back.

"How can you not smell that? It's deadly."

She leaned toward him, and a look of horror crossed her face. "Ohmigawd! It's you!"

"Is not!"

"It is, too. What the heck happened to you?"

He puffed up like a river frog getting ready to sing. "I didn't have time to take a shower this morning, okay?"

"No, no way. I know what you smell like when you miss a shower. Not that bad really, for a guy. But this isn't a missed-shower stink. You smell like a wet dog."

He reached over and rolled down his own car window. Then he roared away from the curb and headed down the street.

"There, happy now?" he asked, quite huffy.

"It's better, as long as the air's circulating." She looked him over. The flushed face, the clenched jaw, the eyes that wouldn't meet hers. "Seriously, Dirk," she said. "What did you do to yourself today?"

"Nothing. And if it's all the same to you,

I'd rather not discuss the way I smell."

"If it's all the same to you," she muttered, "I'd rather not *smell* the way you smell."

"What?"

"Nothing. Just drive to wherever we're going to. And this time, I don't even mind if you speed. I just want out of this car."

"We're going to Wellman's again. I'm going to get in his face about the identity change and ask him about being with Karen the night Maria was killed."

"I thought you were going to wait and find out if he's in some FBI protection program."

"I heard from Ryan about an hour ago. He and John already checked on it, and he's not in any witness program."

"Wow, they work fast!"

"They sure do. And they offered to check out the Island View Hotel where Karen says she and Wellman were that night. I told them, 'sure. If all you guys have to do is play golf and bat a tennis ball around, have at it.' "

"You have such a way with words . . . and people."

"It's a gift."

"You're lucky that Ryan and John and I don't have anything on our own plates right now. You have all this awesome talent at your disposal for free."

"They don't have any hot celebrity bodies to guard at the moment?"

"They're like me; business comes and goes. And unlike me, when they have a job, they get paid big bucks."

"That's how they can afford those awesome cars and that fancy condo up on the hill."

"Bodyguards to the rich and famous . . . yes, it pays better than working for the FBI did, I'm sure."

"Now, if you can get private detecting to pay better than being a cop did, maybe you can move into a condo on the hill and get a fancy car."

"Naw, I like my little house and my Mustang. I'm what's known as a contented woman. I wouldn't change a thing about my life . . . except that awful smell."

"The awful-smell discussion is closed."

# CHAPTER 13

A few minutes later, they arrived at Wellman's house and pulled into his driveway.

"Are you sure he's home?" Savannah asked as they got out of the car.

"Yeah. I called and told him I was coming by . . . warned him not to go anyplace."

"And you figure that did it?"

"Oh, yeah, he's scared of me." He grinned as he took her arm and walked her up the sidewalk to the door. "Isn't everybody?"

"Only those standing downwind of you."

Savannah rang the doorbell and it took some time for Wellman to answer. When he did, he was wearing wet swim trunks and his hair was slicked back and damp. He had a towel thrown around his bare shoulders and a glass in his hand that was half-filled with red juice. The sprig of celery told Savannah it might be a Bloody Mary.

"Hello again," she told him. "Nice day for a swim."

Wellman nodded. "Unless you're looking at the rocks where your wife's body was found," he replied dryly.

"Yeah, right," Dirk said. "Your *wife*. We need to come in and talk about that."

Dirk walked inside without being invited, and Savannah followed close behind him.

"Have you found those missing jewels yet?" Wellman asked. "The store called me twice already today. They want their merchandise or the money right away."

"Let us find out who the murderer is, and then we'll get to working on those stolen gems, if it's all the same to you," Dirk told him.

"Yes, well, before this conversation goes any further, I'd like to go change clothes, if you don't mind too much," Wellman said sarcastically. "I don't fancy sitting around in a wet swimsuit while talking to the police."

"You're just fine like you are," Dirk said. "You knew I was coming and had plenty of time to change if you didn't 'fancy' sitting around in your trunks. Let's go into the backyard. You can sit on your patio furniture if you don't want to get your expensive couch wet."

Dirk headed through the house and out the back door, leaving Wellman little choice but to follow him.

"Be thankful you'll be talking to him out in the fresh air," Savannah told Wellman as they walked out together. "Believe me, it's a blessing."

"What?"

"Never mind."

Dirk was already sitting on one of the deep-cushioned, wicker chairs. He was wearing a half smile, and his eyes sparkled with a grim sort of mischief. It was a look Savannah often saw on his face when he was getting ready to interview someone — and he had something really good on them.

Wellman sat down and took a long, long drink from his glass, nearly emptying it.

"I'd offer you one," he said as he set the glass on the end table next to his chair, "but I know you're on duty, and I'm sure it would be against regulations for you to drink alcohol."

He gave them both contemptuous looks. "And I'm sure that you two follow all the rules to the letter."

"Oh, yeah," Dirk said, "that's us. Rule followers all the way . . . Bobby."

Wellman's face clouded over. "I prefer to go by Robert."

"But you used to go by Bobby. Bobby Martini." Dirk sat back in his chair, lifted his arms, and laced his fingers behind his head. "Tell us about that. Tell us *all-l-l* about that."

"Yeah," Savannah said, "and don't spare any of the gory details. We can take it."

Wellman looked like someone had just poked his backside with a cattle prod. His face flushed nearly as red as his hair and mustache. "That's . . . that's . . . personal and none of your business."

"A murder was committed right here on your property, mister," Dirk told him. "That means you have no personal business. None at all. Get used to it. Until I arrest the killer, your life is a friggen open book. Got that?"

"With numerous really sordid chapters," Savannah added.

Dirk leaned forward in his chair and propped his elbows on his knees, staring at Wellman. "Start talking, and I'm in no mood for any of your bullshit, so give it to me straight."

"Start with the identity change," Savannah said.

Wellman glanced around him, and for a moment, Savannah thought she could see genuine fear in his eyes. Of what, she wasn't sure. Was he expecting the rest of the SCPD to come out of the bushes and arrest him? Or was it something else?

"Okay, okay," he said. "We did have to change our names and assume new identities. But it was for my wife's sake. She —"

"Now there you go," Dirk said, "pissing me off and spewing crap before you even get started."

"What?"

"Don't 'what' us," Dirk told him. "We already know that Maria wasn't your wife. *Gina* was your sister."

Savannah gave Wellman a fake smile. "Do yourself a favor, Martini," she said. "Just assume that whatever you're hiding, we already know all about it. We're just giving you a chance here to tell us your side of things, so that we don't assume the worst about you."

"Yeah," Dirk added. "You don't want us thinking the worst about you. We have really evil imaginations and our worst is pretty bad."

Wellman let out a deep sigh, like a man defeated, and sank down in his chair. "Then if you know Gina was my sister, you know about Vegas and all that mess."

Savannah glanced at Dirk, who was as busy as she was, putting on a poker face.

"Yeah," she said. "I don't really blame you and Gina for leaving there like you did."

He nodded. "We had to. Gus is a really

233

bad guy, I'm telling you. He went crazy when Gina divorced him, beat her up, threatened to kill her. Me, too. And with his connections, he could have done it or had somebody else do it. He would have gotten away with it, too."

"So, why didn't you tell us about Gus right away?" Dirk said. "What if he's the one who killed Maria? He could be long gone by now. All because you didn't give us the heads-up."

"You think I haven't already thought about that?" Again, he looked around him, staring into the shrubs that bordered the sides of the yard. "I didn't want to blow my cover here . . . or whatever you people call it . . . by telling you about my past. And yet, I figure he probably knows where I am now."

"After appearing on those national talk shows, you didn't have much of a cover to blow," Savannah mentioned.

"Yeah, I know. But my agent said I needed the publicity and couldn't afford to pass up the opportunity to appear on national TV. She said she'd make sure nobody gave out my address."

Savannah shook her head. "Once you made your name and face public, you left yourself open. My assistant is good with the

Internet, and she can find anybody in about five minutes."

"But I'm sure you sold a ton of those worthless CDs of yours," Dirk said with a touch of bitterness. "So, I guess it was worth the risk."

Wellman bristled. "Yes, I did sell a ton of them. And they aren't worthless. I've helped countless people achieve their dreams of weight loss and —"

"Save it for the infomercials," Dirk told him with a wave of his hand.

Savannah took her notebook and pen from her purse. "There's one thing I need," she said. "I'm not sure how to spell Gus's last name. Could you clear that up for me?"

She mentally crossed her fingers that it wasn't something like "Smith" or "Brown."

Wellman nodded. "Yeah, okay. You spell it A-V-A-N-T-I-S."

"Oh, thanks. I thought maybe Avantis had an 'E' on the end. That's helpful."

Out of the corner of her eye, she saw Dirk smirk. Her "gee, how do you spell that?" routine was one of his favorites. And he, himself, couldn't pull it off. It required a soft, smooth, Southern accent and a certain amount of eyelash batting.

Their partnership worked so well because they firmly believed in delegation of duties.

He was in charge of scowling, whining about little aches and pains, and moaning about slow-moving traffic. She handled all eyelash batting, dimple deepening, and hip-swinging sashaying.

Each went with their strengths.

"Anyway," Wellman continued, "once Gina got killed and those news crews were all over the place here, the whole world found out where I live. So, I figure even if it wasn't Gina's ex who killed her, he knows where I am now."

"And you figure he'll show up?" Dirk asked. "If he was mad at her for leaving him, why come after you?"

Wellman picked up his empty Bloody Mary glass and went through the motions of taking one last sip. Savannah suspected his mouth was pretty dry, considering the line of questioning.

"Oh, I don't know," he said. "I never liked Gus, and he knew it. He probably figured I'd encouraged her to leave him."

"Did you?" Dirk asked.

"Yeah. I did."

"How long ago was all this?" Savannah said.

"About three years."

Dirk drummed his fingers on the arm of the chair, thinking. "And you believe that he's still mad enough about her leaving him that he'd travel here from Las Vegas, murder her, and then wait around and kill you, too?"

"He might be."

"Okay." It was obvious that Dirk didn't buy it. "How about we talk about a couple of suspects a little closer to home. Like Brian Mahoney and all that hush money you paid him not to turn you in for having sex with your patient."

"Or, should we say 'patients'?" Savannah said.

When Wellman didn't reply, Dirk added, "An open book, my man. Remember? That's what your life is now."

Savannah waggled one eyebrow. "Steamy sex scenes and all."

"I like the ladies," Wellman said with a shrug. "There's no law against that."

"Actually, when they're your patients, there is," Savannah said. "You could lose your license for something like that."

"You do have a license to lose, right?" asked Dirk. "You're not like one of these television doctors who has an honorary doctorate from some Caribbean 'university' for cat juggling, are you?"

"Dirk!" Savannah gasped. "*Cat* juggling! Please!"

"Sorry. What was I thinking?" He turned

to Wellman. "Tell me where you went and what you did after you left the ball the other night. The truth this time."

"I told you. I came home."

"Eventually, yes, you did. But I want to hear about where you stopped along the way, who you met, what you did. You can abbreviate the 'what you did' part. Some details I can live without. I doubt you know any tricks I don't know."

Savannah stifled a snicker. It could be argued that anybody with as active a sex life as Wellman might actually have a few tips for a guy like Dirk, whose idea of a big date was spending the night staking out some scumbag's apartment building with Savannah.

Wellman wasn't an attractive man by any means. Both his face and physique were quite mundane.

Then she reminded herself that money was quite the aphrodisiac to a lot of women, and, of course, it never hurt to slip the word "doctor" into your pick up line, either.

"I'm telling you, I came straight home," Wellman said. "Once I got here, I looked around for my wife and then went to bed."

"But you'd already been to bed . . . a hotel bed . . . with another one of your patients," Dirk said.

"No!"

"That's what Karen Burns says," Savannah told him. "Does the Island View Hotel ring a bell?"

Wellman sat there, saying nothing, with perspiration starting to pop out on his forehead and upper lip.

The morning fog had burned away, and the sun was warm, to be sure. But for a guy sitting there in wet swim trunks, his hair still damp, Savannah decided he was doing an abnormal amount of sweating.

But when she glanced over at Dirk, she noticed that his face, too, was strangely flushed, as though he'd spent the day at the beach — not just a matter of minutes on Wellman's back patio.

*Must be hotter than I think,* she told herself. *That or these guys are pretty worked up.*

"Look," she said to Wellman, "I can understand why you'd hide the fact that you were at a hotel with a woman who's your patient. Especially since you were pretending to be married to your sister — which scores pretty darned high on the ick meter, too. But the gal's giving you an alibi on a night when you bloody well need one. You'd be pretty stupid not to take it."

That seemed to click with Wellman. He slowly nodded his head. "Okay. I stopped by the hotel on my way home. Spent most of the night with Karen. But nothing sexual at all happened. . . ."

"Of course not," Savannah said. "You two probably just held hands, sipped tea, nibbled ladyfingers, and chatted about politics there in your favorite suite."

"All that tea sipping." Dirk snickered. "That's probably how she got pregnant, huh? Dude, you should've slipped a condom on your ladyfinger."

# Chapter 14

"Are you feeling all right?" Savannah asked Dirk when they got back into the car.

"Yeah, why?" he replied.

"Because you're looking pretty flushed to me. Do you have a fever?"

She leaned over and placed her hand on his forehead. He felt cool to the touch.

"No, I'm okay." He glanced at his reflection in the mirror and frowned a bit. "What do you mean, 'flushed'? Do you really think I look . . . you know . . . red?"

"Not red exactly. More like a weird shade of orange."

He reached for his sunglasses that were lying on the dash, and she caught a good look at his hands.

"Dirk! Your palms! Holy cow, boy! What have you done to yourself?"

"Huh? What are you talking about?" he said, curling his fingers into fists and trying to tuck them under his thighs.

"What in tarnation?" she said. "You have orange palms. Your elbows are this weird, dark color, and your face is starting to look like an Oompa-Loompa!"

"A what?"

"An Oompa-Loompa, one of those little orange guys in *Willy Wonka and the Chocolate Factory!* That's exactly what you look like . . . only older and taller and not as cute!"

He yanked down his visor and stared at his image in the vanity mirror. "Oh, shit! I do!"

Turning around in his seat, he reached into the back floorboard. He grabbed a bottle of water and a bunch of old fast-food napkins.

Most hadn't been used.

He dumped half of the bottle of water onto the handful of napkins and began to scrub at his face with the sodden wad.

"Dirk, have you gone plum crazy out of your mind? What the heck are you doing, boy?"

"Rubbing this junk off before it gets any worse."

"Ohmigawd!" she said. "You've got that fake tanning junk on you!"

"I do not."

"Oh, don't lie to me. I thought I recognized that stink. My sister, Marietta, uses that fake bake lotion all the time . . . the cheap crap. Makes her smell like a wet dog. A wet dog that rolled in cow manure."

She started to laugh. And the louder she laughed, the madder he got and the more frantically he scrubbed.

"That's not going to help," she said between giggle fits. "It'll make it worse . . . all streaky. You'll be a striped, blotchy Oompa-Loompa."

"Stop laughing. It's not funny! I have to look good for —"

"For what?" She was instantly all ears.

"Nothing!"

"No, no, no! You almost said it. Now spit it out. What's with all this dieting, working out, and now the fake tan?"

He put down the napkins for a moment and gave her a suspicious, piercing look. "What working out? What about me working out?"

She caught her breath. "I didn't say anything about you working out. Have you been working out?"

Tossing the clump of sogginess onto the back floorboard, he said, "What I have or haven't been doing is nobody's business. And so what if I decided to do some stuff to improve my personal appearance? Since when is that some sort of crime?"

"What's her name?"

His mouth dropped open, and he stared at her. "What's whose name?"

"The girl who you're getting all gussied up for."

"Gussied? Who the hell's gussied?"

"You're dieting, going to a fancy hair cutter, putting on sunless tanning lotion, working out at a gym —"

"Who said I've been working out?"

"Um . . . you said something about it."

"No, I didn't. How would you know that I've —"

His cell phone began to chime, and the phrase, "not a moment too soon" raced through Savannah's mind.

When he hesitated, she said, "You'd better shake a leg and answer that. Could be something important about the case."

He pulled his phone from his pocket and looked down at the caller ID. "It's Ryan," he said.

"Well, find out what he wants, quick!"

He gave her a suspicious look but answered the phone. "Coulter."

He listened, then frowned. "Really? Are you sure? Hm-m-m. That's not what I expected. Okay, thanks a lot, buddy. We owe you one. Yeah, I'll . . . uh . . . see you later

244

about that . . . um . . . right. Bye."

Dirk hung up the phone and turned to Savannah. "They weren't there," he said.

"Who wasn't where?"

"Ryan and John just left the Island View Hotel. They know the manager personally, and they talked to him about Wellman and Karen Burns."

"Okay, and . . . ?"

"And the manager knows them well. Said they've come there a lot and always ask for the same suite. But they weren't there the night Maria was killed."

"Was he sure? They weren't just in and out for an in and out?"

"Nope. Ryan said he swears he was on duty the whole night and didn't see them. They looked over the hotel registry, even checked the security surveillance tape of the lobby. Not a sign of them."

"She lied to us." Savannah felt a hot wave of anger sweep through her. She hated being lied to. And no matter how often it happened — which was all day and all night when she'd been a cop — she never got used to it.

She was convinced that, someday, someone was going to tell her a whopper, and she was going to take off one of her loafers and beat them stupid with it.

"And we bought it," Dirk said. "Well . . . *you* bought it. *I* had my doubts."

"Oh, you did not. You believed her, too. And you know what that means."

"That we're going to make her pay."

"Big time."

Once again, Dirk dropped Savannah off at her house and turned down the offer of a free meal. And as before, he disappeared with a mumbled explanation that made no sense at all. Something about needing to "go talk to Ryan about something" and "having an appointment that the station house set up."

No sooner had he pulled out of her driveway than she had called Ryan to see if he would confirm that Dirk was dropping by, as he'd said he was. If her guys all had some sort of secret, she definitely wanted to be in on it.

But Ryan didn't pick up, and she couldn't bring herself to leave a message on his machine that said, "If you know what's going on with Dirk, you have to tell me, because I'm so nosy that I have to know absolutely everybody's business or I'll burst my britches."

After all, the better part of virtue was being discreet about one's vices.

Once she had greeted the kitties, she found a note from Tammy and Gran, saying they were gone to Santa Monica, as they had mentioned before.

Left alone to her own devices, Savannah nibbled on leftovers from the refrigerator, fed tidbits to the cats, and thought about the case. Mostly, she wondered about the fact that Karen Burns had covered for Wellman. Was she supplying an alibi for him or maybe for herself?

She recalled how reluctant Wellman had been to say he had been at the hotel with Burns. She found it a bit strange that he had "admitted" to something that wasn't true.

Although she had leaned on him pretty heavily, pointing out the value of an alibi for a guy who was under suspicion for murder.

Hearing the phone ring in the living room, she left her munching and mulling in the kitchen and went to answer it.

Tammy was on the other end.

"Hi, Savannah," she said. "Guess what Gran and I just did!"

"You just rode the carousel."

"Oh, how did you know?"

"I'm a detective. And I know you and my granny. How was it?"

"Wonderful, we're going to ride it again in a minute. I just wanted to call you and tell you about Bonnie Saperstein."

"Bonnie Saperstein. Hm-m-m . . . that rings a bell."

"I told you about her before. I found all these articles on the Internet where she's blasting Wellman for his so-called weight loss program. She's a doctor in Twin Oaks who does the same sort of work he does, only she's legitimate."

"Wait a minute. Karen Burns told us that she's going to her now. Wellman told her that it wasn't a good idea for them to see each other right now. And apparently she's trying to drop some weight to fit into a wedding gown."

"Well, I did some more reading and found out that Dr. Saperstein really hates Wellman. It's really obvious in her writings and some interviews she's done about him. It might be worth having a talk with her. She might have some insights into him and what he's doing."

"True," Savannah said. "And Dirk left me here at home, high and dry, to go run some mystery errand again."

"Uh-oh." Tammy giggled. "Dirk never misses work for anything. She must be a real hottie."

"And do you think that's funny?" Savannah asked, completely mirth-free.

"Um-m, no. Not really."

"Me, either."

There was a long, uncomfortable silence.

"I think I'll go ride the carousel again. Right away."

"Good idea."

A few miles inland from San Carmelita, nestled in the foothills, sat the small community of Twin Oaks. The town had been named for two large oak trees that grew atop a big hill to the east of the community.

But other than those landmark trees, a small museum dedicated to the Native Americans who had originally inhabited the area, and one exceptional Mexican restaurant, Twin Oaks didn't have much of a reputation for anything. And the residents liked it that way.

The only crimes that were committed — at least, on a regular basis — happened once a year in the springtime. That's when the graduating high school class would climb the hill by moonlight, all the way up to the trees, drink their illegally obtained booze, maybe spawn a baby or two, and stagger back down.

Savannah didn't particularly like Twin

Oaks, mostly because it was hot. Situated inland as it was, the town had no ocean breezes to cool its residents. The hills blocked the onshore flow. And that often made a twenty-degree difference in the two towns.

Seventy-six felt a lot better than ninety-six on a summer's day.

And Savannah could feel the difference as she drove through the center of town looking for Dr. Bonnie Saperstein's office.

Savannah had found the doctor's number and address in the phone book, but she hadn't called before coming. She had decided to just risk it and see if she could catch Saperstein at work.

If she called, she risked being told no. It was a lot harder to turn down someone who was standing in front of you, smiling a down-homey Southern smile and talking sweet.

And if the doctor wasn't in, she was still better off having made the drive than sitting at home. There, she'd be obsessing about what Dirk was up to and feeling sorry for herself that Tammy was riding the carousel with her grandmother and she wasn't.

She found the building — a small but attractive structure with a distinctly southwest design. The plaster walls were painted a delicate terra cotta, and, like Savannah's house, the roof had red Spanish tiles. The heavy wooden door was arched on top and stained a dark walnut. Geraniums flourished in pots hanging from the eaves.

Beside the building was a parking lot, and Savannah noticed that two cars were sitting there — a small compact and a large, black Bentley.

"Ah, maybe the doctor is in after all," she said to herself. "And if the Bentley is hers, it looks like she's sold a few CDs, too."

Glancing down at her watch, Savannah saw that it was ten minutes till three. If Dr. Saperstein's appointments began on the hour, she might be finishing with someone very soon.

Savannah decided to wait in the lot and watch.

Sure enough, she was right. In less than five minutes, a young woman, who was maybe in her early twenties, came out of the building, got into the compact, and drove away.

As Savannah debated whether to go on in, another woman walked out, closing and locking the door behind her. She was attractive, middle-aged, with salt and pepper hair held back at the nape of her neck with a silver barrette. She wore a simple white tank top and white slacks with a teal blue, gauzy wrap thrown loosely around her shoulders.

Once the door to the building was secured, she headed toward the Bentley and Savannah's Mustang. Savannah got out of her car and met her midway across the parking lot.

"Dr. Saperstein?" Savannah asked.

The woman smiled, and as she walked closer, Savannah could see that her eyes were the same beautiful shade of blue as her shawl.

"Yes, I'm Bonnie Saperstein. May I help you?"

Savannah extended her hand, and the doctor shook it warmly and firmly. "My name is Savannah Reid," she told her. "I'm a private investigator from San Carmelita. I'm looking into a matter — the death of Maria Wellman, Dr. Robert Wellman's . . . uh . . . wife. Could I possibly buy you a cup of coffee? I'd love to hear your opinion of Dr. Wellman."

The smile disappeared from Bonnie Saperstein's face, and a fire burned in her eyes with an intensity that Savannah had to admit was a bit scary.

"Oh, you don't have to buy me coffee," the woman said. "Let *me* buy *you* some coffee. I have quite a lot to say about Robert Wellman."

# CHAPTER 15

Savannah sat with Dr. Bonnie Saperstein in a cozy horseshoe-shaped booth in La Rosita Cantina and sipped her virgin margarita, wishing it had lost its virginity at the hands of the bartender, the way Bonnie's had.

There were advantages to being off duty.

But whether her margarita had the zip of tequila or not, it still had a salted rim and the tangy citrus taste. And as she looked around the cantina, she savored the ambiance of the place, tequila buzz or not.

The gleaming white stucco walls were decorated with brilliantly colored sombreros, serapes, and matador pictures. Patterns of light danced on the copper-topped tables with their tin luminaries all hand punched with delicate designs. Piñatas in various animal forms hung from the ceiling in each corner, all lending the place the laid-back, festive air of Mexico. The music of the Gipsy Kings filled the onion-and-pepper-scented air.

And the enormous bowl of guacamole and accompanying corn chips in the center of the table didn't hurt, either.

"This is a nice midday treat," Savannah said as she scooped some of the creamy dip onto a warm chip. "I'm glad I happened to catch you coming out of your office."

Bonnie Saperstein gave her a sly, knowing grin. "And how long did you have to hang out there in the parking lot before you 'happened' to catch me?"

"Just five or ten minutes. Not long at all as stakeouts go."

Bonnie chuckled. "It must be fascinating, what you do."

"Stakeouts and report writing aren't all they're cracked up to be. But if you catch a bad guy, or gal, and get justice for the victims and their families, it's pretty satisfying." Savannah took a sip from her margarita, then licked the salt off her upper lip. "Tell me about what *you* do. Hypnosis for weight loss and addiction recovery . . . now *that* sounds fascinating."

"The human mind is fascinating. I never get tired of seeing what we do, how we struggle, the coping mechanisms we invent just to get through this adventure called 'life.' "

Savannah decided to dive right in, even at the risk of ruining the instant rapport they had established. "Dr. Saperstein," she said, "does hypnosis really work?"

"Absolutely."

"So, what Wellman's doing . . . selling people those weight loss CDs . . . in your opinion, that's all legit?"

Saperstein's demeanor changed in an instant. And, once again, Savannah saw a deep and potent rage flare in her eyes.

"Hold on," she said. "I said hypnosis works. For a practitioner who knows how to use it, it can be a powerful tool. When used with other forms of therapy, it can make all the difference for some patients."

"But Robert Wellman isn't one of those practitioners?"

"Robert Wellman is a leech, feeding on people who have enough sorrow and difficulties already. The last thing they need is the false hope of a quick fix for their complex problems. He's far worse than a thief who robs people in a dark alley."

Savannah leaned back in her seat, instinctively distancing herself from the waves of anger that were coming at her from across the table. She found herself wondering why Saperstein felt so intensely about the topic. To disapprove of a colleague was one thing,

256

but this degree of hostility . . . ?

"What is it about his approach that upsets you most?" Savannah asked her.

Bonnie thought for a moment before answering. "I suppose it's the fact that he's selling half-truths. And half a lie is worse than a lie."

Savannah nodded. "I agree with that. You can see a lie coming a mile off, but a half-lie can suck you in."

"Exactly. And he's sucking people in by the thousands. He's telling them that by listening to him, they can instantly reprogram their subconscious minds and lose weight."

"And they can't?"

"Not by listening, once or twice, to the junk he's selling. No."

"But don't you sell tapes and CDs and DVDs yourself?"

"I do. And on my tapes I, also, guide my listener through relaxation techniques and visualizations. I talk to them about them releasing the extra weight, surrendering it to the universe, letting go of painful memories, and self-limiting, defeatist attitudes."

"That sounds like the sort of things he says, too."

"Yes, he does. But the difference between Wellman and me is — I also have my patients visualize themselves eating wholesome food in healthy portions, daily moving their bodies in some form of exercise that they love, and actively reducing stress in their lives. I encourage them to examine their life priorities and rearrange them so that food isn't their best friend and consolation."

She took a deep breath and a long drink from her margarita. Savannah watched her, thinking that here was a woman who was, indeed, passionate about her work. And she decided that she genuinely liked Dr. Bonnie Saperstein.

"What Wellman is selling," Bonnie continued, "is magic thinking, a hurtful fantasy. He's not just robbing them of their money. It's far worse than that. He's setting them up for more self-loathing when they fail . . . again . . . like they've failed so many times before."

Savannah nodded, understanding. "And the last thing anyone needs when they're trying to make a major change for the better in their life is more discouragement and self-loathing."

"Yes. Because, no matter how much we all would like to think otherwise, nobody is going to lose weight and keep it off without changing what they eat and how much they move. Everything else is a magician's smoke and mirrors."

"So, I guess it's safe to assume that you hate Robert Wellman?"

"Yes. I do." She closed her eyes for a moment and seemed to be making an effort to quiet herself. "There are very few people on this earth whom I even dislike, but I despise him. And not just for the reasons we've just discussed. He's a vile man and a disgrace to our profession on so many levels."

*And speaking of disgraceful conduct . . .* Savannah thought. "I understand that a former client of his is now a patient of yours. Karen Burns."

"I'm sorry, Savannah, but I can't discuss any of my patients with you."

"I understand, and I won't ask you to. But I'd like to tell you what I know about her, okay?"

Bonnie nodded. "Go ahead."

"She says that she's been having a sexual relationship with Wellman. She also tells us that she's pregnant with his baby."

Bonnie said nothing, but she didn't look at all surprised. Apparently, this wasn't news to her.

"It seems she's ass-over-teakettle in love with him," Savannah said. "Go figure."

Bonnie shrugged. "Not all romances are the storybook kind . . . with knights on

259

white horses and fairy tale endings."

"That's for sure. A lot of those knights on horses turn out to be donkeys' behinds."

Both women helped themselves to another guacamole-laden chip. Then Savannah said, "You have to wonder how people get drawn into these situations . . . spending their money and pinning their hopes on Wellman's scam materials."

She thought of Karen Burns, the baby she was carrying in her belly, and the father of that child who wouldn't even tell his lover his real name. She thought of Lydia Mahoney and her scarred lip. "You wonder why they stay with a guy long after they find out he's a monster."

"Each person is different. If you talk to one hundred people, you'll find they have one hundred reasons why they allow themselves to be deceived by the cheats of this world. Most of them are in terrible pain and looking outside themselves for relief. My job is to turn their search inward."

"And I suppose Karen Burns is in terrible pain. I met her mother. Sheez-z-z, what a mouth on that one!"

Dr. Saperstein didn't reply to that, either, but again, Savannah could tell it was old news to her.

"Here's what I'm wondering," Savannah

said. "I'm wondering if Robert Wellman murdered our victim. And I'm wondering if Karen Burns is unstable enough to either help him do it or at least provide a false alibi for him."

Bonnie was silent for a long time as she stared into the frosty drink in her hand. Finally, she said, "I can't tell you anything specific about Karen. Even if it weren't illegal, I wouldn't do it. My patients trust me with their deepest secrets, and to me that's a sacred trust. But I'll tell you what I know about women . . . at least some of them."

"Okay," Savannah said. "That would be helpful."

"Some women . . . for myriad, sad reasons . . . have terribly low self-esteem. They hate their lives, and they want a way out. They look for a man to provide that new life."

Savannah nodded. "Oh, I know the story all too well. Prince Charming comes riding through the forest glen on that white steed of his, red cape flapping in the breeze, and he carries them away to his castle in the clouds. That's a pretty popular fantasy. We heard it all the time growing up as little girls."

"Yes, but once we become big girls, there are no more excuses. It's time to get real and figure out how things really are. We have to figure out our own life plans, not just look for some guy who will allow us to attach ourselves to him and *his* dreams."

"But some women never make that distinction, between fairy tales and life. It's deeply engrained in us from the start."

"So true. And when certain women receive attention from a man — especially one who's rich or powerful — they start to believe that their wonderful, new life has arrived. That perfect man is going to sweep them into his arms and take them to his world, a utopia of his making, where they'll always have enough money, be young, be healthy, be beautiful and slender."

"And when it doesn't work out . . ."

"When the dream starts to fall apart, these women become desperate. Their fear takes over — that terrible fear of being stuck in their pain like they were before. Only now it's worse because, once again, they're without hope. They'll do almost anything to hold it together."

Savannah leaned across the table and looked deep into the doctor's eyes. "They'll do *anything?*" she said.

Bonnie Saperstein returned the steady look without flinching. "I truly believe . . . some of them will do *anything.*"

262

# CHAPTER 16

"Other than your front room and your backyard, this here park is my favorite place in California," Gran told Savannah as they sat together in folding lawn chairs in the shade of an enormous oak tree and watched the town's citizens enjoying the downtown park.

An hour earlier, they had tossed the lawn chairs into the Mustang's trunk, grabbed a couple of cold sodas from the refrigerator and a big zip-shut bag full of Savannah's home-baked, chocolate chip and pecan cookies, and taken off for the park.

Now they sat, enjoying each other, their snacks, and the park's ambiance. All around them, children and dogs chased Frisbees and balls, wieners and hamburgers cooked on the barbecue pits, kids dug in sandboxes, and lovers lazed around on the grass, exchanging hugs and kisses.

All was well in San Carmelita. At least on

this square block.

Across the street sat the old mission in all of its ancient glory. One of a chain of twenty-one missions that had been built along the Pacific coast by the Franciscan friars, the San Carmelita Mission had stood in gentle, quiet dignity for over two hundred years. Her strong, thick, adobe walls had withstood earthquakes, fires, and even a tidal wave, though they hadn't protected the church treasures from pirates in her early years.

She had been lovingly restored after each catastrophe — man-made and natural — and her gleaming white walls, dark beams, red-tile roof, and lofty bell tower drew tourists by the thousands every year. Everyone wanted a picture of themselves with their arm around the statue of the founder, Padre Serra.

It also didn't hurt that the mission was only a few blocks from some of the most beautiful beaches in Southern California.

"I just feel close to the Lord when I'm sitting here under this tree, lookin' at that church," Gran told Savannah. "What a work of faith a building like that is. The people who accomplished that, all those years ago, must have been truly devoted to God."

Savannah thought of all the Native Americans who had been forced into slavery and died under harsh conditions building that structure. But she decided not to say anything. Why ruin it for Gran?

"I'm tickled that I'm getting to spend some quality time with you," Savannah said. "I feel like either you or I have been on the run since you got here. Me investigating this case with Dirk and you gattin' around with either Tammy or Ryan and John."

"Don't you worry about me," Gran said. "I've been having myself a good time. Riding that merry-go-round was the most fun I've had in ages. That's about the prettiest thing I've ever seen in my life — 'cept you on the day you was born."

Savannah leaned over and took Gran's hand in hers. "Ah," she said, "don't make me cry. I'm PMSing, and it wouldn't take much for me to tear up."

"Well, it's true, Savannah girl. You made me a grandma. That's a mighty special moment in any woman's life."

Savannah did a bit of mental math. "Oh, mercy," she said. "I just realized something. When I was born, you were younger than I am now! That's a scary thought."

Gran laughed. "Not to me. It was the most natural thing in the world. I was ready for it."

"You didn't mind becoming a grandma?"

Gran squeezed her hand. "I thought I might mind a little bit, before you were born. But once you were here, I looked into that beautiful little face of yours, you wrapped those tiny sweet fingers around my pinky, and I knew — I sure as shootin' didn't mind becoming *your* grandma."

Savannah thought about the dining table there at Gran's house, where she had eaten most of her meals as a child. It was actually a dining table sandwiched between two card tables, one on each end.

She thought of all the piles of laundry, mountains of it, that had been done every single day. Except Sunday. Sunday was sacred and everyone rested on the Sabbath.

At least, as much as a family with nine children could rest.

Much of that laundry wasn't permanent press fabric, which mean that either Gran or Savannah spent many hours standing at the ironing board, steaming and pressing clothes on steamy, oppressive Georgia summer days.

And it had to be done because no Reid kid went to school dirty or wrinkled. Gran wouldn't abide it.

The washing machine and the clothesline were always filled with dresses, jeans, shirts, blouses, and underwear galore that had seen better days. Some of the clothes had seen better years, as they were handed down from one kid to the next and to the next.

Receiving a new outfit was usually reserved for a Christmas present or a birthday gift.

She thought of what it must have cost in money, time, and energy to buy and prepare enough food to cover that table three times a day and fill the bellies of nine perpetually famished children. "I don't know how you did it," she said. "Raising all of us like that."

"*We* did it. *You* and me and Pa . . . till he took sick."

Savannah was tempted to argue with her, but then she remembered a heck of a lot of potato mashing and dish washing. Not to mention all that time spent gardening and selling any extra vegetables and fruits to other folks in town. Anything to make an extra dollar was part of the job description when you were the firstborn in a big family.

"Well, that's what happens when you're the oldest," Savannah said. *And your mother's too busy hefting drinks in the local bar to mess with a stove or an ironing board,* she added to herself. "I'm sorry Shirley put you in that position," she said. "Leaving you to raise her brood."

"Don't you ever apologize to me for that," Gran said in her best pseudostern voice. "I'm sorry Shirley didn't do right by you kids, but as for me? She did me a favor. I wouldn't have missed it for the world."

"Not even when Marietta had boyfriends climbing through the bedroom window at all times of the night?"

"I could've done without that."

"Or when Macon let the air out of the pastor's tires when he came calling that Sunday afternoon?"

"Please, don't remind me. I prefer to remember those days through a rosy pink haze."

"Called denial?"

"It works for me. Don't mess with it."

Savannah laughed, then squinted her eyes, looking across the expanse of green grass at a figure walking toward them. "I declare," she said, "I do believe that's Dirk, coming our way."

"I reckon it is. What do you suppose he's doing here?"

"I can tell by his face that something's wrong," Savannah said. "And knowing him, he's just gotta complain to somebody about it or he'll have a conniption."

"He hunted you down and came over here just so's he'd have somebody to gripe to?"

268

"Yeap. That's Dirk for you."

"Why didn't he just call you up on the phone?"

"It's not as much fun as bellyaching in person."

Dirk hurried up to them, and he certainly did look disgruntled about something.

Some kid threw a Frisbee that struck him squarely on the chest, and he didn't even pause for a moment to yell at them. So Savannah knew it had to be bad.

"Man, I am so bummed," he announced when he reached them. Turning to Gran, he gave her a brief smile and a nod. "Hi, Granny. Good to see you."

"Good to see you, too, sugar." Gran gave him a closer look. "Boy, you feeling okay? Your color's a bit offish there. Kinda orange."

"So I've heard." His frown firmly back in place, he turned back to Savannah. "This just stinks. Wait'll you hear this."

"Sitting here with bated breath," she mumbled as she took a chocolate chip cookie from the bag and handed it to Gran.

She offered him one, and his face lit up as he reached for it. Then he reconsidered and sadly shook his head. "No, thanks," he said.

"Yeah, right. How could I forget? You're dieting." Savannah sighed. "Okay. Suit yourself. That's all the more for us."

She re-zipped the bag. "How did you track us down anyway?"

"I called your house, and Tammy ratted you out."

"Good ol' Tammy. I'll have to thank her for that. So, what's up? Did you lose your reading glasses again? Got a stain on your leather jacket? Forgot to buy toilet paper when you went to the grocery store last night?"

He shook his head and plopped down on the grass beside their chairs. "That judge, Dalano? She wouldn't give me a search warrant for Wellman's house."

Savannah shrugged. "That's not so surprising. Judge Dalano hates you."

"She does?"

"Sure. Haven't you noticed?"

He looked crestfallen. "How do you know that? How can you tell?"

Savannah munched on the cookie. "Every time you testify in front of her bench, she glares at you."

"She does?"

"*Glares.* Major nasty looks the whole time you're on the stand. And haven't you ever noticed that she always rules against any motions the prosecutor makes when you're up there?"

"I did notice she's a bit of a hard ass. Oops, sorry, Gran."

Savannah brushed some crumbs off her chest. "Only when you're on the stand."

"Really?"

"Yep. Rest of the time — she's a marshmallow, a real sweetheart."

"Well, I'll be damned. Sorry, Gran."

Granny nodded, granting absolution.

"Why do you suppose that is?" Dirk asked.

"It probably goes back to that time when you were testifying in the *Hinze v. Johnson* case. You said something on the stand about how you thought women shouldn't be judges because they're moody."

"Yeah? So?"

"She was the sitting judge on that case."

He sighed and shook his head. "And you think she held that against me?"

Savannah nodded. "Call it a hunch."

"Well, that just proves my point. She was probably moody that day."

"And today, too?"

"Apparently, denying me a search warrant when it's obvious I've got cause for one."

"What cause do you have?" Granny wanted to know.

"He's living under an assumed name. He lied about his relationship to the victim, pretending — even legally, on paper — that

271

she was his wife. That's some sort of fraud right there. And then his wife . . . or rather his sister . . . gets murdered on his property, and he's got somebody giving him a fake alibi for the night of the killing. Now, ain't that enough for me to get a search warrant, if the judge was being reasonable?"

"And wasn't out to get you 'cause she hates you," Savannah added.

Granny thought it over, then nodded. "Yes, I'd say she put the kibosh on that 'un outta pure dee spite."

"I know I would have," Savannah said.

"You would have turned down the warrant because of what I said?"

"Darned tootin'. Call me 'moody' in my own courtroom, I'd have slapped you with a contempt of court charge . . . and then I'd have just plain slapped you. I'd show you 'moody.' "

Dirk grunted, but then he gave Savannah a little grin. To Granny he said, "How did a nice, sweet lady like you raise a nasty, mouthy broad like this one?"

"I used to be just like her," Gran said proudly. " 'Cept I've mellowed a bit."

Dirk chuckled, then looked around. "Have you ladies had dinner yet?"

"Nope," Gran replied. "All she's fed me is

these cookies. I'm growin' faint from hunger."

"How's about I buy you two dinner?"

Savannah nearly choked on her cookie. Dirk offering to buy two meals in forty-eight hours? She couldn't believe it!

He nodded toward the other side of the park. "I saw a roach coach over there. And they're selling three hot dogs for a dollar. It'll be my treat."

Half an hour later, they had downed their dogs, and Dirk had even bought a second round.

He and Savannah were still sitting at the picnic table, finishing theirs. But Gran had wandered over to the sandbox, where she was digging in the sand with some children.

"You'd think she'd have had her fill of kids," Savannah said, watching her grandmother with love shining in her eyes. "But look at her . . . over eighty years old, but still playing with children."

"She's beautiful," Dirk said simply.

Then he gave Savannah a warm, affectionate look that she couldn't quite understand.

As she finished the last bite of her hot dog and licked the ketchup off her thumb, she said to him, "If you think I'm sleeping with you tonight just because you bought me dinner, you're in for a disappointment."

He shrugged. "I've been disappointed before. I can stand it."

"I'm sure you have." She glanced over toward Gran to make sure she was still out of earshot. "But I could still make it up to you. . . ."

"Oh?" He leaned across the table toward her, a mischievous smile on his face. "I'm listening."

"How badly do you want Wellman's place searched?"

He raised one eyebrow, then cleared his throat. "Um . . . it would be nice. There may not be anything there, but I'd sleep better if I knew that for sure."

"But, of course, you being an officer of the law, one of San Carmelita's finest . . . it would be unthinkable for you to sully your reputation, dirty your hands with such an unlawful thing as breaking and entering."

"And if I made a case against him and later it came out that I'd done something like that, the whole thing could get thrown out of court."

"Especially if it was Judge Dalano."

"And if she was moody that day."

They sat in silence for a while, mulling it over.

Savannah wadded their hotdog wrappers

274

into a ball and tossed it into a nearby garbage can.

"What do you figure our buddy, Wellman, is gonna be doing tonight?" she said.

"What time?"

She looked up at the sky. "Well, it'll be good and dark in about an hour."

He glanced at his watch. "So, maybe from about seven thirty to about eight thirty?"

"Yeah. About then."

"I think he's gonna be down at the station house, answering some new questions I've got."

"You've got new questions?"

"No, but I will have by then."

Gran had stood up and brushed the sand off her skirt, and she was walking back to them.

"Sh-h-h," Savannah said. "Here comes Granny. Don't you dare let her get wind of this."

"Yeah, she'll get pretty mad if she finds out you're planning to do something illegal. She'll try to stop you."

"Oh, ple-e-ez. You don't know my granny very well. She'll wanna go along."

# CHAPTER 17

"I'm sure glad you boys were available to join me on this," Savannah told Ryan as he boosted her over the window ledge and into Robert Wellman/Bobby Martini's utility room.

For one precarious moment, she got her pants pocket caught on the washing machine knob, but then she freed herself and continued on her way.

John had already climbed inside, and Ryan followed close behind her.

"Ow-w-w," she said, banging her knee on the edge of the dryer. "Remind me next time just to pick the lock like a respectable private investigator."

"At least this time you didn't climb through the bathroom window and slip in the bathtub," Ryan reminded her as he lightly jumped from the top of the washer onto the floor.

Agility was such a plus while breaking and

entering.

John shone his penlight onto his wrist. "It's now half-seven," he said. "That gives us an hour to do our dirty work."

Savannah patted the cell phone she had clipped to her belt. "Dirk'll call us the minute Wellman leaves the station. And it's at least a ten-, fifteen-minute drive. We'll be fine."

"I'm just glad there aren't any dogs," John said as he led them from the utility room into the kitchen.

Savannah snickered. "Or cats as vicious as mine?"

"Cleo and Diamante vicious?" Ryan said. "Maybe if you tried to pry their Kitty Vittles out of their mouths."

"True. Attacking an intruder would involve getting their rumps off their window perch, and that would be too much to ask."

Leaving the house lights off, they used their penlights to see as they walked around the kitchen, opening a few drawers and cupboards.

Ryan paid special attention to the area near the telephone, thumbing through some envelopes stacked there. "Nothing but bills," he said.

"Is there a phone bill there?" Savannah asked.

"As a matter of fact, yes. An old one."

"Get the account number."

Ryan took a miniature voice recorder from his pocket and read the number into it.

Savannah opened the refrigerator door and peeked inside. "Nothing in here but condiments and beer," she said. "Wellman and Dirk have more in common than we thought."

"No voice messages," John said, checking the machine. "Either he doesn't get a lot of calls or he's deleted them all."

From the kitchen they went into the dining room, then the living room.

"There's nothing here worth writing home about," Savannah said. "My front room is more scandalous than this. At least I've got some juicy romance novels on my reading stand."

"Let's go upstairs and check out the bedrooms." Ryan headed for the foyer and the staircase.

Savannah followed him. "I've gotta admit that I'm a little afraid to."

"Why, love?" John asked. "Are you nervous that he'll pop in on us unannounced?"

"No, Dirk's got that covered. I'm afraid I'm going to find out that he and his sister shared a bedroom and then I'm going to have to go home and poke out my mind's eye."

"It wouldn't do any good," Ryan said. "You'd still see it. It's a brain thing."

"True. Thanks."

At the top of the staircase, a hallway stretched in both directions. Savannah went to the left, the guys to the right.

The moment she opened the first door, her mind was set at ease. She swept the beam from her flashlight around the room, taking in the lavender walls, the canopy bed with its frilly, satin spread, the tables draped with lace-trimmed linen cloths. Delicate, feminine knickknacks covered most of the horizontal surfaces.

She went back to the door and called down the hallway, "Hey, fellas. I found her bedroom. I'm not humming the theme to *Deliverance* in my head anymore."

"We're so happy for you, darling," John called back.

"Yeah, we found his room," Ryan said. "He's a slob, but nothing too sinister looking."

A few minutes later, they converged in the hallway at the top of the stairs. Even in the dim light, Savannah could see they looked as discouraged as she felt.

"I'm hate to say it, but I think we might

have committed a felony for nothing," she told them.

"You might be right," Ryan said.

"Although . . ." John was playing his light along the ceiling. "I'd wager that this house has a sizable attic. We haven't checked the garage yet. Let's do that and see if we can find an access there."

Savannah checked her watch. "Okay," she said, "but we'd better shake some fanny. Time's a wastin'!"

Once the trio was in the garage, John took less than a minute to find the door on the ceiling. "Brilliant!" he exclaimed as he grabbed the cord that was hanging down and gave it a pull.

The trap door opened, and the stairs unfolded neatly before them.

"Well done, old boy," Ryan said, slapping him on the back.

Savannah looked up at the pitch black hole in the ceiling and felt a little shudder run over her. "And since you're the one who thought of this," she said, "it's only fair you should be the first to go up."

John started up the ladder, but he paused just before sticking his head into the opening. "A chap tends to regret all those slicer-dicer movies he's seen at a moment like this," he said.

"I doubt there's anybody up there with an axe or a sword, waiting to lop off your head, if that's what you're worried about," Ryan said.

Still standing at the foot of the ladder, Savannah told him, "Don't worry. If it comes tumbling down, I'll catch it, and save it for you. I'm sure they can sew it back on in the ER."

"How very witty you two are. So funny I can hardly stand you," John said as he disappeared into the darkness.

Ryan was the next one to vanish into the black hole.

Savannah didn't mind at all that the rule "ladies first" had been put aside for the moment.

As she climbed the highest stairs and stepped onto the attic floor, she heard John sneezing.

"Bloody hell, it's quite a shambles up here," he said.

"I guess Wellman doesn't make it up here when he's doing his weekly dusting," Ryan added.

Savannah saw what they meant when she joined them in the middle of what was, indeed, a very large attic. Because of the contemporary lines of the house, the roof was at odd angles, sloping first one way and then the other . . . not at all like a traditional attic.

She headed for a nearby area where most of the stored junk was piled.

Ryan was already checking out the dusty collection of furniture that included everything from a sofa with gold and avocado green stripes and a matching love seat, to a dark, Mediterranean-style bedroom suite, circa 1975.

"I can't say much for their former taste in furniture," he said. "And you have to wonder why they brought all this junk with them when they moved."

"Let alone dragged it all up here," John added.

Savannah flipped the lid of a cardboard box open and looked inside. "We've got old bottles of shampoo, half rolls of toilet paper, and used razors. I'd say they may have moved in a hurry and just threw everything in sight into boxes."

"I tend to agree," John said. "We have old newspapers here from Las Vegas, dated three years ago."

Tucked into a far corner, away from the heap and sitting by itself, was an oversized trunk that caught Savannah's attention.

"Hey, boys . . . lookie, lookie," she said.

"An old trunk."

"An old trunk in an attic," Ryan replied. "Cool."

"It probably has a body in it," John told them. Then he chuckled. "Sorry. I really must swear off those revolting movies. They're my secret vice."

"Not so secret anymore." Savannah dropped to her knees in front of the chest. She handed her flashlight to Ryan, then slowly lifted the lid.

The hinges actually creaked as she opened it. She giggled and said, "How very Nancy Drew/Hardy Boy-ish. Tammy would love this."

"Why didn't you invite her along?" John asked.

"I never ask her to come when I'm committing a crime. It's a personal standard I have — not contributing to the delinquency of a minor."

"She's not a kid," Ryan said. "She's well into her twenties."

"As far as I'm concerned, she's *my* kid. She'll be my kid when she's seventy."

Savannah leaned over the edge of the trunk to look inside, and Ryan shone both lights into it.

"What the heck is this stuff?" Savannah said, trying to make sense of the strange shapes she was seeing.

John shed his own light into the depths, and she saw something smooth and crystalline, glowing in the far corner of the box.

"It's a skull," she said. "A glass skull. Ooo-o, creepy!"

"And we've got some sort of knife over here." Ryan pointed to a dagger, resting in a lidless box, lined with red velvet. A black pentagram was carved into the bone handle.

"And a Ouija board," John said. "Fascinating."

Savannah picked up a small pouch made of black velvet and loosened its drawstring. Reaching inside, she pulled out several polished stones and a large amethyst crystal.

"What is this stuff?" she said. "Witchcraft paraphernalia?"

"It's a bit theatrical to be the real thing," John said.

They both gave him strange looks. He added, "Not that I'd know from *personal* experience."

"Of course not," Savannah said. "Haven't painted your body blue and danced naked in the moonlight lately?"

"Only in my misspent youth."

Ryan handed Savannah back her flashlight, then reached down and picked up a small mechanical apparatus of some kind. It looked like a cross between a cell phone and a television remote control.

"What's that?" Savannah asked.

"I think it's an electromagnetic field meter. Looks like it records temperatures, too."

"And this," John said, pointing to a long, black tube, "is an infrared, night vision camera."

"Hey, look at this . . . a ghost box!" Ryan replaced the meter and grabbed something that resembled a transistor radio.

"A ghost box? What the heck's a ghost box?" Savannah asked, feeling another little chill run through her.

She couldn't help it. She, too, had seen her share of gory movies. And Gran had been known to entertain the kids with a few hair-raising ghost stories in her day, too.

"A ghost box is a modern-day type of séance tool," Ryan said. "It's a radio that's been modified to continually scan station to station and back again. Some people ask the spirit world questions and then listen to the voices that come through the scanner. They claim to hear answers from the ghosts, who are speaking to them through the box."

Savannah thought it over for half a second. "That's stupid," she said. "They're hearing disc jockeys and talk show hosts."

Ryan laughed. "That's what you and I believe, but there are folks who think otherwise."

Again, John remained conspicuously silent.

They gave him another look.

"I'm not going to say a word," he told them. "Look at where we're standing . . . in a dark attic, staring into a chest full of strange, esoteric objects. I'm not interested in getting on the bad side of any spirits, if that's quite all right with you two."

"Good point," Savannah agreed. "You know, Granny's a great believer in 'haunts,' as she calls them. She won't go near a place if anybody even suggested there might be a ghost in there."

"I'd rather discuss the subject of ghosts and 'haunts' later, by the light of the noonday sun," John told her.

Ryan lifted a large, cobalt blue bottle with a cork stopper and read the label. "Purification water." He thought for a while, then said, "You guys, this stuff in this chest . . . it's séance equipment, ghost-hunting tools."

"You think our lad, Wellman, was a ghost hunter?" John asked.

"More like Bobby Martini was." Savannah's brain whirred, and she could feel some of the bits and pieces coming together.

"He's a scam artist now, selling people something they desperately need, something fake that costs an arm and a leg. I'll bet you that he was one in Vegas, too, again . . . selling people a fake service, claiming to connect them to their dead loved ones."

"Or maybe he really was connecting," John said. "You have to remain open-minded about these things."

Savannah sniffed. "Believe me, I've spent time with Wellman. There may be deep-minded spiritualists with esoteric knowledge of the great Beyond. But he ain't one of them. He's a bullshitter who's out to fleece anybody he can."

She waved an arm around, indicating the general contents of the attic. "And it looks to me like he had to leave town in a hurry."

"And move to a new area and change his identity," Ryan added.

"Who was he running from?" Savannah mused. "The law? Bad guys?"

"When people run," John said, "it's frequently from both."

Savannah was about to close the lid on Wellman's former activities when she noticed several simple shoe boxes in the bottom of the chest, below some night goggles and a voice recorder.

She reached down and dug one of them

out. "So, what's in here?" she said. "Running shoes, like it says on the box, or Dorothy's magic ruby slippers?"

But when she raised the lid, it wasn't red she saw, but green. Lots and lots of green.

"Wow!" she said. "Would you look at this, boys?"

"We're looking! We're looking!" But Ryan was already reaching for the second box.

John pulled out a third.

When all the boxes were open, and the contents revealed, neither Savannah nor the guys could even speak for a few moments.

Finally, Savannah said, "I guess paying off a blackmailer here or there wouldn't present much of a problem to good ol' Dr. Wellman."

"These are all hundred dollar bills," John said, taking out one handful of the notes and thumbing through them.

"There are hundreds of thousands of dollars here," Ryan replied. "I can't believe he came by this money honestly."

"Either he's a big-time crook or an extremely nervous investor." Savannah put the lid back on the box and replaced it in the bottom of the chest.

"If he stole this money from somebody, you know they've been looking for him," John said.

"And he's recently been on national television, promoting his weight loss program." Ryan placed his box in the chest next to Savannah's. "He had to know that would put him at risk . . . maybe Maria, too. Especially if she was part of the rip-off."

"Some people just can't resist the allure of so-called stardom," Savannah said. "They'll sell their momma for the chance at immortality — appearing on a hemorrhoid cream commercial."

A buzzing sound made them all jump. John nearly dropped the box he was holding.

"It's my phone," she said. She grabbed it off her belt and looked at the tiny screen that was glowing green in the dark. "It's Dirk."

Holding the phone to her ear, she said, "Hi. Is he on his way?" She nodded to Ryan and John. "When did he leave? Okay, we're outta here." She listened, then snickered. "Oh, yeah. We found some good stuff."

John and Ryan started making ghostly "o-o-o-o" sounds and laughing.

"The boys are just being goofy," she said. "Meet us back at my house, and we'll fill you in on all the gruesome details."

# CHAPTER 18

As Savannah, Ryan, and John hurried around the side of the Wellman house, she stubbed her toe on something in the dark. She suppressed the urge to scream.

Burglars didn't scream while in the act of burgling.

She was pretty sure that was some sort of rule.

"You okay?" Ryan asked, taking her hand.

"Yeah," she whispered. "It was just my foot. I've got another one."

When they reached the front yard, they paused and listened before walking into the open, better-lit area.

The last thing they wanted was to run into some neighbor out for a nightly stroll with his dog — a curious neighbor who might wonder why they were sneaking around Wellman's yard, wearing dark clothes, with guilty looks on their faces.

When they thought the coast was clear,

they walked briskly across the front yard, heading for the road. Savannah's Mustang was parked about half a block down and on the opposite side.

But when they reached the sidewalk, Savannah looked up and saw a figure standing in the shadows of some tall oleander bushes, directly across the street.

He, too, was wearing dark clothes, and he appeared to be watching the front of Wellman's house.

"Hey," she whispered to the guys. "Over there."

"Yeah, I see him," Ryan said. "Just keep walking. We haven't done anything wrong . . ."

"Except break into somebody's house," Savannah replied.

"Other than that."

"And if we get caught," John added, "I'm sure Judge Dalano will understand when we're on trial before her bench."

Abruptly, the man in the bushes turned around and began to hurry down the sidewalk away from them. He got into a red, midsized sedan that was parked near the Mustang and sped away.

Ryan pulled his digital recorder out of his pocket, pressed a button, and recited the license plate number into it.

"I wonder who that chap was," John said as they got into the Mustang.

"And what he was doing." Savannah started the car.

"Whatever it was," Ryan said from the back seat, "he was up to no good."

Savannah laughed. "Like us?"

"Naw, probably not as bad as us."

When Savannah, Ryan, and John returned to her house, Dirk was waiting in his Buick in the driveway. And when Savannah ushered them all inside the house, she cautioned them to keep their voices low.

"If you wake Gran, we'll all have a bunch of explaining to do," she told them.

The note she had left for Gran, saying that she had gone out on a short errand and would be back soon, was still lying in the middle of the coffee table. Savannah breathed a sigh of relief as she snatched it up and tossed it into a wastebasket.

"Good," she said. "Granny hasn't gotten up. I was afraid she'd come downstairs for something to eat and realize I was gone and then get all worried. But what she doesn't know won't cause me a heap of grief."

"And what is it exactly that I'm not supposed to know?" asked a voice behind Savannah.

She turned to see Gran coming down the stairs, wearing her flannel nightgown and a pink, chenille robe. On her feet were the fluffy, pink slippers that Savannah had given her for Mother's Day.

"Uh-oh, Van," Dirk said, snickering. "You're busted."

Suddenly, Savannah felt like a five-year-old, holding a handful of one of her brothers' or sisters' birthday cake . . . an hour before the party.

"Gran!" she said, far too cheerfully. "You came downstairs just in the nick of time. Come sit a spell and listen while Ryan and I fill Dirk in on all we've been up to tonight."

"Yes," Granny said, giving Savannah a deeply suspicious look. "That's a fine idea. Let's all-l-l hear what you've been up to."

It took Savannah, John, and Ryan over an hour to fill Dirk and Gran in on all the details of their house search.

Gran was scandalized over the Ouija board, dagger, and crystal skull.

"That sounds like black magic junk to me," she said. "I'll betcha that those people were into devil worship, virgin sacrifices, and the whole shebang!"

"I doubt they sacrificed virgins," Savan-

293

nah said, teasing her. "Remember, this probably took place in Las Vegas . . . sin city."

"True." Gran nodded her head and added with all seriousness, "I'd expect there's a serious shortage of chaste maidens in that town."

"I'm sure all those strange objects were props," Ryan tried to reassure Gran. "Stuff to lend authenticity to their sham exorcisms. I have a feeling that when we dig deeper into Wellman's activities, we'll find out that he made all that money by swindling people. Not unlike what he does now."

John agreed. "He probably offered to rid their houses of unhappy spirits for a price. A big price. That's how the scam's been run for centuries."

Savannah got up to refresh everyone's coffee cups and the plate of brownies. When she poured a top-off into Dirk's mug, she said, "Right now, I'm more concerned about that guy we saw when we were leaving Wellman's. I'm telling you, he was hinky. I could feel it coming off of him in waves."

"She's right about that," John said. "He saw us and scurried away like a wharf rat."

"Well, you should be findin' out shortly." Gran shook her head as Savannah tried to refill her cup. "No, thank you, darlin'. My eyeballs are swimmin' in my head as it is."

Dirk got out his cell phone and stared at it. "Yeah, that gal at the station desk should have gotten back to me by now. What's it been — ?"

"Five minutes," Savannah supplied.

"— Since I called her and gave her that plate number to run."

"It takes so long to type all those numbers and letters into the computer. And then she's got to press 'Enter' and all that. It might take six minutes." Savannah resisted the urge to splash hot coffee on his lap.

"I think I'll give her a call," he said, toying with the phone. "Tell her I need it today and not when she gets around to it next week."

"Yeah, why don't you do that?" Savannah said. "That way we won't hear from her until Christmas . . . next year."

His phone began to ring. He smiled and said, "See. It pays to be impatient. She picked up on my 'hurry up' vibes."

"And called you anyway."

He answered the phone and listened as the woman on the other end gave him the information. "Hm-m-m . . . a rental," he said. "I guess that's not too surprising." He paused as she told him more. "Really? You did? Hey, good job. So, what's the name?"

Everyone in the room sat, silent, hanging on his every word. Savannah hovered over him with the coffeepot, her pulse rate increasing by the moment.

He smiled, looking quite satisfied. "Good job . . . uh . . . Cheryl . . . oh . . . um, Deirdre. Sorry, sorta sounds alike, you know. Bye."

"It's a rental," he said, snapping the phone closed. "And she managed to get hold of somebody at the national office who looked up the dude who rented it."

"And?" Savannah said, nudging his leg with her foot.

"A guy from Las Vegas. Gus Avantis."

"The former brother-in-law! Wow! That's heavy!" Savannah nearly dropped the pot. Instead, she set it down on a plate on the coffee table, then sank into her favorite chair, her mind racing.

Ryan and the others were impressed, too. "Wellman told you that his sister's life had been threatened by her ex, right?" he asked.

Dirk nodded. "He certainly wouldn't be the first ex-husband to kill his old lady."

"Three years later, though?" John asked. "That seems like a long time to hold a grudge."

Gran shook her head. "I've seen the way some men are when a woman leaves them.

They hate her and everybody associated with her for the rest of their lives. They feel like they lost some big, all-fired important game, and they can't stand to lose — especially to a woman. They never get over it."

"Who'd want a woman who doesn't want you?" Dirk said.

"Oh, you'd be surprised." Gran sniffed. "I reckon it's not so much that they want her, but that they can't stand the thought that some other fella might have her. They figure she's theirs, like their shotgun, their pickup, their hound dog."

Ryan leaned forward, his elbows on his knees, fingers laced. He had a concerned look on his face. "You know, if this Avantis killed Maria — and we have to at least entertain the possibility that he did — Wellman could be in danger right now. Why would Avantis be hanging around outside Wellman's house, acting suspicious, if he meant him no harm?"

"Good point," Dirk said. "I could call him and warn him. I'm sure he'd be thrilled to hear from me for the third time today . . . since we had such a pleasant talk earlier."

"You did?" Granny asked.

"No, I'm being facetious. He hardly answered my questions at all, and when I started asking him about what he did in Vegas before he moved here, he clammed up and used the 'L' word."

"What's the 'L' word?" Gran wanted to know. "Is that some sort of foul language?"

"In a police department, it's the worst," Savannah told her. " 'L' is for 'lawyer.' He invoked his right to have an attorney present while being questioned."

"A cop would rather be called anything in the book than hear that," Dirk added.

"I think you'd better call him," Savannah said. "Who cares if he wants to hear from you? You're not asking him out on a date. You're warning him that his former brother-in-law is watching him . . . probably with evil intentions."

Dirk took his notebook from his pocket, found the number, and punched it into his phone. He waited a long time, then said, "Yeah, Wellman, it's Coulter. Give me a call back as soon as you get this. Don't worry about the time. It's important."

When he hung up, Savannah said, "Do you think he has his phone turned off or he's just avoiding you?"

"Wouldn't you avoid me if you were him?"

"Heck, I avoid you, and I'm me."

"I'm calling him at his house number, too. If that Gus dude is hiding in the bushes there on his property, he needs to know it."

"And maybe go spend the night at a hotel," Savannah said. "I'm sure Karen Burns would be happy to join him at the Island View Hotel. Their special suite might be available."

An hour after her company had all left, as soon as she and Gran were in bed, Savannah's phone rang with Dirk's ringtone. She picked it up from her nightstand.

"Just can't get enough of me, huh?" she said into the receiver as she pulled the quilt up around her chin and tucked Cleopatra into the crook of her elbow.

Diamante was keeping her feet warm.

"Guess where I am?" Dirk said on the other end.

"Sitting in front of Wellman's house."

"How did you know?"

"I know you."

"I rang the doorbell, and he didn't answer. I can't tell if his car's in the garage or not. I don't see any lights on."

"You did all you could, Dirk. It's midnight. Go home and go to bed."

"Naw, that's okay. I think I'll just sit here for a while . . . just in case Wellman comes home or Avantis shows up."

Savannah smiled, thinking that she could

forgive a guy some social blunders and the occasional crankiness, considering. He might be impatient while waiting for someone to run a plate number. But, on the other hand, he would stand guard outside the house of a guy he detested, late at night, when he was exhausted.

"You're a good guy, Detective Dirko," she said.

"Well, don't let it get out. If people start thinking of me as a nice guy, they'll try to run over me."

"Don't worry, buddy. It'll never happen. Not while I'm around to set 'em straight."

"Good night, sweetheart."

"Nighty-night, darlin'."

# CHAPTER 19

Usually, Tammy radiated sunshine and light. She was one of the most upbeat and positive spirits Savannah had ever had the privilege to know.

But today there were thunderclouds above her head.

Savannah could practically see the torrential rain and lightning strikes over the desk in the corner of her living room.

It wasn't a good day in the Reid household.

"I'm in the doghouse with Tammy," Savannah whispered to Gran in the kitchen as they stirred up a pitcher of sweet tea.

"Yep. She's in a big ol' huff in there."

"She's not talking to me. And when Tammy's not talking, that's a really bad sign."

"She spoke to me all nice and polite when she first came in. But then she sat down at that computer and started peckin' away, and she ain't bobbed up for air since."

"She's mad that we didn't take her along when we broke into Wellman's last night."

"Well, can't blame her for that. I'm pretty miffed that you didn't take me, too."

Gran lifted her chin a notch and strolled out of the kitchen, glass of tea in hand, a certain tightness in her walk that signaled a sure case of Twisted Knickers Syndrome.

Savannah sighed and whispered, "Oh, Lord, just take me now. I'm weary, and I wanna go home."

She looked down at the two beautiful black cats at her feet. She had just fed them two kitty treats each, and they were still licking their whiskers. "You girls still love Mommy, right?" she said.

Cleo stuck her tail in the air and walked away, followed by her sister.

"That's it. Eat my treats and then leave me to go sit on your perch and watch birds. I'm just a food supply and something warm to sleep next to at night. You might as well be men."

She looked in the refrigerator and found Tammy's bottle of organic green tea. She emptied it into one of her best crystal tumblers and added a lemon slice, ice cubes, and a sprig of fresh mint.

"What a major kiss-up I am. I'm pathetic," she muttered as she carried her own sugared tea and the "healthy crap," as she called it behind Tammy's back, into the living room.

She set it on the desk in front of Tammy, next to the computer keyboard. "There you go, sweet cheeks," she said. "And before you ask — yes, the ice cubes were made from filtered water."

Tammy grumbled some unintelligible, half-syllable acknowledgment, but kept on typing . . . extremely vigorously.

Savannah winced, thinking that if she didn't make up with the kid soon, she'd have to buy another keyboard. This one was taking a beating.

"Whatcha working on there?" she asked, looking over Tammy's shoulder.

"Stuff."

"O-o-okay."

She walked away and would have sat down in her favorite chair, but Gran was sitting in it, her *True Informer* in front of her face.

Savannah strongly suspected Gran had chosen that chair out of pure spite. Granny actually preferred the rocker.

Savannah took a seat on the end of the sofa, nearest Gran, slipped off her loafers, and propped her feet on the coffee table.

She took a long drink from her tea, then said, "So, what's it going to take to get you girls to speak to me again?"

Silence reigned supreme in the room . . . except for Tammy's abuse of the keyboard and Gran's rustling of *Informer* pages.

"Come on now," she said to Gran. "I mean, really. We had to climb through the utility room window to get in. I've got a bruise on my hind end where I came down on the washer knob. You're over eighty years old. Did you really have a hankerin' to climb through a utility-room window?"

Without lowering her paper, Gran said, "If you can do it, I can do it. I'll have you know I'm a mighty spry eighty. I still put in a full garden every spring."

"I know you do. Everybody in the county knows what a fine garden you have every year and —"

"And I always put in twenty-four beefsteak tomato plants. How long's it been, missy, since *you* tied up twenty-four beefsteak tomato plants?"

"Well, not since I left home back in —"

"You're darned tootin' you haven't. It's a chore. And if I can do that, I could go along on a measly little adventure with you . . . if I was invited that is, and not just left a stupid note, saying I wasn't welcome 'cause I was an old lady."

Savannah squirmed. "That's not exactly what I wrote, but . . ."

Tammy stopped typing and whirled around in her chair. "And what's your excuse for not inviting *me?* You can't say I'm not physically able when you know I complete the Santa Barbara Marathon every year and can bench press my weight for three reps."

Savannah held up one hand. "I know, I know, Tams. You're a paragon of physical fitness."

"Then why didn't you invite me to come along? I sit here every day and do the boring stuff and never complain, while you and Dirk get to do all the cool, dangerous, scary stuff."

"Dirk wasn't along."

"You know what I mean. It's always you and some of the guys, and not me, doing the fun stuff." Her lip protruded like a petulant toddler's. "And this time was especially bad, because you found some really neat stuff."

"Devil black magic stuff," Gran interjected from behind her newspaper.

"Yeah . . . in *an old chest* in an *attic.* It doesn't get any better than that, and I missed it!"

"How's about I take both of you to Disneyland next week?" Savannah pleaded.

"You think that can make up for a chest

full of spooky stuff in an attic?" Tammy tossed her head, blonde hair flying. "Not on your life."

Gran dropped her paper. "Disneyland? Hey, I'd call it even!"

Savannah's phone began to ring. She reached over and grabbed it off the end table. "It's Dirk," she said. "And not a moment too soon. Hello."

"Hi."

She could tell from that one word that something was wrong. Badly wrong. "What's up?"

"You know that strip club on Mission Street, next to Saul's Pawn Shop?"

"Naughty Nonnina's?"

"Yeah. You gotta get over here."

"What's up?"

"I have to go. See ya."

*Click.* He hung up, leaving her looking at the phone and wondering.

"What's going on?" Tammy wanted to know.

Even a pissy Tammy was a nosy Tammy.

"Dirk wants me to get over to Naughty Nonnina's right away. Something's definitely up."

"Naughty Nonnina's? Isn't that a strip club?"

"Hm-m-ph. Fan dancers," Gran said, her

nose once again buried in her paper.

Savannah hurried into the kitchen and tossed her tea into the sink. When she returned to the living room, Tammy was on her feet and was wearing such a sweet, hopeful look on her pretty face that Savannah couldn't resist.

"Would you two ladies like to come along with me?" she asked.

"Yes!" Tammy's response was instantaneous.

Gran waited a couple of seconds. "No, I'm okay with the Disneyland bribe. You two younguns run along and have a good time. I'll stay here and finish reading my *Informer.*"

She folded the paper just so and settled in for a nice, long read.

As Savannah and Tammy grabbed their purses and headed for the door, Savannah heard her say, "I just found out that one of my favorite actors is gay. I wonder if he knows Ryan and John?"

On the way to Naughty Nonnina's, Tammy was happier, but still uncharacteristically quiet for her. As Savannah drove, she kept stealing sideways looks at her, and she could tell that something was still wrong with her young friend.

"Would you feel better if you yelled at me some more about last night?" Savannah asked her.

"No, I already made my point," was her low-key reply. "I don't have anything more to add . . . except that when you exclude me that way, I don't feel like you respect me. You know, as a fellow investigator."

Savannah reached over and put her hand on her knee. "Oh, sugar, don't say that. I have enormous respect for you. You're an amazing woman!"

"Do you really think of me as a woman?"

"Of course I do. But maybe, unfortunately for you, I think of you as a little sister. And that has more to do with me than you. I just step into that big-sister role out of habit. It's a bad habit, I know. I don't blame you one bit for being aggravated with me."

Tammy put her hand over Savannah's and gave it a squeeze. "Don't apologize. I love it that you think of me as your sister. I wouldn't have it any other way."

"Good, 'cause I don't think I can change that part of who I am. Granny drilled it into me to 'look out for the younguns,' and I don't think I'll ever get that out of my head."

"That's okay . . . since you're taking me along with you today."

"So, we're friends again."

"No. We're sisters. That's better." She squeezed Savannah's hand. "Some sisters biology gives you; other ones, your heart chooses."

"That's for sure."

"And now that we've made up, I've got something good to tell you," Tammy said with a sly grin.

"What's that?"

"I found some stuff on the Web about Wellman, back when he was Bobby Martini."

"Oh, yeah? What's that?"

"He was under investigation for fraud there in Las Vegas . . . him and his sister, and her husband, Gustav Avantis."

"Really? Wow. You read that on the Internet?"

"Yes. They had a pretty successful business going there with that ghost-busting thing. Bobby — they called him 'Little Bobby' — and Gus were supposedly the techno experts, picking up ghost voices on their equipment, measuring spirit 'frequencies' and all that. And Maria claimed to be a medium, channeling those who had passed on."

Savannah turned onto Mission Street, heading toward the east end of town and Nonnina's. "But there's nothing criminal about ghost busting and saying you're a medium . . . whether you really are or not."

"The criminal part was — they started telling people that the ghosts would harm them if they didn't pay big bucks to have them 'cleansed' from their houses."

"Oh, that *is* ugly."

"Yeah, they'd tell these people that evil spirits had taken over their houses. And for the right price, they could set up these machines and send out frequencies that the ghosts wouldn't like, and Maria would talk to them, and they'd leave."

Savannah thought of the shoe boxes stuffed with cash. "And apparently, quite a few people believed them and forked over the big bucks."

"How can people be that foolish, to believe something like that?"

"Folks are taught all sorts of things growing up," Savannah said. "And believing something foolish doesn't make you a bad person. Taking advantage of people who are a bit too trusting — that's something else."

"Will Dirk be able to go after him for it?"

"I doubt it. Dirk already checked to see if Wellman had any outstanding warrants, even as Bobby Martini, but he didn't. Just because he and the others were being investigated doesn't mean any charges were ever brought."

"That's probably why they closed up shop and left . . . to avoid getting prosecuted, I mean."

"Could be," Savannah said, "But I find it interesting that Gus didn't come with them. Maybe Wellman was telling the truth when he said that Gina left Gus because he was a bad guy."

Tammy thought that over for a while as they rode along. And Savannah watched her, thinking how pretty she was with the sunlight shining on her glossy blonde hair, her face screwed up in a certain childlike concentration.

No. No matter how much she tried, Savannah knew she would never think of Tammy as anything other than a beloved little sister, someone to watch over and protect.

"So, schnookums," she said, "what do you think about this whole rigmarole?"

"I think," Tammy replied, "that if I was under investigation in Las Vegas for cheating a bunch of people out of a lot of money, and if I was leaving my husband anyway, and he wasn't a nice guy — that might be a good time to change my name and move to another state."

"And I," Savannah said, "think you're right."

Savannah pointed up ahead. "That's Naughty Nonnina's up there."

"The pink building with the silhouette of the woman with oversized hooters painted on the front?"

"That would be the one."

"Are the owners Italian?"

That one stumped Savannah. "Uh . . . I can't really say. Why?"

"I was just wondering, because 'Nonnina' is Italian for 'little grandmother.' "

Savannah gave her a startled sideways look. "Really? Are you sure?"

"Yeah, I'm sure."

"Naughty little grandma? Yuck."

"Really."

As they drove closer, Savannah looked for Dirk's Buick and didn't see it. But she did see blue and red flashes of light coming from the space in between the strip joint and building next to it.

"You know," she told Tammy, "I was hoping that maybe Dirk had found Gus Avantis and figured out some reason to arrest him."

"That looks like a lot of activity back there in the alley for a simple arrest," Tammy said, "unless he really resisted."

Savannah pulled the Mustang over to the curb in front of Nonnina's. She glanced in her mirror before opening the door to get out, and she caught sight of a large white van headed their way.

As it passed them, she saw the coroner's seal on the side.

"Uh-oh," she said. "Dr. Liu and her team are here. This can't be good."

# CHAPTER 20

"Wow, déjà vu all over again," Savannah said as she and Tammy ducked under the yellow perimeter tape and entered the area the police had cordoned off.

One handsome, young patrolman started toward them, holding his hand up in his best traffic-cop fashion. But when he recognized Savannah, he nodded and smiled.

She gave him a brief wave and a mouthed "thanks," then turned her attention to the business at hand.

In the center of the protected scene was a new, black Mercedes sedan, and on the ground next to it was a yellow tarp. Savannah would have recognized the shape under the tarp anywhere. It was a body.

"Who do you suppose it is?" Tammy asked. Her voice sounded a little shaky.

For all her bravado and eagerness to be in the middle of the action, Savannah could tell she was nervous.

"I don't know who it is," Savannah said, although it was running through her mind that she wouldn't be surprised to hear that Roxanne Rosen did a bit of moonlighting as a dancer at Nonnina's.

"There's Dirk over there," Tammy said, "talking to that cop."

No sooner had Tammy spoken than Dirk spotted them. He quickly ended his conversation with the officer and walked over to them.

He looked mildly surprised to see Tammy with Savannah, but he didn't mention it.

"What's up?" Savannah asked him. "And who's that?"

Nodding toward the tarp, he said, "Take a look."

He didn't have to say it twice. Savannah walked over to the car and the body beside it, bracing herself, as always.

Having seen terrible sights when she hadn't prepared herself, she had learned to guard her psyche as best she could. Although she had also learned that there wasn't really any way to protect one's heart and mind from the aftermath of violence.

She pulled a pair of surgical gloves from her purse and slipped them on. Then she knelt on one knee beside the tarp.

But before she raised the corner, she

turned to Tammy, who was standing right behind her.

"You okay?" she asked her.

She nodded, looking a little sick, her arms crossed over her chest.

"Why don't you go back and talk to Dirk?" Savannah said. "I'll look first, and then I'll tell you how bad it is."

"No, that's okay. Let's just do it."

"All right." Savannah lowered her voice, "But if you think there's any chance you're going to get sick, run fast and get to the other side of the tape before you . . . you know . . ."

"Add my DNA to the crime scene?"

"Exactly."

Savannah turned back to the body and raised the corner of the tarp. In her peripheral vision she could see several cops who were standing nearby moving closer to get a better look.

It took her mind a few seconds to process what she was seeing, because there was so much blood and the flesh of the face was so badly damaged.

She heard Tammy gasp, and one of the cops said, "Damn! Somebody sure made hamburger out of him."

As she continued to pull the tarp farther back, she saw that it was, indeed, a male.

He was wearing a purple polo shirt.

"He has red hair," Tammy said. "Do you think it's Wellman?"

"It's Wellman," Dirk replied. Savannah looked up and saw that he was standing next to Tammy, his hand on her shoulder. "He had his wallet in his pocket. Several pieces of ID and quite a bit of cash, too."

"Ugly," Savannah said. "Looks like somebody hit him in the head with something long and hard . . . and a lot more times than necessary to do the job."

"A rage killing," Tammy added. Her pretty, young face, usually lit with a smile, registered her sadness and horror.

"Yeah," Dirk said. "Somebody sure as hell wanted him dead."

"And it looks like they enjoyed doing it, too." Savannah glanced around. On the blacktop about a yard away, near the vehicle's front driver's side tire, was a large screwdriver. Next to it, someone had placed a bright orange, plastic evidence marker. And about two feet from the screwdriver was a hammer, which had its own marker.

The tire was flat, a deep puncture in its side.

"Well, they weren't the least bit subtle about that, huh?" she said. "They give the guy a flat tire and make sure he knows they

317

did it." She turned to Dirk. "This *is* Wellman's vehicle, right?"

He nodded.

Tammy was standing close to the car, sighting down the side of the front fender. "I think I see blood spatter there near the tire well," she said. "It's hard to tell on the black paint, but you can see it from here."

Savannah looked at the area from the angle she had suggested and agreed with her. "Yeah, that's spatter, all right. I'll bet he was leaning over, looking at his flat tire, when he got the first blow."

Dirk said, "I figure that's why they punched the tire in the first place . . . to get him into position to get whacked."

"You poke a hole in my tire and leave the screwdriver and hammer beside it in plain view," Savannah said, "you'd have my attention. I'd be sure to lean over and investigate."

"What do you suppose they hit him with?" Tammy said, wincing as she looked at the body's ruined face. "The hammer?"

"I doubt it," Savannah told her. "Not unless they wiped it down afterward. It looks clean."

"My best guess . . ." Dirk said dryly, ". . . is the bloody crowbar we found laying on the ground halfway down the alley."

"Ouch," Savannah said. "That's a nasty, I-mean-business sort of a weapon."

"We saw Dr. Liu's van arriving when we pulled up out front," Tammy told him. "Maybe they can lift a print off it."

"One can hope." Dirk knelt beside the body and carefully, respectfully replaced the tarp. Then he stood and stepped closer to Savannah.

When he looked at her, she saw a deep sadness in his eyes that touched her heart.

"I blew it, Van," he whispered, so that no one else could hear. "I watched his house most of the night and tried to warn him, but . . ."

"You don't know Avantis did this," Savannah said, as she reached over and put her hand on his shoulder. "And even if he did, you don't know that you could have prevented it."

He sighed, looking bone-deep weary. "Maybe I could have, maybe I couldn't. But I'll tell you one thing. I'm gonna find that son of a bitch, and if he did do it, I'm gonna nail his ass to the nearest wall."

"I'll hold him still while you do it."

An hour later, Savannah was in her car, headed for G & K Tot Heaven. On the seat beside her was a picture of Gus Avantis, his

Nevada driver's license photo . . . courtesy of Dirk.

Dirk had gone to the morgue with Dr. Liu and the mortal remains of Robert Wellman aka Bobby Martini. Dirk seemed to think that if he made a nuisance of himself, loitering just outside her autopsy suite, he might get faster results.

Savannah had sent Tammy along with him to referee any fights that might break out between him and the temperamental medical examiner.

"If Karen's going to find out that the father of her unborn child has been murdered," Savannah had told Dirk at the scene, "I want it to come from me, not the newscaster on channel two."

So, she was headed to Karen and Gertrude's daycare center to inform her of the tragic truth.

And she wasn't looking forward to it. Informing victims' families was the hardest thing she had been forced to do in a life filled with difficult tasks.

As she parked the Mustang in front of the house, she noticed that many of the decrepit toys were gone from the yard: the broken down swing, the overturned slide, the two-wheeled tricycle. While the place still appeared shabby and depressing, at least the dangerous, damaged equipment was gone.

She doubted that Gertrude and Karen had just suddenly decided, out of the goodness of their hearts, to spiffy up the place. She smiled, self-satisfied that her phone call to Social Services had produced such an immediate effect.

On the curb, waiting for trash pickup, was a heap of long-past-their-prime toys and child-care items.

Yes, somebody at G & K Tot Heaven had been busy . . . whether they liked it or not.

As she walked up the sidewalk to the front door, she could hear Gertrude Burns's shrill voice, drifting through the open windows.

"Where's the kid's damned teddy bear? The one with the blue ribbon around its neck?"

"I threw it out with everything else," was the response, screamed from the other end of the house. "They said get rid of the mess . . . I put it in the trash can."

"You what? Are you crazy?"

"It's garbage. What's the big deal?"

"The kid won't go to sleep without that stupid bear. But of course, you wouldn't know that because you never take care of your own brats. That bear had better be out there or, by God, I'll . . ."

The front door swung open, and a fury

dressed in black with red glasses came charging out. Gertrude stopped abruptly in the middle of the sidewalk when she saw Savannah.

"What the hell are you doing here again?" she demanded.

"I'm here to see your daughter," Savannah told her.

"Oh yeah? Well, I think you're here to snoop again. I think you're the one who made that 'anonymous' phone call to Social Services about *absolutely nothing!* You got us closed down over some old toys . . . like it's bad for kids to play with toys that aren't spanking new!"

Rather than engage her, Savannah simply tried to walk past her. But Gertrude would have none of it. She reached out and took Savannah by the upper arm, digging her fingers into her flesh.

"It was you," Gertrude said. "Wasn't it."

Savannah fixed her with an icy stare and said in a deadly even tone, "You need to take your hand off me this instant. I'm not some poor, helpless child you can manhandle."

When Gertrude didn't respond immediately, Savannah added, "This is your last warning before I knock the tar outta you. Your choice."

Gertrude seemed to understand, because she released her grip on Savannah. But she said, "If I find out it was you who called them, I'm going to —"

"It was me. I made the call. And you'll do nothing about it, except make this place a safer, better environment for the children in your charge."

Savannah sidestepped her and walked on up to the half-open front door.

In her peripheral vision, she saw Gertrude huff and puff for a moment or two. Then she stomped away in the direction of the overloaded garbage can and pile of discards . . . no doubt to rescue a teddy bear with a blue ribbon around its neck.

Savannah steeled herself, dreading what was ahead. Then she knocked on the door a couple of times, stuck her head inside, and shouted, "Karen? Karen . . . it's Savannah Reid. I need to talk to you."

# CHAPTER 21

Karen Burns took the news even harder than Savannah had feared she would. She sat on the living room sofa, her face in her hands, rocking back and forth and wailing.

"He can't be dead," she sobbed. "Not murdered! No, no, no!"

"I'm so sorry," Savannah said as she sat down beside her and patted the woman on the back. "I really am. Please, I know this is awful, but try your best to calm yourself, for your baby's sake. It's not good for it for you to be so upset."

Gertrude walked into the room and cast a disapproving scowl her daughter's way. She had a baby in her arms. The little toddler, Stevie, was holding on to her leg. "I don't know what you're bawling about," she snapped. "It's not like he was going to marry you anyway."

"Gertrude, stop." Savannah shot her a warning look. "You're not helping."

"Well, it's true. He wasn't going to do the right thing by her. He was a scumbag, chasing women all the time. Even with his wife out of the picture, he wasn't going to marry her. Did she tell you he told her to have an abortion? I'll bet she didn't mention that little detail."

"Mom, please," Karen said through her tears. "I can't take it right now. Just shut up."

"Do you hear the way she talks to me?" Gertrude shook her head, disgusted.

"And where do you suppose she learned it?" Savannah muttered to herself.

She reached into her purse and produced a handful of tissues for Karen. Then she took Gus Avantis's picture out, as well.

Holding it in front of Karen, she said, "Dry your eyes, sweetie, and take a look at this picture. Try and think really hard . . . have you ever seen him before?"

Karen did as she was told. After a long look, she said, "No, why?"

"Just asking." Savannah stuffed the photo back into her purse. "Did you ever hear Dr. Wellman mention the name Gus Avantis?"

"No, why?" Her eyes widened, and she looked as though she were about to be sick. "Is that him? Is that who you think killed my Robert?"

"At this point," Savannah said, "he's just a person of interest. We have a few questions we'd like to ask him."

"Who is he?" Gertrude wanted to know. "The husband of some other woman Wellman screwed?"

Savannah rose and walked over to Gertrude, who was still standing on the other side of the room, holding the baby.

"Your daughter just received some horrific news," Savannah told her. "Now would be a good time for you to look deep, deep inside and see if you can find some kindness in your heart to offer her."

Gertrude shrugged. "She picks losers. Every damned time, she goes for the scumbags. And this is what happens. It's not my fault she's all brokenhearted again. It's hers."

"Well . . ." Savannah sighed. "As long as you dug deep."

Then she headed out the door.

She desperately needed a breath of fresh air.

Savannah met Dirk in the parking lot of the Patty Cake Bakery. But when she left her Mustang and climbed into his Buick, she found him drinking black coffee . . . and only black coffee. The small pink bag on the dash held one lone pastry. And there were no tell-tale sugar crumbs around his mouth or on the front of his shirt.

"That one's yours," he said, pointing to the sack. "An apple fritter."

"Thanks," she said. "You still dieting?"

"Yeah. I don't know how you gals do this all the time. It's not just the being hungry part; it's feeling weak and cranky and depressed. Dieting sucks."

"You're darned right it sucks. Been there, done that, lost, and gained it all back, plus some more. That's why this gal don't do it no more. How long do you figure you'll be on this diet of yours?"

He glanced at his watch. "Thirty-four more hours."

"You've got it figured out down to the *hour?* What kind of diet is that?"

"A stupid one, the last one I'm ever doing." He rubbed his hand wearily over his eyes. "Boy, sitting out in front of Wellman's house last night instead of sleeping, that really messed me up."

"No sleep, no food. It'll be the death of you, you don't watch out. You're too old for that sort of abuse. And speaking of young and feisty, where's Tammy?"

"I dropped her back at your house. She's doing some computer work for us, trying to find out who manufactured that hammer and screwdriver and crowbar. Caitlin at the lab said they're all new, hardly a mark on them."

"So, if somebody bought all three locally at the same time, and we can find out what store carries those brands, we might be able to —"

"That's right. And I really want to find this killer. Dr. Liu said Wellman was hit in the head, hard, at least twelve times."

"Whoa. That's a lot of anger."

"Yeah. The guy didn't have a chance. I mean, he wasn't a great human being, but still . . ."

"No prints on any of those items?"

"Not even a smudged print."

"So, they were wearing some sort of gloves. You can't wipe the prints off and not the blood, too."

"Yeah, and the crow bar had blood, skin, and hair on it. Grim."

She nodded. "And as premeditated as it gets."

"I put an APB out on Avantis. If he's still in town, somebody's gonna see him."

Savannah leaned down to set her purse on the floorboard beside her feet, and she saw a bag. It was a white sack with the distinct logo of a fox dressed in a top hat and tails.

"Hey, what's this?" she asked, reaching for it.

But before she could touch it, he snatched the bag off the floor and clutched it to his chest.

"Nothing," he said. "It's nothing at all."

"That's from that classy men's boutique downtown. Ryan and John shop there!"

Before she could stop him, he had jumped out of the car, run to the back, opened the trunk, and thrown the bag inside.

When he climbed back into the driver's seat, his face was flushed and he was breathing hard.

"What the dickens is going on around here?" she said. "You went shopping at The Fancy Fox? Since when does that store carry faded Harley-Davidson T-shirts and worn out bomber jackets?"

"I'm not discussing this with you. Subject closed."

"This subject is so-o-o open! Since when do you shop *anywhere*, let alone *there?* They charge more for one shirt than you've spent on clothes the whole time I've known you."

"That's not true. I buy myself seven new pairs of underwear and socks every Christmas, and I throw out the old ones."

"Whoopee! Ralph Lauren, look out!"

"Who's that?"

"Come on. What's with this business of you —"

Her cell phone began to buzz. She knew from the ring it was Tammy, and so did Dirk. He looked extremely relieved for the interruption.

"Better get that," he said. "She might've found something for us."

Savannah gave him an evil look but flipped her phone open. "Hi, buttercup. What's shakin'?"

Tammy sounded excited. "I'm still working on that hammer, screwdriver, crowbar thing, but I used that account number that Ryan gave me . . . the one for Wellman's phone. And I hacked into his records."

"Oh, yeah? Anything good?"

"You said Wellman got a couple of phone calls in a row when you were talking to him there at the house. And he wouldn't take them in front of you, turned his phone off. Remember?"

"Sure. The first one was at five forty-six."

"That's right. You told me about that. Well, I checked that call and the one right after it. They were both from Gustav Avantis."

Savannah raised one eyebrow. "Really? Well, ain't that just mighty interesting?"

"Yeah, I thought Dirk would want to know that. He's really upset about letting Avantis get to Wellman . . . if he did, that is."

"I know. He's sitting here beside me. We're getting ready to go . . . somewhere . . . He hasn't told me where yet."

"Oh, you guys having another fight?"

"I don't know. It's hard to say if it's a new one or the continuation of an old one. After a while, they just sorta all run together."

"Oo-kay. Well, have fun."

Savannah gave Dirk a sideways glance. His pouty face was firmly in place. "Not likely," she said, "but thanks anyway."

He didn't tell her where they were going until they were pulling into the parking lot of a decrepit motel on the edge of town.

"Roxanne Rosen's staying here now," he said as he killed the engine. "She got kicked out of her apartment for not paying her rent. I want to ask her if she knows Avantis."

"Why would she know him? I doubt that he just walked up to her and introduced himself. 'Hi, I'm Gus Avantis, your former boss's brother-in-law. I was wondering if you'd tell me where he lives or where he likes to hang out in the evenings, 'cause I'm gonna bash him over the head with a

331

crowbar.' "

"Yeah, I know. But I have to do something. I'll go nuts if I just sit around and wait for somebody out there to nail him on that APB."

"Yes, 'wait' is your least favorite word."

They left the car and walked up to room 106. The peeling paint on the door and the number six that was dangling upside down was in keeping with the rest of the motel's décor. The Geranium Inn had seen better days . . . back when its guests had arrived on the backs of wooly mammoths.

It took awhile for Roxanne to answer the door, and when she did, she looked almost as bedraggled as her lodgings. Her hair hung down, limp and dirty, and her eyes were brown . . . no longer that suspicious shade of aqua. Her jeans and tank top looked like she had slept in them.

"Oh, it's you two," she said with even less enthusiasm than she had shown when greeting them the last time.

"Your roommate told me you'd moved here," Dirk said.

"She always did have a big mouth."

"Can we come in?" Savannah asked. "We've got something to tell you."

"I already heard. I know the bartender at Nonnina's. It was Wellman out there in the alley, right?"

"Yes, it was," Dirk replied.

"I didn't do anything to him. Just like I didn't do anything to Maria, except whip her ass, which she totally deserved."

"We don't think you did," Savannah said. She reached into her purse and pulled out Avantis's picture. She shoved it under Roxanne's nose. "We just want to know if you've seen this guy. Take a good look and think hard."

"I don't have to think hard. I'd know him anywhere. He bought me a screwdriver last night."

Sitting on the corner of Roxanne's unmade bed, Savannah tried to breathe through her ears. The stench of stale cigarette smoke, mixed with eau de unwashed body, was enough to put a vulture off his food.

On the opposite corner of the bed, Dirk sat, looking equally thrilled with his surroundings.

They both had a thing about motel rooms. Having seen far too many of such rooms, and knowing how much biological evidence was "deposited" on the bedspreads, carpets, walls, and even curtains, neither of them spent any more time in one than was absolutely necessary.

But the information Roxanne was giving them made it worthwhile. She was perched on a flimsy plastic chair, only a foot from them.

The rooms at the Geranium Inn were as spacious as they were spotless.

"I got to Rick's a little early," she was saying, "before my girlfriends. I was sitting at the bar, and this guy comes up and offers to buy me a drink. We sat there, talking, and the subject of Dr. Wellman came up. He said it was a shame, the doctor's wife getting murdered like that. He seemed to want to talk about it a lot. At one point, I thought he might even be a reporter or something."

"What sort of things did he ask you?" Dirk wanted to know.

"Oh . . . what you cops had said to me, whether there were any suspects yet, what sort of evidence you had . . . stuff like that." She ran her fingers through her thick hair, as if trying to make a feeble attempt at grooming. It didn't help. "And," she added, "he asked me out."

"On a date?" Dirk sounded surprised.

"Yeah, on a date. I didn't look like this at the time," Roxanne snapped back.

"Did you go out with him?" Dirk said.

"No. He was old enough to be my dad

and ugly and kinda creepy, too."

"So, you told him no, and then what?" Savannah asked.

"He gave me his number and then he left."

Dirk perked up. "He gave you his phone number?"

"Yes. He scribbled it on a bar napkin, like they all do, and gave it to me, and then he left."

Savannah felt her own spirits rising. "Do you still have the number?"

"Naw, I threw it out."

"Oh."

"Over there in the garbage can, I think."

Savannah was torn. A garbage can? A possible lead on their prime suspect? A disgusting, *motel* garbage can?

She could see the battle registering on Dirk's face, too.

"You're the one getting paid here, not me," she told him.

He mumbled some intelligible complaint under his breath, stood, and reached into the inside pocket of his bomber jacket. He pulled out a pair of surgical gloves and put them on.

Squatting by the garbage can, he began to sort through its contents. Savannah felt a surge of sympathy for him when he pulled out a tampon applicator, but he pitched it back in and a moment later came up with a rumpled paper napkin. He handed it to Roxanne.

"Is that it?" he asked.

Roxanne nodded. "That's it."

Savannah leaned forward and placed her hand on Roxanne's knee.

"We're going to ask you for a favor, Roxie, a really big favor."

"What's in it for me?"

Savannah gave her a sappy smile. "The deep, abiding satisfaction of knowing that you've cooperated with law enforcement, that you're a good citizen, a valuable member of society."

Roxanne looked doubtful.

Dirk cleared his throat. "I could probably scrounge up fifty bucks for you out of the station's petty cash."

Roxanne grinned. "Now you're talking."

# CHAPTER 22

"This place is just as ugly as it was the last time we were here," Savannah said as she stared at the purple and turquoise striping on the front of Rick's Disco.

Dirk peered through the confetti of smashed bugs on his windshield and nodded. "You have to admit, I take you to all the best places."

"Yep. You never cease to broaden my horizons."

He nudged her with his elbow. "You'd rather be here right now than at the top of the Eiffel Tower."

She chuckled. "That's true. How sick is that?"

"It's not sick. It's refreshing. You're one of a kind, Van."

"Hey, don't look now," she said, "but that's our boy. Just in time for his date with the little cutie who changed her mind . . . only it's us and our ugly mugs instead."

Dirk watched the red sedan as it turned into Rick's parking lot and pulled into a space close to the building. "You sure it's him?"

The driver got out and started to walk toward the door.

"Yes, I'm sure. That's the car I saw in front of Wellman's and the dude who was watching the house. It's the guy in the license photo. Let's get 'em!"

As they hurried across the parking lot to intercept their suspect before he could reach the door, Savannah felt a surge of adrenaline hit her system, her heart pound, her breath quicken.

"Yes," she said, more to herself than to Dirk. "Way better than the Eiffel Tower!"

In one of the police station's interrogation rooms, known as a "sweat box," Savannah sat on one side of the table with Dirk, fairly perspiration-free . . . and Gus Avantis sat on the other side, sweating like a pig at a luau.

She couldn't really blame the guy. If Dirk had been leaning across the table, looking at her that way, she'd be sweating, too.

Dirk might not be the sharpest ball on the billiard table, but he had the art of interrogation down pat.

"Don't tell me everything was hunky-dory between you and your ex-wife," Dirk was saying. "Ex-wives don't flee the area and hide out and change their names when the divorce was amicable."

"Okay, okay . . . so we weren't best buddies afterward. But that doesn't mean I killed her."

Savannah studied their suspect closely, thinking that, even under the best of circumstances, Gus Avantis wouldn't be considered an attractive man by most women. He was average height, a bit on the heavy side, especially in the jowls and belly. And his face was crisscrossed with a mapwork of purple, broken veins that were thickest on his rather bulbous nose.

And he was nervous and slightly bug-eyed, which didn't enhance his appearance by any means.

He spoke with a high, almost girlish voice, and kept licking his lips. She was sure they were dry.

Most people experienced a shortage of spit when being interrogated by Detective Dirk Coulter.

"You smashed your ex-brother-in-law in the head with a crowbar," Dirk was practically shouting at his subject. "You hit him again and again and again, until you were damned sure that he was as dead as his sister at the bottom of that cliff. I've got a capital case here against you, dude. You're going to get the needle for this. Premeditated, double homicide."

Savannah wasn't all that sure that, even if they could get an indictment against Avantis, it would be considered a capital offense. But then, something she *did* know for sure was that cops don't have to tell the truth in an interrogation room. The general public seemed to think they did. She knew better.

"Look, Gus," she said, getting ready to play her "down-home, sweet Southern belle" to Dirk's cantankerous "bad cop." "We know that Robert and Maria . . . or should we say, Bobby and Gina . . . didn't do the right thing by you. They split town with all that equipment that you had for your ghost-busting business. Not to mention all the cash."

Bingo. She could tell by the way his already bugged eyes popped open even farther that she had scored with that one.

"And we sure don't blame you for getting pissed about that. Anybody would be. They disappear without a trace. Then the next thing you know, you're watching TV and there's that son-of-a-bitch brother-in-law on the screen, looking all tidy and prosperous. He's running a whole new game and obviously making money hand over fist. That's gonna ruin anybody's day."

"And you come here to confront him, get your money and your stuff back, and get even." Dirk was practically spitting as he talked, his eyes red with rage, veins throbbing on his forehead.

And it was all a big act.

Many times, Savannah had watched him pitching a fit, raising high heaven, convincing the subject of an interrogation that he was a rabid pit bull, only to walk out of the room and calmly suggest that they go get a burger, fries, and a chocolate shake.

But, fortunately, Gus Avantis didn't know it was an act, and he was caving fast.

"Okay, okay," he said. "We weren't good friends and yeah, I was pissed that Gina ran off, Bobby, too, and took my half of everything with them. And when I saw him on television, sure, it burned my ass. But I didn't come here until after I heard that my ex-wife had been killed. I didn't even know where they lived until I saw it on the news."

"Yeah, right," Dirk said. "Tell us another one before that one gets cold. You killed your ex and her brother, too."

"That's not true! I wouldn't hurt Gina. I loved her. When I heard she'd been murdered, I figured he did it. The two of them never did get along all that well. I came out here to find out what happened to her."

"And to get your Ouija board, and your crystal skull, and your shoe boxes full of cash," Savannah added.

His eyes gleamed at the mention of the money. For the first time since they'd brought him in, he had half a smile on his face. "They still have it? I figured they'd mowed through it all by now. Cool."

"It ain't *that* cool," Dirk said. "It's not like you're getting your mitts on any of it."

"But it's mine! Mine!" It was Gus's turn to look maniacal. "I came here for two things . . . to find out what happened to a woman who used to be my wife, and to get my money and stuff back."

"But not necessarily in that order," Dirk said. "And you forgot to mention 'revenge.' "

"No! I didn't kill nobody! I swear on my mother's grave, I didn't lay a hand on them."

The questioning continued for another hour, but Gustav Avantis didn't budge one bit on any element of his story.

As Savannah and Dirk were leaving the station house, walking toward the Buick,

Savannah said to Dirk, "You know, if you don't come up with something in the next twenty-four hours, you're going to have to turn him loose."

"Yeah. I know." As he opened her car door, he glanced back at the building. "I'm starting to have my doubts that it's him. He swore on his mother's grave."

Savannah chuckled as she slid into the passenger's seat. "Big deal. A lot of guys swear on their mommies' graves . . . and their moms aren't even dead."

No sooner had they pulled into the Burger Bonanza's lot than Savannah's phone rang, playing Tammy's cheerful song.

"It's the kiddo," she said.

"It better not be anything that's gonna interfere with me getting a Super Duper under my belt. Interrogating always makes me hungry."

"Yeah, a guy can work up an appetite, wringing the sweat outta people." She answered the phone. "Hey, sweetie face. What's up?"

"I think I know which store they bought the stuff in!" was the effervescent response.

"Oh, yeah?"

"Yeah! We're in luck. The hammer's not a regular hammer. It's a Stout Guy, stock

343

number 35780901B. Most of the stores sell stock number 35780901A, but not number 35780901B. The 'B' model has a special handle that's slightly curved and . . ."

Savannah was starting to glaze over. She had noticed that the older she got, the fewer details she could retain in her brain for any period of time. She had also noticed that she had to resist the urge to strangle wordy people far more frequently.

Fortunately for Tammy, she was on the other end of a phone line and not standing in front of her in the flesh . . . with a squeezable neck.

"So, which store sells this special 'B' series hammer, Tam?" she asked, trying not to sound homicidal or even impatient.

It wasn't easy.

"The same store that sells that model crowbar and that screwdriver. Although all the stores in the area sell that particular screwdriver because it's a Trusty Tool brand, model number 253-346-102-TTSW . . ."

"Tamitha, honey, which store sells all those items?"

"Three Brothers Hardware on East Main Street . . . down by the bowling alley."

"Thank you, darlin'. And excellent work there!"

"Is everything okay? You sound a bit irked.

Is ol' Dirko getting on your nerves again?"

"Yep, that's it. You guessed it. But I'll be fine. Thanks again. Bye-bye for now."

When she hung up the phone, Dirk gave her a smirk. "One of these days she's gonna prattle on like that a little too long and the top of your head's gonna blow off."

"It might happen. It truly might."

"So, what do you want with your cheeseburger? A shake or a soda?"

"Forget both. We have to go see Three Brothers about a fricken hammer with a serial number as long as your crowbar."

"I think my brother, Ted, sold that hammer," Fred, the hardware man, said. "Or it might have been Jed."

"Are you guys triplets?" Savannah asked, leaning on the counter. Her calves were still sore from all that tippy-toe standing while spying on Dirk at the gym. And there had been four customers in line when she and Dirk had arrived.

Who would have thought the tiny, privately owned store would have so much business?

"No, we're not triplets. Why do you ask?" he said, wiping his hands on the canvas apron tied around his waist.

"Uh . . . Fred, Ted, Jed . . . never mind."

Savannah produced Gus Avantis's photo from her purse for what felt like the umpteenth time in the past few hours. "Have you seen this guy?"

He studied the picture long and hard before answering. "Nope, can't say that I have. But I just got back from a fishing trip this morning, and my brother, Jed, he's been gone fishing, so if this is the guy who you think might have bought that hammer, you'd need to ask Ted, 'cause he's the one who maybe sold it to him."

"Okay," Dirk said, looking as frazzled as Savannah was feeling. "Let's talk to Ted."

"Ted's gone fishing. It's his turn."

Savannah gripped the edge of the counter. She didn't look down to check, but she was pretty sure her knuckles were white.

"Maybe we could get Ted on his cell phone?" she suggested. "I realize it might be an intrusion on his vacation, but this really is important."

"We never take our cell phones with us when we're fishing. Phones and fishing don't go together."

"Fred," she said, using her softest, sweetest Southern drawl. "My friend and I . . . we've got one nerve left between us, and it's unravelin' fast and furious. So, please just make this as easy on us as you can . . . Is there any way that you could look at your records and tell us if — in the past few days — a customer came in here and bought that special hammer?"

"And they might have bought a crowbar and a screwdriver, too," Dirk added.

Fred yawned . . . obviously still quite relaxed from his fishing vacation. "I suppose I could check through all the merchant copies of all of our receipts from the past few days. It's gonna take awhile. But you two look like patient folks. You won't mind waiting, huh?"

Savannah helped Fred check the receipts, and Dirk sold some nails and a roll of masking tape, and an hour and a half later, their cumulative efforts were rewarded.

"Well, hey there, look at this," Fred said in the same even, lackluster tone that he would have used to announce the daily arrival of the postman at his mailbox. He held up a bit of paper to show them. "This might be what you two are looking for. We had somebody buy four items: that hammer that you were so interested in, a crowbar, a screwdriver, and a pair of workman's gloves. Does that interest you?"

He waved the receipt under Savannah's nose, and she snatched it out of his hand.

"These things were bought yesterday morning at ten forty-eight," she told Dirk.

He rushed around the counter and over to them, where they sat at a small desk in the corner, the receipts stacked in neat piles on the table before them.

"Yesterday morning. That's perfect," he said. "How did they pay for the stuff? Cash? Credit card?"

Fred peered at the receipt in Savannah's hand. "Card. See right there? It shows the last four digits on their account — three-one-three-seven. It was a debit card."

"Listen to me, Fred." Savannah leaned across the desk and fixed him with her most sincere blue-eyed gaze — the one she used when she most sincerely wanted to weasel something out of somebody. "You have to find out for me whose card that is. You just have to."

Fred gazed back, spellbound by her blue eyes . . . not to mention the amount of cleavage she was showing by bending over so far.

*Hey,* she thought, *what the heck. It works for Patty the baker.*

"I have to check my records," he said, still mesmerized by the most intense female attention he had received in his adulthood. "I think I can do that online."

"Would you do that, Fred? Would you do that for me, *right away?*"

"I'm not as good on a computer as Jed or Ted are, but I'll give it my best shot."

"Oh . . . thank you, darlin'. I thank you from the bottom of my heart."

Fred cast one more quick glance downward, toward the region of her heart, then shot up out of his chair. "I'll get right on it."

Nearly stumbling over his own feet, he scrambled across the room and through a door in the back, slamming it behind him.

"Sheez," Dirk said, shaking his head. "You sure know how to work those . . . uh . . . feminine wiles of yours."

"We should all use what the good Lord gave us. The good Lord and Victoria's Secret's latest push-'em-up-and-mash-'em-together bra."

# CHAPTER 23

As Dirk pulled up to the curb across the street from G & K Tot Heaven, Savannah shook her head and said, "You could've knocked me over with a goose feather when that Fred guy said the name on that credit card was Karen Burns. Just goes to show you, you can't trust nobody in this world, not even an expectant mother. What's this world comin' to?"

Dirk picked up the folder off the dashboard that had the precious document inside — the one he had groveled to get.

Apologizing profusely and repeatedly to Judge Dalano hadn't been easy. But Dirk never let a thing like simple male pride stand in the way of him and a search warrant.

"At least I got this," he said, giving the folder a loving pat. "I thought for a while there her honor was going to lift the back of

350

her robe and make me kiss her hiney. Literally."

"Naw, she knew you'd like that. The idea was to punish you, not reward you."

She looked at the house with all the discarded, broken-down toys still piled on the curb for pick up, and she felt a shudder go through her.

"I still can't believe this. Karen was the last person I'd figured for a murderer. Maybe killing Maria would make sense to get her out of the way, thinking she was Wellman's wife. But why the doctor? With him dead she doesn't even have a chance of getting child-support payments."

"He probably told her one too many times to go get an abortion. Heck, I've seen women who'd kill a man because he looked twice at their best friend. If he broke it off with her, told her to get lost, and her pregnant . . . there's no telling what she'd do."

"Well, let's go see what we can find in that house. The purchase at the hardware store was pretty incriminating, but a diamond and sapphire necklace . . . now that would be the cherry on the banana split."

"Oh, this just gets better and better!" Karen Burns said, tears and mascara running in black streaks down her face, when they knocked on her door and showed her their search warrant. "So now what? I'm going to be arrested — and me pregnant? You're going to throw a mother-to-be in jail?"

Dirk scowled and walked past her into the house. "I don't 'throw' mothers-to-be *anywhere.* But there's a good chance you might get your butt nicely, gently, politely escorted to jail."

"You're not going to find anything in this house that'll prove that I killed anybody, because I didn't!" She tossed a plastic dump truck and a doll off the end of the sofa and plopped herself down on it. Then she grabbed a handful of tissues from the end table next to her and blew her nose loudly.

"We're not here just because we don't like the color of your eyes or the cut of your hair," Savannah told her. "We know all about your little shopping spree at Three Brothers Hardware."

"What shopping spree? I haven't shopped for anything for ages. I haven't even had enough money to buy maternity clothes. Not that I need them yet."

She placed her hand on her only slightly enlarged tummy and patted it.

Savannah had to agree with her there. She still had a lovely figure and didn't mind showing it off with the tight, black sweater dress she was wearing. Savannah thought about the fact that this woman was seeing weight loss specialists to lose all those "excess pounds," and for a moment, she felt sorry for her.

So many women — naturally buoyant, joyful spirits — were crushed under society's pressure to remain as thin as preadolescent girls.

She thought of Gertrude Burns's harsh words to her daughter, and she felt an added surge of sympathy for the woman on the sofa. But then she remembered Wellman's crushed and mangled face . . . and all vestiges of sympathy disappeared.

Walking over to the coffee table, where a black leather purse lay, she said, "So, how much do you want to bet me, Karen, that inside this purse I'm going to find a debit card that ends with the numbers three-one-three-seven?"

Karen stopped crying instantly, like a toggle switch had been thrown. Fear and anger replaced the frantic, victim look.

"How do you know my debit card number?"

"You'd be surprised what we know about you." Savannah picked up the purse.

Karen leaned over and tried to snatch it

out of her hand. "You can't go through my purse!"

"Darlin', that warrant says we can go through your panties drawer if we've got a notion to do it. So, you just sit back there on the couch and chill out. 'Cause it's gonna happen whether you like it or not."

Savannah handed the purse to Dirk. Officially, *he* was the one with the warrant. But she didn't feel the need to fill Karen Burns in on the particulars of search-and-seizure law.

It took Dirk less than thirty seconds to have the debit card in his hand. An unnaturally cheerful look on his face, he held it up for all to see. "Three-one-three-seven. And, ladies and gentlemen of the jury, we would like to present the prosecution's exhibit number one."

Two hours later, Dirk was less cheerful.

So was Savannah.

They were sweaty and tired and depressed, having scoured the premises thoroughly without finding anything other than the debit card.

Less than ten minutes into their task, Dirk had declared the property "a friggen dump." And coming from a guy who lived in a rusted-out trailer with milk crates and rickety TV trays for furniture, that was quite an indictment.

They paused for a break in the kitchen, after searching every cereal box and potato chip bag in hopes of finding Rodeo Drive jewelry.

Going through the trash, looking for a Three Brothers Hardware bag or receipt, had been the worst. Dumpster diving was Savannah's least favorite part of any search.

"As fun as this is," she told Dirk while they washed their hands at the kitchen sink, using plenty of soap and hot water, "I'm starting to think we might as well give up the ghost. I don't think we're going to come up with anything else."

"I'm afraid you're right." He looked around for something to wipe his hands on. When he picked up the corner of a dishtowel and saw crusty strands of dried spaghetti with red sauce stuck to it, he tossed it back onto the counter and used his shirttail instead.

They heard the sound of a car's engine, and the rattling clanking of the garage door opening. A moment later, a shrill, too-familiar voice drifted into the kitchen.

"Get your asses out of this car right now or you won't be getting any candy. I mean it. You touch your sister again, I swear I'll slug you!"

"Gertrude's home," Dirk said to Savannah.

"Oh, goodie gumdrop. I knew we should've left ten minutes ago."

The door leading from the kitchen to the garage opened, and children poured through. Little ones with round, rosy faces and a couple of elementary school–aged boys streamed in, carrying assorted toys and snacks.

Gertrude followed, a baby in one arm, two bags of groceries in the other. "You wanna get in here and help me, you lazy sack of —" she screamed, choking on her words when she saw Savannah and Dirk in her kitchen.

"What the hell are you doing in my house . . . again?" she shouted.

Dirk gave her a nasty look, but he reached over and took the bags from her. Setting them on the kitchen counter, he said, "We have a search warrant for your property, Mrs. Burns. In fact, we've just finished a rather thorough search and were about to leave. But now that you've been thoughtful enough to pull your car into the garage, it's officially on the premises and subject to be searched as well."

"Mighty thoughtful of you," Savannah

murmured as she reached out and stroked the soft curls of the munchkin nearest her.

"You're not looking in my car for anything," Gertrude said, puffing herself up into an impressive amount of woman, glaring at them through her bright red frames.

"Your car is getting searched," Savannah told her. "Your daughter is under suspicion for killing Robert Wellman, maybe even Maria, too. So, we're leaving no rock unturned."

"My daughter? Suspicion of killing . . . ? What?" she sputtered. She whirled around and stomped into the living room.

Savannah and Dirk could hear her screaming at Karen, even as they went into the garage.

"What the hell have you done now, you stupid, fat cow? It's not enough that you get yourself knocked up by a married man . . . you've got to go and kill somebody, too!"

Ten minutes later, Savannah and Dirk walked back into the house to find Gertrude and Karen still arguing in the living room. Karen was half-sitting, half-lying on one end of the couch, curled into a fetal position, sobbing hysterically. Gertrude sat on the other end, arms crossed over her chest. Savannah could practically see the smoke curling out of her ears.

The baby lay on the sofa between them. It was crying, too.

Just one big happy family.

Instinctively, Savannah walked to the sofa, leaned over the wailing Karen, and picked up the crying baby.

"What do you think you're doing?" Gertrude snapped.

"Comforting this child," Savannah said. "Since nobody else is."

"Well, we've got a thing or two on our minds around here, what with you two talking about arresting my daughter for murder!"

"Oh, we're going to do more than talk about it," Dirk said. He held up two brown evidence bags. "We just found a plastic sack stuffed under the driver's seat of her car with Three Brothers Hardware printed on it. And inside, guess what we found? A receipt for a screwdriver, a hammer, a crowbar, and a pair of workman's gloves."

He waited for that information to sink in.

It did. Karen curled into a tighter ball and shrieked even louder. Gertrude's face turned from red to purple.

"And . . . oh, yeah . . ." he continued, ". . . did I mention that we found the bloody gloves under the driver's seat next to the bag?"

"Y'all oughta take out the trash more often," Savannah said as she cuddled the baby expertly against her chest. " 'Neatness is next to godliness,' as Gran says, and it gets rid of incriminating evidence, too."

Dirk set the brown bags on the coffee table, then reached behind him and pulled a pair of handcuffs from his belt. "Karen Burns, you're under arrest for the murder of Robert Wellman . . . er . . . Bobby Martini. You have the right to remain silent. . . ."

Savannah and Dirk had to practically carry their suspect to his car. Her legs were too wobbly to support her . . . or at least, she gave that impression as she stumbled along, with one of her captors lifting her under each arm.

"I don't want to have my baby in jail!" she screeched, sounding a lot like her mother.

"Maybe you should have thought about your baby when you were smashing its father on the head with a crowbar," Savannah told her. "You made mincemeat out of that man, Karen. You can't do that and just go on living your life like nothing happened."

"And I'm gonna get you for killing Gina Martini, too," Dirk said. "I haven't figured out how yet, but I will."

"Who's . . . who's Gina Martini?"

Savannah sighed, feeling troubled, uneasy about something, even though an arrest had just been made. "I just wish we'd been able to find that jewelry," she said.

"What jewelry? Who's Gina? I don't know what you people are talking about!" Karen screamed as Dirk opened the back door of the Buick.

Savannah watched as Dirk seated her inside and secured her seat belt. She watched, and she wrestled with a feeling that something was wrong.

Over the years, she had seen countless people arrested . . . most of them guilty, some of them innocent.

The innocent had a certain air of disbelief about them, as though they simply couldn't comprehend what was happening to them. The guilty usually put up a fuss initially, then displayed a sullen resignation to the whole process.

Karen was a study in incredulity. She was in a state of terrified shock.

"What's the matter?" Dirk asked Savannah as he closed the door.

"She didn't do it."

"What do you mean she didn't do it? I've got her card, the receipt and bag in her car. The bloody gloves!"

But Savannah wasn't listening to him. She was already headed back to the house.

She walked across the street, past the pile of discarded toys on the curb, and up the sidewalk. When she reached the front door, she didn't bother to knock, just walked on in.

She strode past a startled Gertrude, who was in the middle of doling out sweets to the children.

She walked straight through the house to a bedroom she had already checked before . . . one of the kids' rooms.

Once inside, she hurried over to the unmade bed with the Spiderman sheets and picked up the ragged teddy bear with the blue ribbon around its neck.

"There you are," she said, looking into his faded eyes.

"What are you doing with my bear?" asked a small, timid voice behind her.

She turned and saw a little boy standing there, his eyes wide with concern.

Squeezing the stuffed animal, she could feel the hard lumps just under the fur of its

361

belly . . . right near the center seam where it was sewn.

"I'm going to have to take your bear to the toy doctor," she told the child. "He ate something he really shouldn't have. But I promise you I'll bring him back to you."

"Double-dog promise?" the boy asked.

"*Triple*-dog promise."

With the bear's owner's blessing, Savannah carried teddy back into the living room. When Gertrude saw the toy in her hand, her face fell.

"What are you doing with that?"

"You know," Savannah told her. "You know exactly what's inside this bear because you put it there. It's a diamond and sapphire necklace. And judging from the lumps on his butt, I'd say there's a pair of earrings in there, too. The ones you snatched off a dead" — she glanced around and saw several young faces watching intently — "that you removed from a deceased female . . . a corpse."

"I did not."

"You did. That's why you threw such a hissy fit the other day when Karen pitched it into the garbage."

Gertrude didn't reply, just glared at her through her red rims.

"And not only that," Savannah continued,

362

"but you were perfectly willing to let your daughter, your *pregnant* daughter, be arrested for something you did."

"She did it! It was all her. She put that stuff inside that bear and sewed it back up! It was her!"

"No, she didn't. But I'm going to enjoy telling the jury what a peach of a mother you are, accusing her to me like that."

Dirk came charging through the front door, a confused and worried look on his face.

"What are you doing?" he asked Savannah. "I don't have a cage in the Buick. I had to handcuff her to the door handle so that I could follow you in here to see what . . . What's going on?"

"The jewels are inside this bear," Savannah told him. "And Gertrude here put them there. She also killed Wellman. When the lab gets around to dusting that bag, it'll be her prints they find on it, not Karen's. And if that's not enough, you'll find her DNA inside those gloves. I'm sure her hands were sweating something fierce when she was killing Wellman. Beating somebody to death is mighty hard work."

Dirk was flabbergasted, Gertrude morose.

"I didn't steal that stuff off her dead body," she said in a strangely flat, monotone voice. "They were laying on her dressing table in her bedroom. She'd already taken them off."

Neither Dirk nor Savannah spoke. They just held their breath and listened.

"I found them after . . . after we had our fight there in the yard and she fell. I went through the house because I wanted to see what he lived like. How we were going to be living after . . . once she was dead and he married Karen. And that's when I saw them laying there. She was dead anyway. I wouldn't rob a dead body."

"Well, at least you've got your standards," Savannah muttered.

"But you'd beat a man to death with a crowbar," Dirk added. "Set him up to bend over and look at his tire, and then smash him in the head . . . over and over."

"He lied to my daughter." Gertrude gave a casual shrug. "He said he was married and he wasn't. He said he loved her and he didn't. He said he'd set her and me and all of us up somewhere and pay all our bills. I was really looking forward to that."

"I'll bet you were," Savannah said.

"A nice big house for all these kids. Somebody to help me take care of them. It was going to be great. But then he backed out. Told her all he'd do is pay for the abortion. He let us down. Disappointed us. He shouldn't have done that."

Dirk nodded. "Apparently not."

Savannah looked around the room at the wide-eyed little ones and wondered what was going to become of them.

She remembered every moment of that day, so many years ago, when she and her siblings had been removed from her mother's care and placed with Granny Reid.

That had been the beginning of Savannah's childhood. Before that, she had never been allowed to be a child.

Her heart ached for Gertrude Burns's grandchildren.

Not everyone was blessed to have a Granny Reid.

# CHAPTER 24

The sun was setting as Dirk drove Savannah homeward. Again, they had taken their favorite route along the foothills and were enjoying the sweet, citrus smells of the orange and lemon groves enhanced by the evening dew.

"I wonder how that Karen gal is going to function now, on her own, without her mother to take care of her," Dirk said.

"She's getting to learn some long-overdue life lessons," Savannah agreed. "No doubt about that. It's a shame. 'Cause when a body puts off the learning, the lessons get a lot tougher. And her pregnant — that makes it way harder. Life's not going to be easy for either of those women for a long time."

"Do you think Karen knew her mother had done it?" Dirk asked.

"She might have suspected. I don't know for sure. I really don't think Karen was in on it. I could tell she really was in love with

366

Wellman. I don't see the appeal, personally, but there's no accounting for taste."

"Or a lack of it."

They drove along in silence for a while, both enjoying the break from all the stressful activities of the past few days.

If there was anything better than having a case to work on, it was having one wrapped up.

"I think this is a first for me," Dirk said. "Instead of the wrath of a woman scorned it was a prospective mother-in-law scorned."

Savannah nodded. "I think Dr. Bonnie Saperstein was right about how some women think a man is going to change their lives forever, make them whole and happy. Then when that fantasy gets snatched away, they'll do anything to get it back."

"She's a nasty, rotten old broad. That's for sure. You gotta wonder if she was always that way. Like was she just born mean?"

Savannah gazed into the darkening orchards around her, breathed in the fragrant air that was streaming through the car window. "No," she said. "I can't believe that. But I do look at those little kids, growing up in a house where that sort of crap goes on . . . how do they really have a chance to learn anything different?"

Her cell phone buzzed, and she looked to

see who it was. "Brian Mahoney?" she said. "Why the heck would that tallywhacker be calling me?"

She didn't sound particularly friendly when she answered, "Yes?"

"Sa . . . Sa . . . Savannah?" The woman on the other end was crying so hard that she could hardly speak.

"Lydia?"

"Yes. It's me. You said I could call you if . . ."

"Of course. What's going on? Where are you?"

"I'm down at the gate, the one that leads into Spirit Hills."

"And what's happening?"

"He hurt me again. Pretty bad. I couldn't take it. I grabbed his cell phone and snuck out the back way and ran."

"Good for you, girl!"

"Can you help me?"

"Damn tootin'! You hang tight and we'll be there in five minutes. And if you see Brian, you hide . . . behind a bush somewhere if you need to."

It didn't take them five minutes. Dirk really stepped on the gas, and they were there in four.

When they saw the gatehouse, the first

thing Savannah noticed was that the guard looked scared to death. He was a small, older man in a neatly pressed khaki uniform. He was backed into a corner inside the booth, blocked from any means of escape by the impressive bulk of Brian Mahoney.

Mahoney was screaming at him.

"Where is she? Where is my wife? Don't tell me you didn't see her. She couldn't have gotten out any other way than through there! You tell me where she is or I swear I'll break your scrawny neck!"

He was wearing a dirty, ripped T-shirt and torn jeans. But what distressed Savannah about his attire was the fact that his shirt was spattered with drops of blood.

And she saw no trace of any injury on him.

Somehow, that wasn't particularly surprising. Brian Mahoney struck her as a guy who caused other people's blood to spill more than vice versa.

"Hey, hey, hey!" Dirk yelled as he and Savannah scrambled out of the Buick. "Back off there, Mahoney!"

When Mahoney turned around and saw them, his rage level soared. "You? I'm sick of you two! Get outta here. I've got problems!"

"And you're going to have even more if you don't back away from that guard,"

Savannah told him. "You can't go threatening people like that."

"Yeah? Well, you come on over here yourself, you bitch, and we'll see if it's a threat or a promise."

"Oh, now you've gone and done it," Savannah said, shaking her head. "You just stepped in a fresh cow pie with both feet."

A smoldering Dirk hurried up to Mahoney, a pair of cuffs already in his hand. "Turn around," Dirk told him, "and put your hands behind your back."

"What?" Mahoney gave him a challenging little smirk. "You're going to arrest me? You and who else?"

Savannah felt a shot of apprehension sizzle through her. The guy was big, really big, and all muscles and temper.

She glanced around the nearby shrubs, trying to see any sign of Lydia. At first she didn't see anyone. But then she noticed an oleander bush moving slightly. Through the tangle of dark green leaves and bright pink blossoms she could see something that looked like human skin.

But before she could help Lydia, she had to assist Dirk with Mahoney. Resisters who were over six foot three often presented a problem.

"You better turn around and put your

hands on that wall right now, buddy," Dirk was saying.

"Or what?" Mahoney tossed back.

"You'll be finding out what any minute now. Step away from that guard, and lift your hands. Do it now!"

Savannah walked over to Dirk, and the two of them advanced on Mahoney. To her dismay, he raised his clenched fists from his sides and positioned them in a fighter's stance. And worse, the sick little grin on his face made it obvious that he was enjoying this encounter, rather than being frightened or intimidated as they certainly would have preferred.

Brian Mahoney was a pro at this sort of thing. And Savannah was determined that neither her nor Dirk's blood would be mingling with the drops already on his shirt.

Dirk raised his own fists, cuffs tight in one of them.

She knew he wouldn't draw his weapon unless he absolutely had to. Dirk always preferred wrestling to shooting.

"Look," Dirk was telling him. "All I'm asking you to do is come out of that guard house, turn around, and put your hands behind you. Then I'll cuff you, for your protection and mine, and we'll have a little chat about whatever's goin' on. If everything's hunky-dory, then I'll uncuff you and we'll all be on our merry way. Sound like a plan?"

Mahoney didn't drop his fists or his nasty little grin. "Naw, I don't think so," he said.

"Okay, your choice," Dirk said as he pulled a billy club from the back of his belt and strode toward him.

Savannah rushed forward with him. But when she got almost within grabbing distance of Mahoney, she looked quickly to the left, pointed at the corner of the guardhouse, and said, "Oh, hey, look! It's Lydia!"

As she'd predicted, Mahoney's head whipped around to see what she was pointing to, and a second later, Dirk had one of his arms, and she had the other. They turned him around and slammed him, face first, into the brick wall of the guardhouse.

She grabbed his right hand, while Dirk nabbed the left. And before Brian Mahoney could spit a plug of tobacco, he was cuffed.

"Where is she?" he yelled, seemingly more anxious to see his wife than he was worried about being in the hands of the law.

"You got him?" Savannah asked.

"Yeah," Dirk replied. He pushed Mahoney onto the ground, where he sat down hard on the asphalt. "I'm gonna call a unit with a cage to transport him, though. I don't want him in the back of my Buick."

"Why not?" Savannah said. "He'd fit in with all the other moldy garbage back there."

She leaned closer to Dirk and lowered her voice. "Turn him around so that he's facing the other way."

"Why?"

"Just do it."

"Okay."

Dirk did as she said. And the moment Brian's head was turned, she hurried over to the oleander bush.

She found a shivery Lydia, crouched there, her arms folded over her bare breasts. She was shaking violently and blood was pouring from both sides of her horribly swollen nose.

All she had on was a pair of black lace panties.

She was crying.

"Oh, sugar," Savannah said, crouching beside her. "He messed you up good didn't he, darlin'?"

Lydia simply nodded and continued to cry.

Savannah took off her own linen jacket and started to put it on the woman, who was trembling so badly she could hardly slide her arm into the sleeve.

Glancing over Lydia's body, Savannah searched for other signs of injury. Most noticeable was her left ring finger. It was terribly swollen and dark blue. Savannah could tell just by its strange, grotesque angle that it was broken.

"He . . . he threw me out of the house," Lydia was saying. "He beat me up and then he pushed me out the door, and I didn't have any clothes."

"I'm sorry, sweetie," Savannah told her. "But it's over now. Sergeant Coulter has him in custody now, and he's going to jail. You don't have to be afraid anymore."

Lydia held up her hand. "He tore my wedding ring off my finger. It really hurts."

Savannah was already dialing 911. "I'll bet it does. I'm getting you medical help right now. An ambulance will take you to the hospital, and the doctors will set that for you. You're going to be okay. The worst is over now."

Lydia looked up at her with eyes that were filled with sadness, fear, and pain. But there was another little something there that hadn't been before.

It looked a lot like hope.

"It *is* over, isn't it?" Lydia said. "I can press charges against him, and you guys can send him to jail for hurting me."

"Absolutely."

"And then this whole nightmare could be finished."

Savannah nodded and smiled.

But once she had given the 911 operator all the particulars and hung up, she got to thinking about all the other women — hundreds and hundreds of them — over the years who had been where Lydia was.

"You know, Lydia," she said, her hand on the woman's shoulder. "This will be over if you make it so. You have to testify against that guy, tell the court what he did to you, what he's done to you all these years. You have to help the prosecution convict him of his crimes toward you. And then, once he's behind bars, you have to guard your own life. Really be on guard. Because if you don't, in a year or less, you'll find yourself with another guy just like Brian — different name, different face, but the same situation."

Lydia cried softly. "I've been hit before. By my dad. By other boyfriends. By my ex-husband."

"So, make sure that this is the last time."

Lydia nodded. "I will."

"You have to. You're the only one who can decide that it's over. Never again." She leaned down and patted the woman on the head. "Promise me, Lydia. Promise yourself — right now."

"I promise."

Savannah took heart.

Lydia sounded like she meant it.

Savannah, Dirk, and Granny sat in Savannah's living room, relaxing amid the desolation of a major feast.

The empty glasses, dirty dishes, and serving plates that held only crumbs, all testified that some serious eating had recently been done.

The party was over, and Tammy, John, and Ryan had left, all groaning that they had major bellyaches and would never be hungry again for the rest of their lives. And that was the way Savannah liked her guests to leave. The more miserable they were, the better she, as a Southern hostess, had done her job.

"That must have done your heart good, knowing that woman's going to pay for what she did," Gran said.

"Not as much as you might think," Savannah admitted. "Usually there's a family who's eager for justice for their loved one. But while we were investigating this, we didn't come across anybody who really loved either Bobby or Gina Martini, or gave a hoot that their killer's been arrested. It's sort of a hollow victory."

"Not for me," Dirk said. "I was glad to lock up that sourpuss. Even if nobody liked those people, she didn't have the right to kill them. She's right where she belongs, and I'm happy about it, even if nobody else is."

"I'll tell you what did give me a heap of satisfaction," Savannah said. She drained the last sip from her iced tea, then set the glass on the coffee table. "And that was getting that phone call from Lydia Mahoney this afternoon."

"Mahoney . . ." Gran said. "That name sounds familiar. Isn't she the one who's married to that no-good bum of a cowboy who was blackmailing the doctor?"

"Yes, the one with the tricked-out pickup and the gun rack," Dirk said.

"Dirk's jealous," Savannah said. "He wishes he had that truck."

"I don't want nothin' that guy has." Dirk sniffed. "Especially now. He's gone from living at a Southern-style mansion with big white columns to an eight-foot jail cell."

"You arrested him?" Gran asked.

"Yes, and it was the high point of our day," Savannah replied. "That worthless maggot thumped on his old lady one too many times. He broke her nose and then her finger, ripping her wedding ring off her. Threw her outside with hardly anything on. She high-tailed it outta there and gave me a call. Dirk slapped him in jail and, once she'd given her statement, I took her back home."

Gran smiled and nodded. "That's a fine thing. I bet you that when that woman's head hits the pillow tonight, she'll get the best night's sleep she's had in ages."

"And," Dirk added, "she's pressing charges on him, so we can keep him locked up for a while, give her a chance to resettle somewhere far away from him."

Savannah looked over at her grandmother and saw that Gran had nodded off. She smiled and said, "I'm taking her to Disney-land tomorrow . . . make it up to her for neglecting her so much this past week."

"Something tells me your grandma didn't feel neglected," Dirk replied as he got up from his chair, picked up one of Savannah's afghans, and spread it over Granny's lap, then pulled it up over her shoulders. "She's the type who entertains herself. She's a honey."

"She is. One in a million."

Savannah studied Dirk in the soft, golden lamplight, and thought that Granny wasn't the only honey in the room. Though he wasn't likely to own up to it.

"It was good to see you back on your feed again," she told him, her voice soft and sweet.

"What?"

"Your diet. You seem to be off it tonight. You were chowing down, big time, on those ribs and that potato salad."

"Oh, man . . . I didn't even know how much I'd missed your food. I took that first bite of ribs and almost burst into tears." He cleared his throat. "Wouldn't wanna do that in front of Ryan and John."

"No, absolutely not."

Dirk glanced over at Granny. "You think she's gonna sleep for a while?"

"Oh, she's out. Why?"

" 'Cause there's something I've gotta show you, something about that diet I've been on and the trips to the gym and all that. And I don't want her to see."

Savannah sat up straight in her chair, all ears and eyes. "Sure. What is it?"

"I didn't want to tell you about it at all, but I know if I don't, somebody else will."

She gulped. "Okay."

"And it's not the sort of thing that I want you to hear about secondhand."

"I understand."

He walked over to the desk chair, where

he had hung his leather jacket when he had arrived. He fished around inside the inner pocket and pulled out an envelope.

Savannah felt time slow down, the way it had at times in her life when she was about to hear something huge, something that would change everything. She steeled herself for the revelation.

He said, "I want you to take a look and tell me what you think. And be nice. No wisecracking, okay?"

"Wisecracking? Me? You forget who you're talking to."

"I know exactly who I'm talking to. That's why I'm warning you. I need you to be my sweet, understanding Savannah."

He sat down on the footstool at her feet and held out the small manila envelope. When she reached for it, her hand was shaking. "I'll be good," she said. "If it's important to you, it's important to me."

She opened the envelope and looked inside.

"Pictures?" she asked. "Your big secret is pictures?"

"Actually, the photographer called them 'proofs.'"

She pulled the stack out of the envelope and leaned closer to the lamp beside her.

At first, she wasn't sure what she was seeing. It was a shot of a man, from the waist up, wearing a snug, muscle-hugging, red shirt. He had quite a lot of muscles and was looking particularly good in his red shirt. In fact, he was looking extremely good in that red shirt.

"Oh, my god!" she said. "It's you!"

Even in the dim light, she could see him blushing. "Yeah, yeah, it's me."

She looked at the next one in the stack. In this one, he wasn't wearing any shirt at all. Just some red pants with a wide, black belt, and a red hat with white fur around its edges. His tanned chest and biceps bulged in all the right places.

"Holy moly! It's been way too long since I saw you with your shirt off! You're a hunk, dude!"

"Yeah? Really?"

"Smokin' hot!"

The next picture was more of the same outfit, different position, a definite "come hither" look on his face.

"I don't know if I'd have chosen that particular outfit, but man, you look great! You could be on the cover of a romance novel!"

"The outfit wasn't really my choice. It had to be something Christmas-ish, and I told them no way I was gonna pose with nothing but a sprig of mistletoe over my you-know-what."

"So, this is why you've been dieting and shopping at Ryan and John's stores and working out? You were getting boudoir pictures taken?"

"What's a boo-dwar picture?"

"Naughty pictures to give to your wife or girlfriend. But you don't have a wife or a girlfriend, so . . ." She flipped to the next shot, which looked like he was nude but holding a gift-wrapped box in front of him.

"I told them I'd need an extra-large package for that shot. You know . . . to cover my . . ."

"Don't say it."

"My extra-large package."

She groaned. "I told you not to say it." The last was of him wearing a skin-tight, red tank top, again with all the muscles bulging in the right places. He was holding a giant candy cane at a moderately suggestive angle. "These are great. Really. But why the Christmas theme?"

She looked up and saw that he was grinning, all nervousness gone and smug satisfaction in its place.

"You," he said, "are looking at Mr. December himself. In the glorious flesh."

"Mr. *December?*"

"That's me. Mr. December of the SCPD Charity Hunk Calendar. The proceeds go to disabled officers' kids. It's a really good cause, you know. I couldn't say no."

"They chose you for the Hunk Calendar! Get outta here!"

"Well, don't look so surprised. There're only thirteen guys in the department right now and one of them is Kenny Bates."

"Yeah, I see your point."

"And I knew that when the calendar came out, you'd see it, so . . . I had to tell you."

Savannah sat quietly for a long time, looking at the pictures, her hands no longer trembling.

Finally, she broke the long silence and said, "I thought you'd got yourself a girlfriend. I thought you'd fallen in love with somebody el—" She choked a little. "I mean . . . with somebody."

He looked at her for a long time, his eyes tender, an enigmatic half smile on his face. "Is that what you thought?"

She nodded, not looking at him.

He put out his hand, so she stuffed the photos into the envelope to give them back to him. But when she did, he didn't take them. Instead, he caught her by the wrist and pulled her toward him.

A moment later, they were face-to-face, so

close that she could feel his warm breath on her cheek.

"Let me tell you something, girl," he said, his voice deep and low. "The day that I actually admit that I'm in love . . . you're gonna be the very first to hear it. Nobody else."

She opened her mouth to speak. Nothing came out. So she tried again. "Okay."

He smiled, his eyes searching hers. "And don't you ever forget that."

"Okay."

He took the envelope out of her hand and stood. "I've gotta get going," he said, putting on his bomber jacket. "Do you want me to carry Gran up the stairs to bed?"

"No. Just let her sleep down here. That's what she always does. But hey, before you go . . ."

He turned around and looked at her, a vulnerable, sweet expectancy in his eyes. "Yes . . . ?"

"I know what I want for Christmas."

"What's that, sweetheart?"

"I want an eight by ten of you and your . . . um . . . extra-large package for my nightstand."

He gave her a wicked grin and waggled one eyebrow. "Well, you be a real good little girl, and we'll see what old Santa Claus puts in your stocking."

# ABOUT THE AUTHOR

**G. A. McKevett** is the pseudonym of a well-known author, Sonja Massie. She is currently working on the next Savannah Reid mystery. Readers can visit her website at www.sonjamassie.com.